Loyal as I am to Twyla, I skedaddle from her salon during Claire Buchanan's hair trims. Oh, I adore Claire—who doesn't? But wherever she goes, Luke's sure to follow. Trouble is, he tries to get her attention by revving his Harley, and the vibrations alone shake out my perms and curl my fingernails.

Claire pretends not to notice Luke, of course. She'll jerk down the hood of a hair dryer, turn away from the window and leaf through fashion magazines.

While only a hairdresser knows for sure, my guess is Claire and Luke's shared past was hotter than tamales in August. Makes you wonder whether sparks would fly again if somebody bought him for Claire at the Lost Springs bachelor auction....

Dear Reader,

We just knew you wouldn't want to miss the news event that has all of Wyoming abuzz! There's a herd of eligible bachelors on their way to Lightning Creek—and they're all for sale!

Cowboy, park ranger, rancher, P.I.—they all grew up at Lost Springs Ranch, and every one of these mavericks has his price, so long as the money's going to help keep Lost Springs afloat.

The auction is about to begin! Young and old, every woman in the state wants in on the action, so pony up some cash and join the fun. The man of your dreams might just be up for grabs!

Marsha Zinberg
Editorial Coordinator, HEART OF THE WEST

HITCHED BY CHRISTMAS
Jule
McBride

TORONTO • NEW YORK • LONDON
AMSTERDAM • PARIS • SYDNEY • HAMBURG
STOCKHOLM • ATHENS • TOKYO • MILAN • MADRID
PRAGUE • WARSAW • BUDAPEST • AUCKLAND

Jule McBride is acknowledged as the author of this work.

ISBN 0-373-82590-0

HITCHED BY CHRISTMAS

Copyright © 1999 by Harlequin Books S.A.

This edition published by arrangement with Harlequin Books S.A.

Visit us at www.romance.net

Printed in U.S.A.

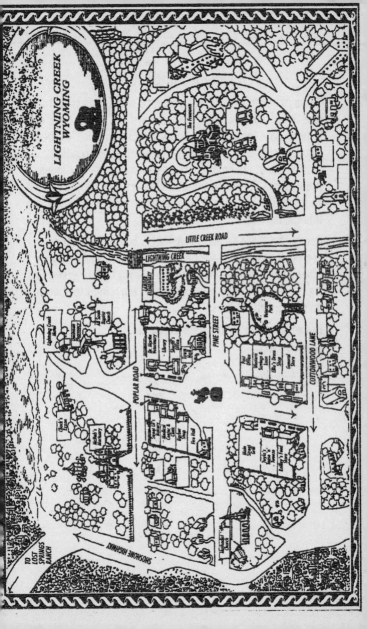

A Note from the Author

Years of reading and loving romance novels has taught me one thing: once the gavel comes down and a sexy hunk's bought, paid for and at a woman's beck and call, he'd better watch out! I've clocked many treasured hours reading stories about bachelor auctions—some split-your-sides funny, some cry-your-eyes-out weepers. I've loved them all, so I couldn't be more thrilled to write such a themed story this Christmas.

Really, there are as many reasons to buy a man as there are reasons to love—or be loved by—one. In *Hitched by Christmas*, a lonely cowboy who's bought by four sisters as a gift turns out to be more than they bargained for because he's a true gift of love.

I'm wishing you such gifts this season.

Merry Christmas,

Jule McBride

To Marsha Zinberg and Susan Sheppard for juggling stories, pulling together threads of the impossible, and making things make sense. For your generous dispensing of editorial Band-Aids that fix all story-things, there simply aren't enough thank-yous.

CHAPTER ONE

LUKE LYDELL NARROWED fierce blue eyes that belied his probable Native American heritage, ruffled a work-callused hand through his jaw-length, arrow-straight jet hair, then surveyed the crowded bleachers where countless women were shouting bids toward an auctioneer's podium. Resituating himself on a foldout metal chair that was about as uncomfortable as a saddle during the last days of fall roundup, Luke turned his attention to the bachelors being auctioned off.

"You might have lost your good looks over the years, Lydell," ribbed one of the guys Luke had grown up with at the Lost Springs Ranch for Boys, "but you haven't lost your bad attitude."

"Well, I sure don't raise Cain and kick butt the way I used to," Luke returned.

"Maybe not." Another whispered voice came over the auctioneer's. "But you were the only guy in the bachelor's auction brochure still wild enough to wear a ripped shirt."

"Shredded." Luke laughed softly, feeling glad the whispered conversation was taking his mind off the one thing he wanted to forget—the announcement of Claire Buchanan's engagement in yesterday's paper.

"And you posed with a bull, no less."

"Great pose," someone commented. "So romantic."

"Lindsay needed a picture," Luke defended calmly, glancing toward where Rex Trowbridge and Lindsay Duncan, the organizers, were watching the bachelor auction from the sidelines, "and that was the only picture I had. Me 'n' Slim Struthers—remember him?—well, we took that picture for the sake of comparison, so potential buyers could see the size of the bull."

"The bull was bigger than you," offered someone mildly.

"Right," replied Luke. "That was the point. The folks were purchasing the bull, not me."

"Well, today you're for sale."

Luke smiled. "I guess I figured one of these women would notice my ripped rags in the brochure and take pity on me. You watch. She'll buy me, take me home and feed me. And then she'll offer to darn my shirts."

"Not in a month of Sundays, Lydell. All these women want us to do is cut their grass, trim their hedges and baby-sit their kids for a weekend."

"If you're lucky, hedge trimming's all they'll want." Luke glanced at the crowd again. "But we'll find out soon enough. We're at their mercy today."

"Ain't that the truth."

Luke's eyes settled on the bachelor who was on the auction block, strutting his stuff. "Well," Luke continued, suddenly feeling vaguely uneasy, "this is for a good cause." All the guys wanted to participate in the bachelor auction, to help raise money for the ranch where they'd grown up. Luke *had* wanted to. Now, seeing the riled-up crowd, he wasn't so sure. Every year at Christmas Luke gave back his fair share to the Lost Springs Ranch for Boys—more than most people knew. Now, still keeping an eye on the women, he said, "Guess I didn't expect the women to be so..."

"Aggressive?"

Luke considered. "That'll do."

They were all different—young and old, rich and poor, and clad in everything from down-home western clothes to fancy frilly sundresses, but they had one thing in common: they were seriously intent on purchasing themselves a man. When Luke's eyes landed on a busty, pretty blonde in a big straw hat who kept placing bids by waving a white bandanna printed with black designs, he couldn't help but say, "What form of surrender do you think she has in mind?"

No one answered because the auctioneer suddenly shouted, "Sold to the wild buncha gals in front!"

"*Which* wild bunch?" Luke joked, watching the gavel come down. Another guy began parading while the crowd buzzed like hornets. *And in the heat of an east Wyoming June, no less.* Luke blew out a mock-wary sigh. "Anybody besides me starting to feel like grade A beefcake?"

"Sure" came the reply. "But if I'm prime rib, what would that make you, Lydell?"

Luke's lips tilted. Ribbing with the men was taking the edge off the more serious worries of investigative work, ranching and the unstoppable lust Luke felt for Claire Buchanan—all of which weren't far from his mind. "I figure I'm a choice tenderloin. Or a filet. Take your pick."

"Dead meat," somebody behind him said succinctly. "That's what we all are. And wearing that outfit, you deserve whatever you get, Luke."

Luke could have said his choice of attire was entirely unintentional, since he'd been stuck up on the north side of the Cross Creek Ranch where he'd been moving cattle since before sunrise, but he only glanced down and assured, "We aim to please."

In the silence that followed, Luke's eyes scanned the crowd again, and for the first time he allowed himself to take a good look at Claire. His eyes drifted over her unusual face, the plump mouth and dusky, smoky blue eyes that were ringed with natural shadows. As far as Luke was concerned, she had absolutely no right to embed herself so firmly in his gray matter, not when she was getting married next Christmas.

Ever since yesterday's announcement of her engagement, Luke had been remembering the past they'd once shared. As he'd haggled over beef prices, ear-tagged cattle and gone over cases for various law enforcement agencies around the area, her face kept swimming before his eyes. Even after all these years, every inch of her was still tangled up inside him like a wild thing caught in barbed wire.

Luke just wished she wasn't about to witness him being auctioned off to some crazy woman who'd use him for God only knew what nefarious purposes. *Now, don't you put the cart before the horse.* If Luke was lucky, maybe he'd be the one man who didn't garner any bids.

Keep dreamin'. Looking at the rowdy crowd, Luke was definitely starting to hope whoever purchased his services would want something simple, such as carpentry work or...

Just not sex. Luke was strong as an ox—six one and lean, his body thick with ropy muscle. Even so, as he stared warily at the hollering she-devils, Luke saw a few women he wasn't sure he could whip in hand-to-hand combat.

Hopefully, it wouldn't come to that. Not that Luke had anything against sex, but he definitely preferred standard dating rituals for the warm-up. And a few of the woman out there looked ready to wrestle a man down and hog-tie him. He winced, realizing it was almost his turn on the auction block and that he had no choice but to put on a show for the ladies. So what if he had to pose and flex a few muscles? The proceeds from this event were going to the Lost Springs Ranch, after all. Still, he felt as if he was about to get eaten alive. He glanced down at the jeans hugging his thighs. "Maybe I should have worn nicer slacks," he found himself saying. What he meant was looser.

"Lydell," someone whispered, "you don't *own* anything we'd refer to as *slacks*."

"True."

But Luke did have better jeans. Fortunately, he was wearing new Tony Llama boots, and his belt buckle was nice—one he'd won years ago at the Cheyenne Frontier Days Rodeo, when he'd ridden a full eight seconds on a nasty bull named Big Harold. Otherwise, his T-shirt had felt sweat-damp and too dirty to wear by the time he'd reached Lost Springs, so he'd left it slung over the seat of his Harley. Now he lifted a hand and rubbed his bare chest, which had turned a dark chestnut from the summer sun, his fingers just touching the red bandanna tied around his neck.

An elbow dug into his rib. "Getting antsy, cowboy?"

Cowboy.

For some reason, the word stung for a second. Not that he didn't love cowboying. But many of the guys who'd been raised with him at Lost Springs had moved on, some heading for cities. While Lost Springs provided a decent, well-maintained place where an orphaned or abandoned kid could get a clean bed and three squares a day, it hadn't been an easy upbringing for any of them. Luke had gotten itchy feet himself, but after doing some traveling, he'd returned home like the prodigal son.

Not that Luke had a proud pa to greet him. Now, as his blue eyes scanned the landscape again, Luke tried to tell himself he'd come back because he missed ranching. And because he could pick up investigative work in Casper from his old cop buddies. And because Lightning Creek, Wyoming, was the closest thing to home a he'd ever known. He tried to tell himself he hadn't returned because of Claire. But that was probably a lie.

His gaze dropped from the big, cloudless, western blue sky, over rolling hills and grasslands, to where heat shimmered on the rock faces, then he looked toward where folks milled near the bleachers, eating corn bread and ribs. He could still see where Twyla from the Tease 'n' Tweeze was raffling off a quilt made by the Converse County Quilt Quorum and the table where Claire had been raffling off two of her oil paintings.

Claire was good. Luke had even secretly bought some of her artwork, including paintings titled *Blue Sage Dreams* and *Lost Springs Ranch*. In the latter, Claire had captured the ranch in fiery twilight. A lone boy wandered in the scrub grass, his small figure dwarfed by the far off silhouette of steep mountains and a western sky that stretched forever. One of his arms was lifted toward the endless sky, and he looked strangely alone and forgotten while the vast sky he reached for seemed to beg eternal questions—where did we come from? Where are we going?

They weren't questions Luke asked often, but when he'd seen the picture, and how the boy reached for the sky as if it held all the answers, Luke had known Claire somehow understood his childhood, maybe even better than he did. Somehow, the woman had managed to paint what Luke could never say in words, and staring at that fiery orange sky, he'd wondered again who his folks were and why, years ago, they'd abandoned him on the doorstep at Lost Springs on a Christmas morning.

And then Luke had found the gallery owner and bought

Claire's painting of the ranch. Ever since, it—and others—
had hung in his living room, out at the cabin.

Not that Claire would ever know.

Right now, she was standing alone, near the bleachers,
looking better in jeans and a plain white T-shirt than any
woman had a right to. Unlike the other women, she seemed
to be somehow apart, like a lone tree standing above the
timberline. She was merely watching the auction with
those perceptive, questioning eyes, looking as still as one
of the figures in the gorgeous pictures she painted. In
Lightning Creek, Wyoming, nothing could hold a candle
to Claire Buchanan.

Hell, nothing in the world could hold a candle to Claire.

She was slender, as tall and pale as a birch tree in winter, and after Luke's eyes traced the curve of her long,
slender neck, his gaze caressed the delicate bones in her
high cheeks that he knew were strangely soft to the touch.
Her fine light tawny hair was pulled back, and a braid
swept around her neck, trailed over a shoulder and down
her chest. Shadows fell in the hollows of her cheeks as
well as around her eyes, making her look strangely wise.
Luke could still barely believe how intimately he'd once
touched her, or how she'd offered herself to him bodily
years ago. It was harder to believe he'd turned her down.

Ever since, they hadn't crossed paths much, though
Lightning Creek was a small town, and avoiding each
other was difficult. In fact, ten years of avoidance had
nearly taken an act of God, and even so, they still wound
up bumping into each other on occasion, like today.

Blowing out a sigh, Luke tried to ignore the June heat
again, but it was the kind of electrical heat that made the
air crackle and that would turn downright sultry come sun-
down. Letting his gaze drift with deceptive casualness past

Claire, Luke calmly studied some sticky-fingered kids eating cotton candy.

"And now for Luke Lydell!"

"Time to root hog or die," Luke murmured under his breath. The last person he wanted to parade himself in front of was Claire, but he'd figured she'd be here, so he'd had months to prepare himself. Luke rose while the auctioneer said, "Let's give him a hand, gals!"

To rousing applause, Luke strutted across the stage while his bio was read. Barely listening, he tried to ignore both Claire and the rising bids as he flexed his biceps. Suddenly, he realized a group of young squealing girls in the middle of the bleachers seemed hell-bent on buying him.

He squinted. Sure enough, it was Claire's four jeans-clad sisters—Emma Jane, Rosie, Vickie and Josie. Luke figured the oldest, Emma Jane, was probably in college by now, while the youngest, Josie, would still be in junior high. Their father, Tex, was with them. One of the few men in the audience, he was smiling broadly at his daughters, his lips curling around an unlit cigar. Repositioning a ten-gallon hat on his head, Tex shoved both hands into the pockets of new-looking jeans. Glancing away, Luke also thought he saw two of Claire's girlfriends, but maybe not. Fact was, Luke didn't know much about Claire's friends; she'd attended a girl's school in Cheyenne during their high school years, only coming home for the summers.

But why would Claire's sisters bid on him?

They'd get him, too, Luke realized uneasily. No doubt, Tex Buchanan was providing them with plenty of cold, hard cash. He would naturally want to make a sizable contribution to the Lost Springs fund-raiser. As Luke paraded for the hooting women, Emma Jane suddenly shrieked such a huge sum that Luke did a double-take.

Josie excitedly shouted another bid.

Frowning, Tex reprimanded his youngest daughter. A seeming family powwow followed, while Josie was reminded that she and Emma Jane weren't at loggerheads; the girls were on the same team and not supposed to bid against each other.

From the area beside the bleachers, Claire was watching her sisters and Tex with growing alarm. Meantime, the competition waved her white bandanna, screaming such an unreasonable amount that Luke stopped flexing his muscles and simply stared. Hell, he thought dryly, if he'd known he could command this kind of money, he'd have willingly sold himself to a woman years ago.

Especially when Emma Jane raised the bid. The competitor whipped off her straw sun hat, slapped it against her thigh and got down to business, shouting yet another offer.

And so it went. The bidding got so high that Luke finally stopped flexing a second time, crossed his arms over his bare chest and merely watched. Just seeing Claire's sisters jump up and down like jackrabbits was starting to make his head hurt, so he was half relieved when they finally won.

Just as he was stepping down, the girls ran up to him. They were all tall and willowy, like Claire, and they had her straight light hair and blue eyes. For a second, they eyed him critically as if he were a horse they were considering putting to stud, then seemingly deciding their purchase was sound, they crowded around him as if he was a mama cat and they were kittens. "Well," Luke said, glancing anxiously toward the bleachers where Tex was deep in conversation with another rancher. "Do you and your pa need some shelves built or something?"

"Shelves!" Josie, the youngest, squealed.

Luke raised an eyebrow. "Or some chores done?"

"Chores!" giggled Vickie.

They all started stammering, but Josie was the worst. She finally managed to say, "Oh, no, Mr. Lydell. We don't need shelves built or any chores done, but since Tex said we could do whatever we wanted with you, Emma Jane came up with the great idea to buy you as a present for someone."

"Does your pa know about this?" asked Luke.

"Of course not!" squealed Josie.

This didn't sound good. Luke stared at Emma Jane, whose long, straight hair accentuated the fact that she was older and taller than her sisters, as slender as a toothpick. "Emma Jane," he said, "you bought me as a present for…?"

Emma Jane sighed. "I'm so sorry. We're getting ahead of ourselves. Let me explain. We bought you for our big sister."

Luke could have choked. "Your sister?"

Vickie nodded enthusiastically. "Our big sis, Claire."

He knew exactly who their sister was. He glanced toward his Harley in the parking grounds, considering escape routes. "I think you'd better have a talk with your pa about this. He's paying, after all."

"He said to do whatever we wanted," Emma Jane defended.

"Tex just said to make sure we got our money's worth," added Rosie.

Josie was studying Luke curiously, with wisdom beyond her years. "You know Claire, don't you?"

Better than you can imagine. Since she was the oldest, Emma Jane probably remembered it, too. Even though Claire had kept the youthful relationship from her parents, Emma Jane might have known Luke and Claire had once had feelings. "Girls," Luke managed to say, "while we've never been formally introduced, I know you all by sight, and I know who your pa is—" Now Luke glanced toward Claire, feeling strangely helpless. She was still standing by the bleachers, looking concerned but pretending not to see him or her sisters.

"Claire's getting married in six months," Emma Jane continued pragmatically.

"We're her bridesmaids," added Vickie.

"We get to wear green velvet gowns with red sashes," Josie put in.

"And the wedding's on Christmas Day," Rosie said with a sigh.

Luke had seen that much in the paper. The rest, he was afraid to ask. He realized they'd all paused, looking at him expectantly, so he said, "And?"

"And you're such a...*cowboy*," Josie said breathlessly, her cheeks turning bright pink.

As if she'd never seen one. "Josie, darlin'," he couldn't help but remind her, "you were born here in Wyoming, so you've seen cowboys."

"Yes, but it looks like you've got some Indian blood, too." Rosie paused, looking mortified. "I mean, Native American—"

"Don't you worry about political correctness." Luke shoved a hand in the back pocket of his jeans, thinking this was no time to discuss politics.

"What Rosie means is that you're so—" Vickie blushed, too. "Well, you know."

Luke was very afraid he did.

"Sexy," Emma Jane continued, sounding particularly grown-up.

Luke wasn't liking the tenor of this conversation one bit, so he held up a staying hand. "Whatever you think I am, girls, please feel free to keep it to yourself. Meantime, what's this line of thinking got to do with me?"

The youngest, Josie, was now too flustered to speak, and Vickie was staring at Luke with eyes the exact dark blue color of Claire's. Because she was college-age, Emma Jane seemed to be the designated spokesperson. She sidled closer, rose on tiptoe, cupped a hand around her mouth and continued in a hushed tone. "See, we bridesmaids need to get Claire a gift," she explained. "And you know how they always have those strippers and such at bachelor parties?"

Luke's eyes widened. "I've—uh—heard that, yeah," he admitted cautiously. "But that's something *guys* used to do, Emma Jane."

She didn't look convinced.

"Used to do," Luke emphasized. "Way in the past."

Josie hadn't heard the whole conversation, but she crossed her arms in dissatisfaction. "We bought you, so you have to do whatever we want."

"Within reason," Luke murmured.

Emma Jane ignored him. "We decided to...*procure* you for Claire because..." The sudden mischievous sparkle in Emma Jane's eyes said she was completely aware he and Claire shared a history. But why would Emma Jane force them to be together now, when Claire had just announced her engagement? Any unfinished business between Luke and Claire was obviously meant to stay that way.

"Yeah, Emma Jane?" Luke prodded, his patience at a minimum. "You procured me because?"

Emma Jane smiled sweetly, leaned closer and very softly whispered, "Because our big sis used to have such a big crush on you, and before her wedding, she deserves a last fling with a dangerous man."

CHAPTER TWO

"I SWEAR, I'M GOING to wring Emma Jane's neck," Claire Buchanan vowed under her breath, her soft husky voice taking the venom out of the threat. "Emma Jane *has* to be the ringleader. Josie, Rosie and Vickie couldn't have come up with this." Only Emma Jane knew Claire had once had feelings for Luke, and Emma Jane was also convinced that Claire's marriage to Clive was going to be a mistake.

"I'm happy about the engagement, sis," Emma Jane had announced loftily yesterday, glancing over the top of a novel with a bare-chested man on the cover. "But I'm not sure you and Clive share enough passion to make it work."

"As if anyone asked your opinion, Emma Jane," Claire had shot back. As far as Emma Jane was concerned, no relationship was worth its salt unless the woman was being continually ravished. Still, all Claire's little sisters were tarred with the same darkly mischievous brush, so naming the key culprit wasn't really the issue. What had the girls been thinking?

We bought you Luke Lydell, they'd said.

"Talk about the gift from hell," Claire whispered on an exasperated sigh, wondering how she could best do damage control. Lifting a hand to push back the damp tendrils of hair that kept escaping her braid and falling onto her forehead, Claire speeded her steps, her long-legged strides bringing her closer to where Luke was waiting for her in the parking grounds, leaning lazily against his motorcycle. *Waiting for me, as if I'm still some little schoolgirl hanging around, wanting his attention.*

If Claire knew what was good for her, she'd let Luke lean his tall, dark, rangy, half-naked body against that fool motorcycle until kingdom come. Or until Christmas, by which time she'd be safely married off to Clive.

Trouble was, after six years of studying art and psychology, Claire still didn't know what was good for her.

Whatever it was, though, it definitely wasn't Luke.

Usually when she felt like this, she'd pause, examine her pique and take ten deep breaths, but just the mention of Luke's name had a way of making her irrational. Ignoring the angry thump of the braid against her back and keeping her furious blue eyes fixed on him, Claire wended around pickup trucks that were pulling from the lot, then passed some cute, rowdy kids who were circling the booths where crafts were being raffled. As she sidestepped an iced-down vat of soft drinks and long-necked beers, the sudden scent of spicey chicken and ribs assaulted her, making her stomach growl, reminding her she was hungry.

"And thank you, global warming," she whispered, wishing sweat wasn't beading on her upper lip. Leave it to fate to have her confronting Luke with dripping armpits. She shoved a hand deeper into the back pocket of her jeans and squinted against the dry clouds of dust stirred by her Justin boots. Her breath suddenly caught, and mortification shot through her. What if Luke thought she'd put her sisters up to this?

Claire quickly assured herself he didn't know she'd once filled notebooks with his name and sketchbooks with drawings of his face, though he damn well knew that their run-ins years ago at the feed store hadn't exactly been accidental. Claire had always gotten Tex's ranch foreman, Ely

Brown, to take her into town with him on Saturdays, since she knew Luke would come with the foreman from Lost Springs.

That was how she'd started talking to him. Not much at first, just enough to realize that Luke knew about more than beef prices and rodeos, and that he happened to share her interest in western art. Just enough that it led to countless stolen kisses, and to longer talks where she'd begun to share her dreams for the future. Just enough that she'd made the girlishly foolish mistake of thinking he wanted a lot more from her than simple conversation.

Now Claire came to a standstill about ten feet away from him. It seemed close enough. Less dangerous. But even from here, all her muscles tensed, and she wound up tossing her head like a prancing mare.

Luke simply stood there, calmly watching her, and Claire suddenly wished she'd worn something other than jeans and a plain white T-shirt. She wished she had more control over her reaction to him, too.

But of course she didn't.

It was hard to say why she was so drawn to him. Just as it was hard to say who he really was or where his folks were from, since he'd been found on the doorstep of the Lost Springs Ranch one Christmas, and no birth record was ever discovered. While the sleek, jaw-length blue-black hair that he tucked behind his ears and his sharply chiseled features announced Native American blood, he had Anglo eyes that were as boldly blue as the cloudless western sky behind him, and he talked like the countless cowboys who'd been his father figures. Already, at thirty, age and the sun's touch were giving Luke a weathered look, making wrinkles form around his eyes and bringing a hard, pragmatic set to a mouth that was usually locked thoughtfully around a toothpick. Claire let her gaze drift over his ropy arms and then his naked torso, which was as smooth as washed stone, made dark and hot by both nature and the sun, and alive with muscle.

Luke *wouldn't* bother wearing a shirt to the auction, Claire thought, feeling a sudden rush of irritation as her eyes dropped to where sun glinted off a rectangular silver belt buckle. Her gaze followed his long legs down to where they were crossed at the ankles, the boot-cut bottoms of his jeans resting easily over new-looking boots. Suddenly, she remembered a time when Luke didn't have such good boots, when they'd been of cracked vinyl, not leather, and dusty and worn down at the heels, and Claire's heart suddenly pulled with an unwanted ache for the little boy he'd once been.

Now his shoulders were strong and broad, his hips lean and narrow, and his stomach flat and dark. His narrowed eyes were a little too hard and watchful, the seemingly lazy pose of his body just a tad too still. *No wonder my sisters bought him.* Her heart pounding, Claire blew out a quick puff of breath, nervously toyed with the engagement ring on her finger and braced herself for the heated annoyance that was bound to mark their encounter. "So, we meet again, Lydell," she forced herself to say.

He nodded. "Hey, Claire."

It had been a good long while since she'd heard Luke's slow, terse cowboy drawl, and something in it made her stomach constrict. Except for a few accidental run-ins, they'd avoided being this physically close for years, and now Claire could swear his eyes held fire, the kind that said he'd thought of her more than he'd ever let on.

She cleared her throat. "Don't worry, Luke, I just hopped over to say I won't be needing your—uh—services." *Hopped.* She'd tried to make it sound as if the long, sweaty trek over here was inconsequential, but she'd only made herself sound ridiculous.

A dark eyebrow lifted. "Do I look worried?"

"No."

His eyes suddenly sparked with devilment. "You *hopped* all the way over here to tell me you're not looking for a man?"

He was right, she realized. She should have gotten into her Jeep and driven home. Maybe she should instruct him to come to the ranch tomorrow to do some chores to fulfill his obligation regarding the auction: she could beg Mama to deal with him. Shoving a hand deeper into the back pocket of her jeans, Claire stared at him for an uncomfortable second. "I didn't say I needed a man, Luke," she assured him. "I *have* a man."

He shrugged as if to remind her that he wasn't responsible for any of this, and somehow, she wished she wasn't quite so aware of how amazingly blue the slivers of his eyes looked against his dark skin. "Well," he said, "those wild little sisters of yours obviously weren't convinced. They think you need a fling with a dangerous Indian."

Her heart hammered, but she wasn't about to let him rile her, nor give in to the urge to close the distance between them. Just what had her fool sisters said? Praying they hadn't really referred to him as a "dangerous Indian," Claire tried not to sound overly concerned. "They said I needed a *what?*"

"You heard. That's why they *procured* me." Luke glanced away and when his eyes seared into hers again, their liquid blue heat ran right through her veins. *"Procured,"* he continued. "I think that's the word Emma Jane used."

"They…" Claire's cheeks suddenly felt boiling hot, and she stared at Luke, taking in his irritating, mildly bemused expression, and how the breeze lifted his fine blue-black hair. "Procured you..."

"Like a stud bull, Claire."

His lips suddenly twitched and, as much as she fought it, Claire almost smiled, herself. Her sisters had said Luke was going to help with some wedding preparations. That was bad enough, but this was worse. "They wanted us to go on a...like a...date?"

Date was definitely better than whatever "stud bull" implied. Still, one look at Luke and Claire's mind started running to hot, musty haylofts and steamy summer nights in the grasslands. Luke wasn't exactly the type to wring his dark, broad, callused hands over midnight curfews imposed by a girl's pa.

That was why Claire had been shocked years ago to find out he cared about western art. Not that he lacked sensitivity. She could see it plainly in his eyes. Eyes she was staring at too intently, she realized. Softening her focus, she barely heard him over the insistent pounding of her heart. He was shaking his head. "Not a date, Claire. They said they were paying for a fling," he continued, his lips still curled in faint bemusement. "There's a difference."

"As if I didn't know." Ignoring the crazy jitters of her insides, Claire shrugged. She wasn't about to allow Luke to rile her passions again, just so he could watch her flounder like a fool. "Well, just consider yourself off the hook."

"Mighty kind of you."

"I'm not *kind*," she tossed back mildly. "I'm engaged."

"So I hear."

He looked as if the news hadn't affected him a bit, and she hated the fact that she wanted it to. Raising her hand, she waved away a buzzing fly more energetically than was necessary. "You could at least say congratulations."

"Congratulations."

Something unexpectedly terse in his tone made her say, "You have a problem with my getting married?"

"None whatsoever. Girls get married."

Girls, she noticed, not women. Now she definitely knew he was trying to goad her. He was thirty, not that much older than she. "I'm twenty-six."

"All grown-up."

"Grown-up enough not to let you take potshots, Luke."

"Sorry," he said, squinting those incredible eyes at her. "But you came barreling over here like you had an ax to grind, Claire."

"Maybe I do."

"Now, don't go having a conniption fit. It's not my fault your sisters bid for me."

She felt more unwanted heat pour into her cheeks. "Well, the way you were parading around, Luke, I guess you were asking for it."

He surveyed her another long moment. "Was I?"

Her heart fluttered as she remembered how good he'd looked flexing his muscles. "Yes," she returned, thinking it was the wrong time to remember they'd been near this spot the last time they'd been together. It was years ago, after another fund-raiser, but even now, Claire could feel both the heat of his kisses and the sting of his rejection. Watching him sober, Claire felt her throat ache with something she couldn't quite name—maybe regret for what she'd once thought they might share, maybe longing.

He said, "Been a while since we've talked, hasn't it?"

Her lips lifted at the corners. "Hmm. And I thought we were just baiting each other."

He chuckled softly.

Suddenly it seemed easier to study her boots than his broad-shouldered, half-naked body, and she toed the dust a second before lifting her gaze again. "Really, Luke... Tex wanted to make a contribution to Lost Springs, and he would have, whether my sisters bought a—a bachelor, or not." Somehow, calling him a bachelor hurt. Wasn't Luke ever lonely, living by himself when he could so easily find a woman to look after him? To love him? Glancing away again, Claire supressed the emotions, taking in the soothing wash of pale summer colors she loved to paint—the cerulean sky, the burnt umber and sienna in the bone-dry arid land. "The way I figure it, Claire," Luke said when she looked at him again, "Tex paid good money for a service so, no matter how we feel about it, we've got no choice but for me to oblige."

The comment was so unexpected that Claire almost burst out laughing. She didn't know what possessed her, but she said, "Whoa. Let me get this straight, Lydell. You're offering stud services?"

He grinned.

Her heart did a three-sixty in her chest and she stared at him, wondering if he was serious, and chastising the part of herself that so desperately wished he was. "What?" she continued, knowing better. "You're seriously saying you want to take me out for a fling?"

Luke was still studying her, and when he spoke, his voice sounded strangely neutral. "Are you *looking* for a fling?"

Years ago that was exactly what she'd wanted from him. Now some perverse streak made her simply say, "Oh, always."

With a mock look of shock, he placed a hand on his bare chest, over his heart. "Thought you were engaged."

"A fling," she repeated. "With my *fiancé*."

His eyes sparked again with humor. "Sure you're not just afraid?"

"Of you? Never."

"Positive?"

"Lydell," she shot back. "I'm not a kid anymore."

The slow way his eyes drifted over her body said he'd noticed. "Is that right?"

Her heart lurched again. For a second, his eyes seemed so intent that she thought he was going to close the distance between them, but he simply turned away. The words were out before she thought them through. "If you insist on doing something for the money, come by the ranch tomorrow. You can do some chores." The missed beat of her heart told her how much she wanted him to come.

"Maybe I will."

That was just like Luke, she thought with a touch of anger. Noncommittal. He always left her dangling.

As he took the T-shirt from the seat of the Harley and tugged it unceremoniously over his head, she watched the play of sunlight on his strong bare back. The shirt was red. Given his fine dark hair, it was a good color for him, not that Claire imagined he paid much attention to his wardrobe. He didn't bother to tuck the shirt in, but threw one of those long, limber legs over the motorcycle the same easy way he'd mount a horse.

It's a wonder you can find the keys, she thought. As she watched him dig them from the front pocket of his sinfully tight faded jeans, Claire allowed herself one final second of blissful longing. If the truth be told, she'd thoroughly enjoyed the performance he'd given on the auction block. Sure, she'd wanted him—what woman wouldn't?—but years ago he'd rejected her, and after that, she'd forced herself to quit dreaming of him. In fact, he hadn't plagued her thoughts for years, and she certainly wouldn't be thinking of him on Christmas, when she married Clive.

So, you did good, girl. He's driving away. Claire sighed again, now with relief. She and Clive were a good match; in fact, he was one of the most desirable men in Lightning Creek. He lacked Luke's undeniable ability to stir her deeper passions, but Clive was even-tempered and good-looking, tall and lanky with dark blond hair and a moustache. Firmly, she told herself Luke was a first crush, nothing more.

But why wasn't he leaving? With her patience now wearing dangerously thin, Claire kept waiting for the familiar roar of the Harley's motor. She knew the sound well. It had grated on her nerves for years, every time Luke brought the bike to town instead of his Jeep. She'd heard its ridiculously loud revving from inside the Roadkill Grill while she was trying to eat lunch, and while she was getting her hair trimmed at Twyla's Tease 'n' Tweeze, and renting videos in the general store.

Sometimes, Claire could swear Luke had bought that motorcycle solely to remind her that they were both still living in Lightning Creek. Fortunately, it worked like a cowbell, and Claire could hear him coming and get out of his way.

Now she thought of Clive and felt a twinge of guilt. But she was mad at him, too. Clive had a mind for only two things—ranching and programming computer software, which was his hobby. Mama said Claire should view his interests as an asset, since Clive was so obviously intent on building the combined fortunes of the Stoddard and Buchanan ranches, but he often broke their plans at the last minute. If Clive had come to the bachelor auction as he'd promised, none of this would have happened.

Luke was straddling the bike and staring at her, his dark

hair and lean body making him look like the consumate warrior, his blue eyes looking even darker now in the sharp summer sun, even from this far away.

"Good seeing you, Luke," she called.

He gunned the motor. "Sure you don't want to take a ride?"

"And where would you be taking me?"

"Around the block."

She knew that was a lie. Nevertheless, reason fled and she unexpectedly found herself walking toward him with a slow, rolling stride, as if going to him were as natural as breathing. Resting a hand on his shoulder for balance, she felt the hot summer sun and the quiver of muscle beneath his shirt, and then she simply, wordlessly slid behind him on the seat, hugging his thighs with hers.

A second later, he gunned the motor again, and it roared through her blood. Just as the breeze lifted his shirt, her arms circled around his waist, and her hands landed where they'd secretly wanted to be—on his bare skin.

LEANING BACK IN A BOOTH in the diner, Luke watched her eat. He'd known better, but he'd ridden like hell for leather, with the Harley's wheels eating up the highway. He hadn't bothered to wonder what in blazes had gotten into him; he'd just ridden into the setting western sun like some wild outlaw, with Claire hugging his waist. He'd imagined loving her from now until Christmas morning— so thoroughly that she'd no longer want to marry Clive Stoddard. But that was just a crazy impulse, one Luke would never heed. When he'd felt Claire relax against his back, he'd known he'd ridden long enough, and that whatever flinty energy lay between them had finally spent itself on the open road.

Of course by then they'd gone all the way to Casper.

They'd been taking it easy ever since, shooting the breeze instead of eyeing each other like frisky horses in springtime. He took a toothpick from a dispenser and chewed on it, staring through a plate-glass window, into the deepening orange twilight until the rattle and clank of the crowded diner drew his attention back inside.

"Meg Ryan," Claire was saying. She was wedged into the corner of an orange booth opposite him, and she was digging into a plate that could easily satisfy three hungry ranch hands. Luke glanced over the fried potatoes and eggs, which she'd doused in ketchup, the stack of flapjacks, which were drowning in blackstrap molasses, and the strip of steak, which she'd brushed with A.1 sauce, using the back of her spoon.

"Did you get enough to eat?" she asked, catching his eye.

He nodded, thoughtfully rolling the toothpick over his tongue. Somehow, the ice had broken, and they were talking to each other like two human beings. They hadn't done it in years. "You always this easy to get along with when there's a heapin' plate of grub in front of you?"

Claire merely lifted a biscuit, swiped it with butter and stared back pointedly. "Meg Ryan," she repeated.

Luke had no idea what she was talking about, but he was beginning to realize that dinner conversation with Claire Buchanan wasn't necessarily linear. "You mean the one in the movies?" Luke thought he'd seen her in something at the Isis Theater in Lightning Creek.

Brushing stray wisps of hair from her forehead with the back of her hand, Claire made a small sound of irritation. "In the bachelor auction brochure, you said you thought the perfect woman was cute, sexy and smart."

If he didn't know Claire was marrying Clive, Luke would have thought she sounded jealous. "I did?"

She nodded, licking molasses off her fork without a touch of guile. "Yeah."

Changing his mind about the toothpick, Luke took it from his mouth and tossed it onto his plate. As he stretched his long legs under the table, still trying to get the road kinks out of them, he pushed the plate aside and squinted, trying to remember. Then it came to him. "Lindsay and Rex made that up. They needed bio materials for the brochure, and I couldn't think of anybody."

Claire's plump lips parted to release a low, throaty laugh. "You don't know who you think is sexy?"

He shrugged. "Not that Meg Ryan woman. She's too cute. I don't go for cute." No, he happened to go for exotic, long-limbed beauties he could never have, like Claire.

"No?"

"Nope."

He glanced away, thinking she really had no idea what she did to him. He loved everything about her—her husky voice, her swollen mouth, her face that belonged on Paris runways instead of on a cattle ranch in Lightning Creek, Wyoming. He loved the serious, smoldering fire in her eyes, how fast she got riled up…and how much she hated herself for losing her temper. As far as Luke knew, she never understood how kind she really was, since she'd never once had a real run-in with truly mean human nature. *The kind of human nature that leaves a baby boy on the snowy steps of a ranch house on Christmas morning.* Given that Claire was getting married this Christmas, Luke suddenly realized that would make the holiday doubly bad for him from now on.

Still looking at her, studying the damp-looking wind-blown tendrils that were curling against her high, flushed cheekbones, Luke wished that once—just once—he'd seen her hair out of that braid and down around her shoulders. And then his chest felt tight because he was remembering riding here with her hugging his waist.

"So, do you like Van Morrison and drive a Jeep Cherokee? The brochure said you did."

You know I do. He nodded. "Yeah, Claire."

She fell silent again. If she noticed him watching her finish her meal, she didn't show it. He decided he liked her lack of pretension, too. She was, by turns, both funny and serious, and she didn't bother with makeup, jewelry or fancy clothes, not that she needed to when she looked so good in a man's white undershirt and jeans. She had both undergraduate and graduate degrees in art and psychology, too, but she'd never started acting like a big-shot. No, she had too much sensitivity to wear smarts and education on her sleeve in a place where so many people weren't nearly as fortunate. It was hard to believe her pretty, long fingers painted work that was sold in countless art galleries and crafts shops in Wyoming. Or that those perceptive eyes saw a world all their own.

But they did. Luke thought again of the haunting painting of Lost Springs that hung in his living room, and of how lonely that boy looked, silhouetted against the fiery sky. "How'd your raffles go?" he suddenly asked.

"They were nice." She was now polishing off a healthy wedge of apple pie. "Twyla and I made twice as much as I thought we would, but not nearly what you guys got from the auction. You should be proud of yourselves. You pulled Lost Springs out of the hole." She glanced away, her eyebrows furrowed with concern. "So many ranches are having trouble lately, though. I've heard it's really rough on some of the smaller places." Carelessly, she swiped a napkin across her mouth. "Anyway, you did good."

"Think so?"

Her eyes met his. "Without a doubt, Luke."

The comment made him feel so good that he was half inclined to tell her about the other charitable work he did, including opening Santa mail and delivering gifts to the boys at Lost Springs at Christmas. Years ago, when some of the other guys who'd been at the auction today realized what Luke doing, they'd begun sending checks to help purchase the gifts. Not that Claire would believe Luke delivered them. Nobody in Lightning Creek had ever guessed the identity of the secret Santa.

Claire started chatting about Lost Springs, talking about the boys she was counseling there part-time, many of whom he knew. "I keep thinking about Brady Spencer. He's so cute that I've sometimes wished I could adopt him myself. But right now, I'm a little worried about him," Claire said as the waitress picked up the money Luke left on the check.

Glancing after the waitress, he said, "'Bout ready?"

Claire nodded, sliding from the booth. As Luke watched her, he fought the feeling that she was sliding right out of his life, and he suddenly remembered the ease of their encounters years ago, during the summer they'd shared. Another sudden urge to claim her welled within him, but he knew they couldn't go back in time. Besides, he could never offer her the kind of life she was going to share with Clive.

Following her, Luke nodded on the way to the door. "Yeah, Brady's got some problems," he agreed, picking up on their conversation. Last year the five-year-old sent a letter asking for Santa to find the parents who'd abandoned him. Luke had pulled out all the stops, using his law enforcement skills to see if he could, but he still had no leads. "But I wouldn't worry too much," Luke continued as he held the door open for Claire. "When a kid's heart's broken there's not much anybody can do. Even if it doesn't always seem like it, those boys appreciate your contributions at the ranch, Claire."

She offered a shrug as they stepped into the soft summer night, a teasing light coming into her eyes. "How do you know what I do at Lost Springs, anyway?"

"I've got a cabin on the place."

"Oh, right. I forgot."

He knew she hadn't. He got the impression she was pretending to know less about him than she did, so she wouldn't seem too interested, though he didn't know why, since she was engaged. "They like having someone looking after the south border of the property." And Luke liked being there. The Lost Springs land was the closest thing he figured he'd ever have to a birthright.

"What?" Claire smiled. "You keep out the riffraff?"

"I don't know about that," he returned, shooting her a wry smile. "It's mostly bears and coyotes."

Pausing with Claire a second on the sidewalk, Luke silently watched the last traces of twilight vanish on the horizon. The moon was a glowing white crescent, the stars bright, their constellations scattered across the black sky. No one was outside. Without the air-conditioning and the clatter from inside the diner, the night seemed hotter, darker and more still. Fireflies and crickets buzzed and chirped.

"Hot out here," Luke commented.

"July'll be worse," Claire said agreeably.

"C'mon." He shouldn't have, but Luke leaned toward her, anyway, suddenly threading his fingers through hers. If she found anything unusual in the touch, she didn't let on as they headed around the side of the diner, where he'd parked. As they walked, she talked about how hard it was to make use of her psychology degrees in Lightning Creek. One day a week, she was working at a Planned Parenthood clinic in Casper; on another, she was doing crafts with kindergarten kids. The rest of the time she painted. "Anyway, the point is that I'm lucky to get to counsel those boys and to do some art therapy at Lost Springs."

Coming to a standstill beside the bike, Luke let her hand drop and said, "Why didn't you ever leave town, Claire?" He'd always thought she would. She'd gone to a girls school, had opportunities and could have worked anywhere.

As she glanced toward the back door of the diner, he studied her face, which was almost lost in the night's shadows. "Lightning Creek's home," she said simply. "How about you? Miss being a state cop?"

He considered a minute. He knew he should get on the bike and get them both out of this dark, quiet alley. With her this close, his mind kept running to forbidden subjects, such as the delicious curves of her mouth. Through the diner's open back door, he could smell the scents of spiced ham and hear the sizzle of steaks frying. Voices chattered from inside the diner and around the corner, but they seemed far away, serving only to wrap him and Claire in their own world.

"Luke?"

He realized he was merely watching her and shook his head. "No, I don't miss it much."

He didn't want to, but when her voice softened, he heard desire and promise in it. "But you got a law enforcement degree at University of Wyoming, right?"

His mouth quirked. "Sitting out on the interstate drinking coffee, talking on a CB and waiting for someone to break the speed limit didn't turn out to be as exciting as I'd hoped."

"Are you still trying to work as a P.I.? That's exciting."

She sure knew a lot about him, but then Lightning Creek was a small town. Word got around. "Not in Lightning Creek."

She chuckled. "No need there. Everybody already knows everybody's business. Especially if you get haircuts at Twyla's."

He nodded appreciation. "It's definitely a one-horse town. But I take cases whenever I can get them. Lately, I'm mostly herding cattle up on Cross Creek." His smile deepened. "Who knows? Maybe more people'll start getting divorced over here in Casper and need me to work surveillance."

"That's the trouble with you, Luke." Claire chuckled impishly. "You need to think big."

"Big?"

She nodded. "Sure. Maybe the folks in Casper'll start murdering one another. You'd really get some good cases then."

He laughed. "Watch it, Claire," he warned. "Old age'll make you cynical."

"I'll take that under advisement."

He listened to her laughter rise and fade, melting into the muted stirrings of the Wyoming night. Over some grassy hills, he saw shadows moving in the darkness, and close by insects buzzed. When his eyes returned to hers, they locked and held—and he unexpectedly felt the full heat of the night. His voice turned husky. "Murder, huh?" he said again. "What a wicked mind you've got, Claire."

Her eyes held his. "You have no idea how wicked."

She was so pretty that he had to fight to calm the sudden swift beats of his heart. Especially when she simply stepped closer, her hand gliding onto his chest.

Your mind might be wicked, Claire. But not as wicked

as mine right now. "Claire," he warned gently, noticing how their bare arms touched, so alive with warmth. *She needs a fling with a dangerous man,* Emma Jane had said.

Now, as Claire's imploring blue eyes fixed on his, Luke wondered if Emma Jane hadn't been right. *I'm not dangerous,* he'd defended a few hours ago. *Oh, I know,* Emma Jane had returned. *But we're paying you to act dangerous.* Right about now, Luke defintely wanted to.

Claire's voice was as soft as the night. "It's been such a long time since we've talked like this, Luke."

And with reason. Claire was one woman he never intended to get involved with. Releasing a faintly exasperated sigh, he cupped her chin. He meant to let go, he really did, but instead he rubbed a rough, work-callused thumb across her swollen-looking lips until they parted. Without even thinking, he dropped the thumb inside, and as he probed the slick, silken warmth of her inner cheek, heat shot to his groin.

The unmistakable desire in her eyes told him she was no longer a young filly. She was fully grown. As he withdrew his thumb, her lips closed over the tip of it in what might have been a kiss. "Luke," she said, a faint, nervous tremor in her voice. "We'd better go, or else…"

His eyes bore into hers. "Or else…" He knew exactly what would happen. They both did.

"We'd better go," she repeated.

"Not before I kiss you once," he found himself whispering. "Just once, Claire." And then his mouth lowered, crushing down and completely capturing hers, his tongue reaching deep. Her hands rose on his chest while his found her waist, and he lengthened the searing kiss he knew they shouldn't share. Her body and tongue melted against him, hot as candle wax. Long, slender legs he well remembered pressured his, and her female heat was worrying his groin.

Whatever warmth had been in the night was now in his blood, whatever kindness in their talk was now tugging at his heart. With every movement of his mouth on hers, his body turned hotter and heavier with need. Only when his control was threatened and he feared he'd take things to the next level, did he force himself to lean back and survey her in the dark. Her blue eyes had turned violet and so vulnerable that guilt flooded him because he knew he was about to hurt her. His voice was deep, roughened by desire. "Come Christmas, you're getting married, Claire."

Her soft, moist mouth slackened. "Why didn't you—" She paused. "Why didn't you want me, Luke? All those years ago…"

He knew it was difficult for her to ask, but he had no business rehashing the past, especially if his intentions weren't serious. "I just…" *Didn't.* It was a lie, but Luke let the word hang in the air.

She looked torn between losing her pride and pursuing the matter. "So, tonight you kissed me because of the bachelor auction, huh?" she ventured coolly. "Because you were *paid?*"

He caught her wrist before she could step back, and the pulse he felt beating rapidly beneath his fingers further fueled his desire. "You know better than that," he said, the words gentle despite the emotions that were threatening to run away like wild horses. "I kissed you for the same reason you kissed me, Claire. Because I wanted to. But you're marrying Clive."

"You hardly have to tell me that," she assured him, looking upset about what they'd just done.

Luke forced himself to let go of her wrist. "And it makes what just happened between us our kiss goodbye." Still tasting her mouth, he felt the pull of her lips as surely as the pull of his need for her love, but he turned away and busied himself with the helmets. Helping her with hers, he pulled the strap tight and then he put on his own. Claire didn't say anything, just watched him mutely with disbelieving, questioning eyes that could have broken his heart if he'd let them.

And then she slid behind him on the seat again.

God only knew what she was thinking. Probably what he was—that it was better to ignore the unaccountable lust between them. On the highway, the night seemed cooler. Luke squinted against the wind, and he felt it blow the fine shafts of hair that hung from under his helmet. He felt other things, too—Claire's hands on his belly, her small breasts pressed against his back. His heart ached when he felt dampness through his shirt, against his shoulder. It made him want to pull to the side of the road and love her exactly how she'd asked him to all those years ago.

Instead, he leaned farther over the handlebars, into the wind, and he tried to tell himself that the dampness he felt wasn't really tears.

"GET," LUKE GROWLED much later. "Just get on out of here." Leaning against his motorcycle for leverage, he tossed a stick toward the shadows moving across the empty, unlit parking grounds at the Lost Springs Ranch. Some wild dogs were out there, Luke guessed. Maybe coyotes. They were probably scavaging leftovers from the food booths. Tomorrow the boys from Lost Springs would come out and pick up the stray pop cans and candy wrappers.

Deciding to ignore the dogs, Luke stared unseeing into the darkness where Claire had vanished. Well, one thing was certain. Luke definitely wasn't showing up at the Buchanans' ranch tomorrow to earn the money Tex was giving to Lost Springs. Luke figured Claire would come up with some story about how she'd made use of him. He sighed again. By the time he'd pulled the bike near her Jeep Wrangler, her helmet was already off. She'd dropped it and simply fled.

Now he felt sick. He was no fool. He understood what was between him and Claire, same as she did. Probably better. It was raw chemistry. It was a man-woman attraction of a sort that would never go away. But why couldn't Claire ever think it through?

Luke thought back to years ago, when she'd asked him to make love to her here, in a secluded wooded spot just off the parking grounds. There had been another fundraiser that day, and along with the Fremonts, some of the wealthiest folks in town had raised college scholarship money for the Lost Springs boys.

Late that afternoon, after Luke was told he'd be one of the recipients who'd attend UW, Claire had found him out here. She'd said she wanted a goodbye kiss since she was leaving for school in Cheyenne, and he'd obliged, walking into the woods with her, as they had many times. At first, they'd sat side by side on a fallen log, just talking, which was nothing unusual. All summer, she'd been turning up at the feed store on Saturdays, and he'd more than noticed her. In fact, he'd spent most Friday nights reading about western art just to impress her, but he'd never thought she could have real feelings for him, not even after their relationship had become more physical. No, Claire had always hung around with the sons of the big ranchers, guys like Clive Stoddard who'd someday stand to inherit land around Lightning Creek.

Because of that, Luke half suspected she was toying with him all summer, but he'd wanted her, and that day, while they were kissing in the woods, he'd touched and kissed her breasts, then slid a hand under her dress, inside her panties and between her legs. Even now, he could remember the nerve-racking desire he'd felt as she shivered beneath his touch, climbing toward release. But he'd never expected her to touch him, too, gliding those slender-fingered hands to his crotch, suddenly cupping him and asking him to please make love to her, right then and there. Overwhelming passion had blindsided him. All his life, he'd felt sure love wasn't in the cards for him, since no loved child was ever abandoned on a doorstep. Claire's words had filled him not just with hope, but with paralyzing fear. What did Luke—an abandoned kid from Lost Springs—know about love? What did he have to give her?

He'd pulled away too swiftly, and in the next heartbeat, Claire had taken his confused vulnerability as rejection and run from the woods, fixing her bra and buttoning her dress as she fled.

Luke had stood there in the woods a minute, feeling as flustered and immeasurably aroused, trying to figure out what had happened.

And then he'd come to his senses and chased after her, only to find himself staring at the tailfins of an antique shiny black Cadillac that Tex Buchanan sometimes drove into town. Luke had stopped breathlessly, his side aching from running so hard, the dust he'd stirred rising into his eyes, and he'd contemplated the fact that shiny cars would always come for girls like Claire Buchanan. Maybe it was better, easier, to simply accept the fact that she was a rich rancher's daughter, and that he was a scholarship boy, a kid from Lost Springs whom they'd been kind enough to help. Sure, she'd been trying to take things to the next step, but that meant pursuing a relationship that would only seriously limit her options in life.

Luke had turned and walked back down the road.

Now, just like then, Luke knew he was doing the right

thing. Gazing up at the moon and the stars, feeling the sultry heat of the night buffet against him, he uttered a soft "damn," then he glanced toward the tree line, where the wild dogs prowled. In a strange way, he felt just like one of those dogs. Rootless and running in the shadows, never in the center of things but always on the outskirts. Once more, he remembered Claire's painting of Lost Springs, how lonely that boy had looked as he tried to touch the sky.

The image was humbling. That day in the woods, Claire had seemed just as unattainable as tonight's moon, love as unreachable as the stars. Now Luke figured that's what happened once a baby was left on a doorstep. He grew into a man who avoided love. How could it be otherwise? Luke had a fierce love of the land, but no piece of ground to call his own, and he had Indian blood, but he didn't even know the name of his tribe. How could a man love a woman when he didn't even know what kind of blood ran in his veins?

Claire didn't understand it yet, but she deserved things Luke could never give her—everything she was going to get come Christmas. Money, land and status. One day, maybe she'd even thank him.

Clive Stoddard was a respected rancher. Soon he'd come into his mighty impressive birthright, since his pa, Evander, was ailing. In addition to being an heir to the Lazy Four, Clive was one of the best cowboys around, too. Because Luke had no doubt Clive would merge his family's ranch with the adjacent Buchanan lands, Luke figured it was only a matter of time until Claire Buchanan Stoddard looked around and saw the bounty before her. Somewhere down the pike, she'd take in the cattle grazing in the grasslands, happily write her children's names in a family Bible that belonged to a man who had a history, and she'd appreciate her husband's wherewithal to build their joint fortunes.

By Christmas, Claire would figure out that things were better this way. She'd be glad Luke hadn't loved her back.

CHAPTER THREE

CLAIRE GLANCED NERVOUSLY around the shopping mall in Casper. It had been months since she'd seen Luke, and now as her gaze settled on Santa, she was doubting the wisdom of coming here looking for him. Her eyes drifted from where the fur ball of Santa's pointed cap rested against his broad chest, and then down the velvet suit to his knee-high black boots, but she still couldn't put her finger on why the man seemed so familiar.

Rereading the sign announcing that Santa was about to take his scheduled lunch break, she skated her fingers over a red velvet queue rope. Beside her, an old codger dressed as an elf was shooing kids past a photographer and toward a white platform decorated with ice-capped papier-mâché mountains and pathways leading to Santa's throne. After each kid was done talking to Santa, a second elf handed out a photo, which was laminated and attached to a key ring.

"About time," Claire suddenly whispered when a twangy voice flowed through the loudspeakers, over the piped-in chorus of "The Little Drummer Boy." "Luke Lydell," said the voice, "could you please meet your party near the North Pole?"

Maybe I shouldn't have paged him, Claire thought. Just hearing his name made her want to turn tail and head back home to the Stop Awhile, but she desperately needed a seasoned ex-cop now, didn't she? She simply didn't have a choice, did she?

"Darn right, I don't," Claire murmured. Right before he'd vanished, Clive had all but called off their wedding, and now Claire needed Luke to help her find him. Oh, Luke acted humble about it, but he reviewed cases for law enforcement agencies, and everybody in Lightning Creek knew that in addition to herding cattle, he'd helped solve murders in both Newcastle and Yellowstone.

"A reg'lar saddled-up detective," Ely Brown out at the Stop Awhile had called him. "Git it? Like an armchair detective, Claire, but differ'nt."

"I get it, Ely," Claire had assured him.

Not that Claire intended to share all the particulars of Clive's disappearance with Luke, she thought, her face coloring. She'd sooner die than let Luke know that Clive might be rejecting her. At the thought, everything inside her suddenly turned watery and her knees weakened with distress. She knew it was pure foolishness, but Claire couldn't help but wonder if there wasn't something wrong with her…something that made men leave.

Slipping from a too-warm parka, she tugged the braid from beneath her collar and glanced toward the doors. Outside, high winds were blowing snow from drifts, making white clouds of mist roll across the parking lot like tumbleweed in a ghost town. She'd just about frozen stiff out there; the flannel-lined denim shirt she'd pulled on over her jeans and turtleneck should have kept her warm enough, but while the Jeep was great for hauling art supplies, it wasn't exactly the best insulated vehicle on the road and air had seeped through the cracks.

"Where are you, Luke," she whispered, her hands still worrying the rope. Earlier today, while she'd been working in her attic studio at the ranch, the idea of soliciting Luke's help had come to her in a flash of inspiration, and she'd charged off half-cocked. She just wished they'd spoken since the bachelor auction last summer, but he'd never shown up at the ranch to work for the money Tex donated to Lost Springs, and Claire hadn't run into him in town. Not that she'd been looking. She'd been an engaged woman, after all. Now, of course, she wasn't so sure about her status.

As she kept watching the crowd, she could only hope Luke had forgotten how she'd flung herself at him after the auction. It wasn't a big deal, anyway. They'd just kissed, and everybody knew kisses came twelve to a dozen.

"Luke Lydell," the voice came again. "Your party's waiting at the North Pole."

His *party.* As if she and Luke were about to have their own private hootenanny. Claire glanced toward Hills Department store, then down the brightly lit corridor leading toward a Christmas tree and food court. Still no Luke. Suddenly getting the strangest feeling that someone was watching her, she darted her eyes to Santa, but he was occupied lifting a little girl onto his lap.

Glancing away, Claire took in the window displays— the red bows on the spurs and saddles in a tack shop, and the fancy hand-tooled Tony Llama boots brimming with stocking stuffers, then she searched the crowd once more, gazing into the tired but happy faces of ranch folks, some of whom had probably driven hours to do last-minute shopping. After a moment, her eyes settled on a cowboy. Seemingly immune to the harsh winter weather, he wore only a plaid flannel shirt and denim vest, and his work-stained gloves were still stuffed into the back pocket of his Levi's.

"Pa!" squealed his daughter, a grade-school girl in pink

bib overalls who flew past Claire, pigtails flying. "Do we git to see Santa now? Can we git my picher lam'nated and give Mama a key ring for Chris'mis?"

The man's leathery face cracked into a smile. His daughter was obviously the apple of his eye, and his dark, watchful eyes that had seen too much of the world suddenly sparkled like black diamonds. "Yes, indeed, darlin'."

As the girl ran toward the long line of kids waiting for Santa, Claire felt a wave of emotion. She'd never forget the long, harsh winters she'd spent on the Stop Awhile when she was a little girl, nor the pent-up excitement brought on by bouts of cabin fever, nor how, every Christmas, Tex and Mama had brought her and her sisters to this mall to see Santa. Back then, Claire couldn't imagine any city in the world bigger than Casper, Wyoming, and the mall, with its sparkling lights, decorations and toys had been pure magic.

She squinted. She could swear Santa had been watching her again, but now he was attending to the boy climbing onto his knees. The boy was wearing a red-checkered shirt, black slacks and a western-style hat, and the toy holster slung around his waist came complete with two six-shooters. Claire frowned. Given his age and white-blond hair, the boy reminded her of Brady Spencer at the Lost Springs ranch. Because Brady started school this year, he was coming to a better understanding about why he was at Lost Springs, and he'd become fixated on finding the folks who'd abandoned him. Claire had been doing everything she could to help him. So had Luke, judging by how much Brady talked about him. Now the boy with Santa began talking excitedly, and Claire slipped the camera she always carried from her parka pocket.

"Mr. Lydell" came the third and final page as she began

taking snapshots, "your party is waiting near the North Pole."

Luke *would* wait until two days before Christmas to do his shopping, Claire thought, feeling a sudden rush of pique, and wondering where he was. The guys in the Cross Creek bunkhouse had sworn he was here. As much as she didn't want to admit it, it was entirely Luke's fault that her own shopping had been finished by August. After seeing him last summer, she'd flung herself into countless activities—Christmas shopping and planning her wedding among them. She'd helped open a hotline for abused women in Casper, too, then she had taken two weeks off from her counseling jobs to drive across the state, taking photographs.

She'd gotten good ones, too, especially of a powwow at a Cheyenne reservation, and of some fly fishers upstate. Now she was all but hiding out in the four-room attic of the ranch house, which contained her studio. Mornings, she'd drive to counseling jobs, and then she'd paint in the afternoons, using the photographs. Some days she braved the cold, sketching the ranch hands as they cut calves from the herd and weaned them, preparing them for the feed lots.

If not for the troubles with Clive, it would have been a wonderful Christmas. The Stop Awhile, so called because it had once been a stagecoach stop, was something to behold, since Tex prided himself on decorating with more lights than anybody else in Wyoming. Fires blazed in a stone fireplace near a ten-foot decorated pine, and scents of Mama's baking sweetened the air. "Why don't you take it easy before the wedding?" people kept asking. "Why not enjoy the last Christmas before you get hitched!"

Because the wedding might be canceled.

As far as everybody else was concerned, it was all over

except for the shouting. Just days from now, on Saturday, in the Methodist church off Shoshone Highway, she'd marry Clive, wearing a white velvet dress her mama had made. Her sisters were to wear emerald green gowns with red sashes, and a musical trio from Laramie was performing. In order to make Christmas week less hectic, they'd already held the rehearsal dinner.

After the wedding, the Buchanans planned to host an old-fashioned hoe-down in the Stop Awhile's brand-new hay barn. Both Tex and Mama had begged her to hold a formal reception, but Claire had been adamant, and Clive agreed. By Christmas night, everybody would want to relax, and this would be a party to remember, where folks could be themselves, wear regular clothes and even join in with the band if they happened to bring a fiddle, blues harp, washboard or saw. People from all around Lightning Creek were supposed to come.

Claire hadn't been able to force herself to send Luke an invitation, even though she knew Clive had invited hands from Cross Creek. How could she? she thought, when regardless of what Luke professed, he cared for her. Not that the invitation mattered now. Her throat tightened as she recalled her and Clive's explosive fight. Well, she wasn't about to break the news to her folks until she'd spoken with Clive again, this time more rationally. Maybe things would work out....

Watching the little girl in pink overalls hop onto Santa's lap, Claire's throat got tighter still. The girl's craggy-faced father watched with proud, shiny eyes that pulled at Claire's heart.

There was nothing like seeing a proud cowboy.

Or wanting a child of your own, Claire thought, envying the man. Claire wanted babies so badly. Driving over here, she kept traitorously thinking that those babies should be hers and Luke's. Of course, she told herself, that was only because she was angry with Clive, and because Luke had once been her fantasy man. Moments later, as the girl jumped down, the elves began cleaning the photo station, preparing for their break.

"What about you, lil' gal?"

"Me?" Repocketing her camera and wondering if she should give up on Luke, Claire glanced at the old wizened elf.

He winked. "You been here for a spell, eyeing Mr. Claus. Ain't every day you can git your picture taken with Santa."

Claire smiled despite the various emotions coursing through her. Had Luke answered the page, seen her and simply walked the other way?

"How's about it, ma'am?" the elf prompted.

She forced a chuckle. "You convinced me."

The elf jerked his head toward the throne. "Go on," he said. "Git. We're about to go on break, but that other elf'll take a picture and make your laminated key chain."

As Claire headed up the stairs to Santa's throne, she decided Tex would love a key chain with her and Santa striking a pose. Only after she'd decided to slip it into his stocking did she realize she hadn't even thought to give the key chain to Clive.

If I find him.

Claire managed a smile as Santa waved her onto his lap, but as she seated herself, she felt oddly unsettled. She'd felt a jolt of…what? *Electricity. Awareness. Desire.* But for *Santa Claus?* She couldn't so much as feel the man's body since it was liberally padded beneath the red suit, and when her eyes darted to his face, she saw little but a fluffy white beard and thick mustache.

His voice was low. "What's your pleasure, ma'am?"

Claire's heart stuttered. For a second, she could swear she was staring into Luke's eyes, but then, a lot of people—Santa Clauses included—had blue eyes. "Pleasure?" she managed to say.

"What would you like for Christmas?"

Smiling for the elf with the camera, Claire said the first thing that came to her mind. "To find Luke Lydell."

She didn't know what happened next. Suddenly, the whole mall seemed to spin upside down.

"My pocketbook!" A woman shouted.

"Git that ornery varmint!" the old elf yelled.

"There he goes!" added the elf photographer.

Santa had already risen to his feet. Tumbling off his knee, Claire landed unceremoniously on the floor, smack on her butt on her parka. From there, she watched in stunned fascination as Santa gave chase, grabbing a teenage boy who turned out to be the purse snatcher. A second later, a mall security guard took over, marching away with the boy.

To a round of adult applause and delighted squeals from young fans, Santa turned around and headed back to the throne, stopping only to lift Claire's key chain from the photo station. Reaching her, he stretched down a long red-velvet-clad arm. Just as her fingers closed around a dark, strong hand that was covered with calluses, Santa yanked, hauling her to her feet. Since the white fur ball of his long pointed cap was resting against his chest, and since Claire had bounced against him, the fur ball teased her nose. She sneezed.

"What?" he teased. "You have an allergy to Santa?"

Those blue eyes were only inches away. Her heart missed a beat. "Luke?" she ventured, keeping her voice low so the kids wouldn't hear.

"Heard you were looking for me, Claire," he returned. "So, I guess you just got your Christmas wish."

IN A BACK ROOM AT HILLS, Luke swiped off the Santa hat and tossed it atop a box containing bulbs, tinsel and wrapping paper, then he started unbuttoning the red velvet jacket. If Claire insisted on watching him undress, it was fine with him, but he wasn't going to stand around here, feeling like a fool, decked out in a Santa suit. Casting a glance toward where his jeans and plaid flannel shirt were folded, Luke shrugged out of the jacket, then a padded vest.

"You have to take the case."

Claire's soft, persuasive voice was barely audible over the nearby sound of shoppers and piped-in Christmas music, but Luke figured he'd be hearing it when she realized she wasn't getting her way. Stepping over a string of lights on the floor, he blew out an exasperated sigh. "There *is* no case, Claire."

"But Clive's disappeared."

Luke didn't buy it. "You said you saw him yesterday."

"He's disappeared *since* then."

Claire had already filled Luke in, scant though the details were, and now he bit back a groan of annoyance. If Claire really thought Clive was missing, she would have called the cops. What was plain as a pikestaff was that Claire wasn't going to leave Luke alone. Ever. When he was younger, Luke had hung on to bucking broncs until he felt his brains loosen inside his skull, but nothing had ever shaken him the way Claire did. He guessed having her get married on Christmas would have been way too easy.

"Darlin'," he said, "you shouldn't have come here." *Not after the way we kissed last summer.*

For an uncomfortable second their eyes met, and Luke became aware they were stuck in a room no bigger than a horse stall. Even worse, they were surrounded by boxes of Christmas decorations, and Christmas wasn't exactly Luke's favorite time of the year.

"I had no choice," Claire assured him.

He scrutinized her. A black turtleneck hugged the slender curve of her neck, and against the dark cotton, her poreless skin looked doubly pale. Either winter or the weak light of the room made her eyes look lighter, too, like blue ice. Realizing his gaze had remained on the soft pout of her cranberry mouth a second too long, Luke came to his senses and nodded toward the door. "Claire," he continued, "if I were you, I'd step outside." He really couldn't believe this. If nothing else, the way they'd parted last summer should have stopped her from coming here.

She didn't budge. Whatever he did, Luke reminded himself, it was for her benefit. Come Christmas, she'd be hitched to one of the richest, most upstanding cowboys in Lightning Creek. Luke frowned. Unless Clive really had disappeared. Feeling angry with himself for letting her arouse his interest, Luke wordlessly rested a hand on the zipper of the velvet pants.

Claire eyes widened. "Oh, you mean I should step outside because—"

When he started pulling down the zipper, she did exactly what he expected—bolted like a startled mare. The next time she spoke, it was through the half-open door. "But I need help," she said, her voice sounding inexplicably tremulous, not that wheedling would work on Luke. "And you owe me."

His lips parted in astonishment. "I what?"

"Owe me. You were supposed to stop by the ranch last

summer and do some chores in return for Tex's contribution to Lost Springs.''

She knew damn well why he hadn't shown up. "We never had any real agreement, Claire."

"Tex made his contribution," she reminded him firmly. "He held up his end of the bargain."

"And you're going to collect mine six months later?"

"Better late than never."

Stepping out of the black boots and velvet pants, Luke grabbed his Levi's and put them on. Then he shoved his feet into some old Justins he'd worn because salt had already marred the leather. It was snowing today, and he didn't want to mess up his Tony Llamas.

Through the door, Claire said, "Your pants are on, right? I heard the zipper again."

Woman, you must have ears like a bat. "What have you got?" Luke shot back. "Zipper sonar? I'm still dressing."

Two steps of her long, jeans-clad legs brought her back inside the room. "You look dressed to me."

Steadfastly ignoring the startled, half-dreamy gaze now aimed at his bare chest, Luke stretched a long arm past her and snatched the flannel shirt. Shrugging into it, he slowly buttoned and tucked it in. Claire had quit talking and was merely watching him.

His eyes caught hers. "Quit staring."

"I'm not staring."

But she was. Grabbing his Stetson, Luke ran a habitual finger over the black brim, then eyed a waist-length shearling jacket he'd left hanging on the doorknob. He sighed. "Look here, Claire. I'm sure Clive's—"

"Gone," she ventured again. "And something could have happened to him."

The soft catch in her voice wasn't lost on Luke, and his gaze sharpened as it traced over the diamond on her finger.

"Happened? What aren't you telling me?" Was Claire's fiancé really in some kind of trouble?

Claire looked wounded. "I'm not witholding information," she declared.

"As if this is a federal case," Luke muttered. Shrugging, he situated the Stetson on his head, working it back and forth to ensure the high winds outside wouldn't blow it off. "'Bout ready?" he asked, nodding toward where she was blocking the door. "I'm aiming to leave, Claire."

"You can't."

Wrong, darlin'. He had to get out of here, even if it meant moving Claire's sweet little butt himself. After all, he was beginning to suspect he knew the real reason Claire was here. *Just lay it on the line.* "Claire," he said, thoughtfully chewing the inside of his cheek. "I know you're getting married on Christmas, and it's natural if you're getting nervous. Maybe you're thinking about that summer we got to know each other, or about last June, after the bachelor auction. Maybe you're wondering about us. Maybe—"

"Maybe you're crazy, Luke!" One of her hands, the one with the engagement ring, unwrapped from the parka and landed on her hip. "What makes you think...?"

That you still want me? Luke eyed her a long moment. *This.* How the tiny room pulsed with the attraction, and how often he'd pushed her away without her taking the hint. Feeling frustrated, he slipped a hand inside his shirt pocket, drew out a toothpick and poked it between his lips. His mouth set grimly around it. "When I saw you out there in the crowd," he said, "I should have known you weren't here doing last-minute Christmas shopping."

"I finished shopping in August."

He shot her a droll glance. "With such a big family, I guess there's a lot to buy." The implication was that he was orphaned and alone, and only when he saw her guilt-stricken expression did Luke realize he'd gone too far.

"That's not *exactly* why I did my shopping early."

"Sorry," he murmured. "Why did you?"

She didn't say anything, just swallowed hard. And that was the worst. Suddenly, Claire the spurned woman was gone, and Claire the artist was soulfully watching him, her steady, perceptive blue eyes gazing from beneath pale eyelashes, as if she was now seeing every Christmas afternoon Luke had ever spent alone. Not that he didn't love his cabin in the far southeast corner of the Lost Springs Ranch, but come Christmas Day, when the other cowboys were with their families, it could get lonely out there with nothing for company but elk and deer. Sometimes Luke wondered at the wisdom of living on land that was a constant reminder his folks had abandoned him. Deep down, he knew he chose to do so because he'd never fully let go of his past. Fortunately Claire's eyes held no pity. Luke couldn't have stood that.

"You owe me, Luke," she continued. "And I need a cop."

"But I'm not a—"

"Ex-cop. Whatever," she said. "And you happen to be the only one I know."

His gaze swept her lips, and his breath caught as he remembered how they'd tasted last summer—wet and warm, like salt water. "You know why I can't help you, Claire. Call Sheriff Hatcher."

"This is a...private matter."

"Then maybe you and Clive should keep it private." Luke was the last person she should involve. Still, he surveyed her, wishing missing-persons cases hadn't always stirred his interest. He'd considered looking for his own folks for years. He wasn't sure why he hadn't. Fear of what he'd find, he guessed. Despite himself he suddenly continued, "Clive was supposed to go to a ranch near Douglas to talk about buying some hay, huh?"

Claire nodded quickly. "The Lazy Four lost some hay in a barn fire earlier this year."

Luke chewed on the toothpick, his mind turning. "I heard." The Stoddards' place wasn't the only one that had such troubles recently.

"After he left Douglas," Claire continued, "he was going up to Sheridan to take a look at some bulls, and then..." She paused, her frown so deep that the thin lines of her eyebrows drew together. "He was supposed to go to Cheyenne and meet with the beef council, or else to Laramie to see some men about grain prices. I forget which."

Luke didn't stop to contemplate the seductive twinge in his voice. "Always pay such close attention to what your fiancé has to say?"

Quick temper flashed in her eyes but vanished immediately. "I'm sorry I can't remember more, but the point is we had a fight, Luke."

Luke was starting to feel too curious for his own good. "I figure you two lovebirds'll work it out when he comes home."

"But it's Wednesday now and we're getting married Saturday."

Luke pondered the fact that Clive was still out cowboying so close to Christmas and his wedding. If Luke was marrying Claire, he'd probably be otherwise occupied. Especially since he'd heard the crew hadn't yet finished the house on the Lazy Four where Clive and Claire were supposed to live. Somehow, Luke assumed Clive would be at the site, motivating the workmen. His eyes narrowed.

"Heard your house isn't finished. Where are you all planning to live, meantime?"

"Really, only the kitchen needs work," Claire returned. "And most of my stuff's already been moved there."

Imagining Claire and Clive living together brought Luke nothing but discomfort, especially since he knew Clive by sight. He was younger than Luke, Claire's age, and good looking, tall, rangy and blond. Luke chewed another minute on the toothpick. "You taking a honeymoon?"

There was something he couldn't quite read in her eyes—regret or wistfulness. "We were supposed to go to San Diego."

We were. The past tense indicated she really thought Clive might be gone. Still, Luke reasoned, maybe Clive was working so he could take extra time off for the trip. Shoving a hand into his back pocket, Luke leaned a shoulder against the wall. "You're afraid he won't show? Is that it?" He searched her eyes, looking for hints of emotion, and found himself thinking she had the eyes of an angel. Sometimes soft and deep as water, the irises were starting to darken now like lapis lazuli.

"It's not that," she said with a frustrated sigh. "But I don't want Tex and Mama—"

"You call your daddy Tex?"

His question took her by surprise, and she tilted her head as if considering. "Yeah. We all do nowadays." She shrugged, squinting as if she were searching for a reason. "I guess Pop just started seeming more like a Tex. His great-granddaddy was originally from Texas, you know."

Luke hadn't, and now he told himself he hadn't asked out of personal curiosity, but only as an interview tactic to put Claire at ease, so she'd offer more information. Not that Luke had any intention of looking for Clive, but he was sure Claire was withholding something. "And you tried to call Clive today?"

She nodded. "He canceled his meetings."

"You say nobody else knows he's gone?"

Shaking her head, Claire anxiously toyed with her braid, pulling it in front. The movement shouldn't have called his attention to her chest, but it did. She didn't have much of one. She was small-breasted, slender and leggy. Catching the tenor of his deeper thoughts, Luke suddenly frowned, repositioned the toothpick in his mouth and trained his mind back on the conversation. "Do you always check up on Clive like this?"

"I'm checking up on him because I'm worried!" she defended.

"You don't look all that worried, Claire."

"Well, I am. And...yesterday, I thought I saw Clive in town. Right in Lightning Creek."

Luke was starting to feel torn. There might be trouble in paradise, but he wasn't chasing all over town, searching for Clive Stoddard. Suddenly, his frown deepened. Luke didn't want to hurt her feelings by offering the suggestion, but he had no choice. "Do you think Clive's having an affair?"

Her eyes widened. "Affair?"

"You know, is he sleeping around?" He wasn't sure which made him feel testier—the idea of Clive hurting Claire because he was fooling around, or imagining Clive fooling around *with* Claire.

"I know what it means to have an affair."

"I bet you know a lot of things," he couldn't help but say, his eyes smoldering as he thought of the things she'd probably shared with Clive. "Well, is he?"

"Why the third degree?"

It was her refusal to answer that convinced him she thought Clive was two-timing her. Luke saw red.

Claire was watching him carefully. Her voice was touched by concern. "Luke?"

"If you want me to help, I've got to ask questions." Trouble was, he was both curious about her relationship with Clive and angered by the things he'd heard. Still, he was beginning to think Clive wouldn't cheat. Since their engagement was announced, Luke had taken an interest in Clive's activities, and the man was reputed to be honest and hard-working.

Relief flooded Claire's features. "You're really going to help me?"

Right now Luke felt pulled every which way but loose. He knew he needed to steer clear of Claire. She could turn things around on a dime; already he felt unaccountably guilty for not doing more for her. "Sorry," he forced himself to say, "I'm real busy, what with Christmas and all."

She sent a dubious glance toward the Santa outfit.

He sighed. "Some of us have to work for a living," he reminded. In fact, he was supposed to inoculate some cattle at Cross Creek later.

"I work," Claire defended.

"But you don't have to."

For a second, he thought she'd react. Dark emotion flashed in her eyes, but then it disappeared. "Well, I understand you're busy," she continued diplomatically. "But do you have to...uh...be Santa this afternoon?"

Luke shook his head. "Another guy comes on after lunch. The security guard here asked me to do this because a group of teenagers have been snatching purses. Now that they've got one of them, he'll probably turn in his buddies."

"You were so good with those little kids...."

"Watch it, Claire," Luke warned. "Flattery won't work on me."

"It's not flattery. It's the truth."

Biting back a sigh, Luke refrained from pointing out that he'd had lots of experience with kids. At Lost Springs, there'd always been younger boys who couldn't tie their shoes or do their homework, and Luke had helped them out when he could. Dealing with kids was second nature.

Unwanted emotion suddenly made his gut constrict. Every time Claire crossed his path, she fueled his fantasies. It had taken months to get last summer's kiss out of his system. Luke had women friends, of course, but nothing special, and he'd always known making love with Claire would be different. Even though she was engaged, he was still looking at her and wondering what it would be like to start a family. He *was* good with kids. Still, he had to consider the morning he'd been left on the porch at Lost Springs, with nothing but a blue-and-white-checkered blanket to keep him warm. Had his mother or father— whoever left him there—known in advance they were going to abandon him? Maybe they'd once wanted kids, too.

Wanted me.

Not that it mattered now. The point was that people never knew themselves until they were tested, Luke included.

"You owe me, Luke," Claire said again.

As she stepped toward him, Luke suddenly wondered if he wouldn't be doing himself a serious favor by helping her. Rumor had it that Clive Stoddard was a fine, upstanding man, not the type to carry on with women. Besides, Luke thought, as his eyes drifted over Claire, no man in his sane mind would choose another over Claire. And how hard could it be to find a guy in Lightning Creek, Wyoming, anyway? If you blinked as you drove through, you'd miss the place. Clive had probably rearranged his schedule due to the holidays. And the sooner Claire found Clive, the sooner she'd be married off, and out of Luke's blood forever.

As she looked at him, Claire tilted her chin more than she needed to, seemingly for the express purpose of making him feel ten feet tall. Luke's remaining resistance weakened. "Well," he said, "I never did come out to your ranch, to do those chores after the bachelor auction."

"And it's Christmas," she put in quickly.

"You've roused the spirit of giving within me," he said dryly. "So, why don't we go out by the Christmas tree and get a cup of coffee? You can tell me where to start."

Claire's voice caught with relief. "Have I ever mentioned that you're my personal Santa, Luke?"

Lifting his shearling jacket from the back of the door, he waved Claire across the threshold. "Nope."

She sighed. "Well, right now you are."

Capturing the toothpick between his teeth, Luke rolled it onto his tongue. "Thanks, darlin'. But after this, can't we just call it even?"

CHAPTER FOUR

"I CAN'T HEAR," Claire whispered in protest.

"I'm on hold, anyway. And you're not even supposed to be here," Luke whispered back, his hand curling around the phone's mouthpiece, covering it just in case Wesley came on the line again. He glanced around the unfinished kitchen of the house Claire would soon share with Clive. Dropping Claire's Jeep at her folks and driving out to the Lazy Four had seemed like the next right step after leaving the mall, but now this whole place was making Luke feel out of sorts. Every time he looked at Claire, he wound up thinking back to the way they'd kissed last summer, and despite all the snow outside, he could still feel the sultry heat from that night and recall how the wet warmth of Claire's mouth had affected him. Putting a fresh toothpick between his lips, he wiggled it under his tongue.

"Luke." Claire released an audible sigh. "What do you mean I'm not supposed to be here?"

"I'm a hired gun, remember?" he returned, trying not to react to her voice, which was so soft a man could float on it. "We walk alone."

Leaning against the counter beside him, Claire tilted her head in a way that drew his gaze down the long curve of her neck. Her shadowy blue eyes looked dubious. "First, you're not charging me," she returned petulantly. "Which means you haven't been hired. And second, you're doing this because you still owe me from the bachelor auction. Besides, you don't even carry a gun.''

"Wrong. There's a Colt Pony Pocketlite in my boot.'' The .380 was so small Luke could hide it in his hand. But Claire was right about one thing. He'd never take her money. Especially not for something so simple as finding a missing fiancé. Even now, after years of supporting himself, accepting Buchanan money would have felt like taking charity. Unwanted memories came to mind of the open cardboard boxes of canned goods, used clothes and toys that folks always dropped at the Lost Springs ranch during the holidays. Like all the boys, Luke had been grateful for the donations, but they'd also served as a sore reminder of his station in life.

"C'mon." Claire's soft pout of a mouth pursed in a way he wanted to take as a dare. "It's my house, Luke."

That it is, he agreed. Giving up, he tilted the phone so she could listen when Wesley returned. Luke had been trying to keep her at arm's length, and now, as Claire leaned beside him, he caught a scent of fancy shampoo that made him want to nuzzle her. At least there was solace in the fact that Claire and Clive's new A-frame looked so uninhabited. The main house at the Lazy Four had Christmas candles in every window, and huge crossed candy canes hung above the entrance gate, but there were no such decorations in here. Drywall and studs were visible in the kitchen, sawdust clung to Luke's boots, and the new furniture in the living room still had plastic wrapped around it. Claire, who didn't have a prissy bone in her body, seemed blissfully oblivious to the mess.

Luke glanced outside. It wasn't yet five o'clock, but it was already dark, and light from the uncovered overhead light fixtures cast reflections in the darkened windows. Staring into an uncurtained picture window that faced a deck and the back of the lot, he took in Claire's tall, slender body. It was definitely a turn-on. His eyes settled where her tight jeans hugged a gorgeous rounded tush. The phone clicked back on. "Luke?"

"Yeah, Wesley," said Luke, picturing his stocky, redheaded friend. "So, you say Clive Stoddard came to the police barracks and told you all this?" Luke prompted. He'd already found Clive's well-worn calendar book and confirmed the cancellation of his appointments, then, against Claire's protests, Luke had called Sheriff Hatcher's office and the state police barracks to make some casual inquiries.

"Yeah," said Wesley. "Like to say, yesterday a feller by that name walks into our barracks. Looks like he's got a bone to pick. Says he wonders if we can't send some boys to interview folks at a coupla mom-and-pop ranches around Lightning Creek."

"You mean like the one I work out at Cross Creek?"

"Naw, Lydell. That'd be a big spread by comparison. I'm talkin' little. Places that are really just farms, like Gomer's Hole or the Flying Swords."

"Never heard of 'em."

As Wesley continued offering names, Luke shoved the phone under his jaw, dug a notebook from his shirt pocket, flipped it open and began writing. "Uh-huh. The Triple T. And you say North Fork's owned by a fellow named Elmer Green?" Realizing Claire's luscious blue eyes were bugging, Luke tilted the phone toward her again. As she leaned to listen, he felt the casual brush of her silken skin by his temple. Shifting his eyes from her profile, he continued, "Is that all the ranches he mentioned?"

"Yeah. Swears up and down that somebody's been forcing people to consider selling land. Suspects that's why there's been more than the average number of tragedies this year—barn fires and the like. Says he questioned some folks personally, and found out they've gotten serious about selling. Turns out some of those places I mentioned have already been sold.''

Luke realized he was studying Claire again. "Nothing wrong with selling land."

"Yeah, but Stoddard claims folks are being run off."

"He say who's behind it?"

"He didn't have a clue, but he was mad. Says the next thing you know, they'll be targeting bigger spreads."

"Places like his," Luke muttered, then felt taken aback by the unexpected venom he'd felt toward the man. Berating himself, Luke shook his head. Clive was going to make Claire happy, so there was no call for jealousy. Still, it grated that Clive had been born with a silver spoon in his mouth, and that in addition to getting the most desirable woman in Lightning Creek, he was heir to a spread the size of the Lazy Four. "What?" Luke suddenly said, realizing he'd experienced an uncharacteristic lapse of attention.

"Turns out Stoddard had a barn fire himself last year. Anyway, I'd never heard of Clive Stoddard 'fore yesterday. As you know, Sheriff Hatcher handles Lightning Creek, so we State boys tend to stick to our own side of the road. Like to say, I even thought the man might just be paranoid. I mean, he looked rich as sin…good vest and boots, you know what I mean?"

Luke's eyes darted around the house Clive was building for Claire, then his eyes settled on the glittering rock on her ring finger. "Sure do. He's the real thing. He's got money."

"Well, like to say, thought he might just be paranoid. You know how loco those rich guys can get, especially when they think they're about to lose a few of their inherited greenbacks.''

"Yeah," Luke managed to say, once more hating the twinge of resentment he felt. What was wrong with him? There were haves and have-nots in this world, and Luke had never cared that he wasn't in the former group. Especially nowadays, since he did better than average financially. Catching Claire's gaze, Luke twisted his lips into a smile. She smiled back, the comments about rich folks not seeming to disturb her in the least. "So, Wesley," Luke continued, "what'd you tell Clive?"

"That we'd call Sheriff Hatcher. I figured we'd go at the case jointly after the holidays." Wesley sighed. "'Course, Stoddard was mad when we didn't get right on it, but he said he understood. You know how it is. With the weather like this, and so many folks traveling to get home for the holidays, we've been instructed to concentrate on safety first. Ain't nobody selling their property on Christmas Day, know what I mean?"

"Yeah. Well, thanks, Wesley." Luke distractedly worked the toothpick between his teeth while his eyes took in an open, airy loft space in the central room beyond. Seeing the open double doors that led to the master bedroom upstairs, his mood further soured, and his gaze returned to the picture window where Claire's reflection was superimposed on the snowy night. "Oh, one more thing, Wesley."

"Shoot, partner."

"Mind running down this number?" Luke rattled off a number he'd seen on a matchbook cover in Clive's home office. The office was the most-used room in the place, but even it was still a mess of unpacked boxes, scattered file folders and disconnected office equipment. Still, Clive would be organized under usual circumstances. He kept

extensive home files on every head of cattle at the Lazy
Four. He obviously had a love of computers, just as Claire
had said, and duplicate records were in the ranch office on
disks. "Really appreciate all the help, Wesley," Luke said
before he hung up the phone.

Still leaning beside him, Claire frowned. "Do you think
Clive went to interview some of those folks on his own,
maybe hoping to help straighten out their troubles before
Christmas? I mean, assuming somebody's been trying to
buy land?"

Luke shrugged. "Possible."

Her frown deepened. "It's just not like Clive, though.
All he ever thinks about is ranching. And computers. He
loves fooling around with them."

She sounded none too happy about that. Luke couldn't
help but raise an eyebrow. Was there more difficulty than
the seemingly inconsequential fight she'd mentioned?
"Trouble in paradise?"

She looked nervous. "Not really. I mean, we did have
that fight...but he must be somewhere on business."

"He probably is." That was better than thinking of
Clive helping his fellow man while he, Luke, was in
Clive's house lusting after his woman. And that *was* what
Luke was doing. Not that the way Claire looked gave him
much choice. He glanced at Claire and sighed, then he
pushed aside his shearling jacket and Stetson, both of
which he'd laid on the newly sanded island countertop. He
circled the island and perched on a stool.

"Want something to drink?" Claire asked. "I've got no
idea what's here, but I figure I can find something."

"Sure." Luke watched as she opened and shut various
cabinets, all of which appeared to be empty. Picking up
the thread of their earlier conversation, he said, "Even if

Clive did question those folks, it doesn't sound particularly dangerous, so I wouldn't worry about him overmuch.''

"Hmm.'' Claire headed for some cardboard boxes that were open on the floor, squatted down and began rooting through them, making pots and pans rattle and clank. "But why would Clive stay in town without telling me?''

Luke had no answer, unless Clive really was seeing another woman. "You're probably right, Claire. So close to Christmas, he must have had trouble keeping his business appointments. Folks leave for the holidays, that kind of thing. There're still people jotted on his calendar who we haven't reached.'' Lifting a hand, Luke took hold of the toothpick and thoughtfully rolled it between a thumb and index finger. "Is Clive usually accountable for his time?''

Claire glanced up from the boxes, a saucepan in her hand, and blew out a quick, exasperated sigh. "Never. He won't even carry a cell phone. If he's working around the ranch, mending fences or riding, he hates to be disturbed. He gets really mad.''

"Has he ever been gone overnight?''

"Once or twice.'' Shrugging, she turned to the boxes again, now lifting some coffee filters and peering beneath them. "Usually we eventually find him up in the barn with a sick calf.''

A sick calf. It was getting harder by the minute to dislike Clive Stoddard.

"Like I said on the way over,'' Claire continued, "Clive's got tons of friends in both Laramie and Cheyenne. I'll give you their names and numbers. With the roads so bad, I guess he might have stopped, which would explain things. Usually I wouldn't worry, but…''

"You had a fight,'' Luke concluded. And her wedding was only days away.

She nodded. "Maybe it's a good sign that I'm not wor-

ried. If something bad happened, I think I'd get a gut feeling."

"I think that's shaky logic."

She shot him a sudden, irresistible smile that remolded
her classic features into something more impish. "I
thought cops relied on hunches."

"Old wives' tale."

But Luke did have a hunch. He and Claire would be
explosive in bed. Pure dynamite. Together they'd blow off
the roof. His gaze lifted to the master bedroom, then he
glanced around. The house suited her, with lots of windows and plenty of room to move. Suddenly, his eyes narrowed. Ever since he'd ridden in through the arched front
gates, the Lazy Four had seemed strangely familiar. Now
Luke thought he knew why. He whistled softly. "This is
the house you designed, Claire."

Seemingly giving up on fixing drinks, Claire stood,
stretching her lithe body in a way that made Luke far too
aware of her. Just watching her aroused him, he admitted,
fighting the telltale tightening of his body. Her eyes lovingly trailed over the unfinished house. "I didn't know if
you'd notice. Told you I'd have this place someday."

Everything inside Luke suddenly ached, and he wished
he'd never come here. "Yeah, you said you would." But
when she'd said it, Luke had been dreaming of building it
for her. Years ago, when they'd met at the feed store, he'd
watched her use up whole sketchbooks, drawing plans for
this house. He couldn't believe he'd only now recognized
it.

She was smiling at him. "Things always turn out dif-
ferently from how you imagine them," she said. "You
helped, you know."

"Not really." But during those long, hot summer afternoons in town, while she waited for Ely to finish his busi-

ness, Luke had pored over the sketches, offering suggestions. "You added a deck," he said. "More windows. But it's still your dream place."

"It will be, if it's ever finished." She shrugged. "Clive wanted something bigger, more like the main house."

Luke shook his head. "A colonial?"

She nodded. "All white. I didn't like the idea."

It wouldn't be to Luke's taste, either. Forcing himself to push away images of her and Clive together, Luke said, "I guess you used your feminine wiles on Clive, so he'd build the place."

Claire's laughter brought a mischievous sparkle to her eyes; she looked positively delighted. "How'd you guess?"

Luke shrugged. "You've got a way with men, Claire."

She tilted her head, eyeing him. "You really think so?"

He met her gaze. "You're forcing me to repeat it?"

"Not forcing." When her voice softened, he was sure she was thinking of that day in the woods when they'd come so close to making love, and he felt heat running through his bloodstream. "I don't think I could force you to do anything, Luke," she continued, another sudden smile tugging at her lips. "But I guess I'm daring you."

"Dares are another matter," he assured her. "So, let me just say it again. You definitely have a way with men."

"You aren't so bad with women, either," she returned. A silence fell, and just when it became uncomfortable, she swooped down, this time pulling a bottle from a box. "How about some Wild Turkey? Since I'm such a siren, I figure I can charm you into having a shot with me. Or would that muddle your deductive mind?"

"Looks lethal." Luke surveyed the whiskey. "But I have a strange method of thinking. Since I put things in the back of my mind and just let them stew, I figure I can handle a shot.''

"I'll pour," she offered helpfully. "All you have to do is drink.''

"Drinking sounds like a lot of exertion, but Wild Turkey might be worth the effort.''

She chuckled. "So, you think by not thinking, huh?''

"That's a way of putting it.'' Luke cracked another smile, running a hand absently along the countertop, lifting his Stetson by the brim, then setting it back down. "After I knock one back, maybe I'll walk around outside. The drink ought to warm me up enough.'' With the new snowfall, Clive wouldn't have left footprints, but it didn't hurt to look.

As Claire pulled up two shot glasses and the bottle, Luke suddenly wondered if the fight with Clive was more serious than she'd let on. Claire definitely wasn't telling him everything, but he knew her well enough to suspect that questioning her wouldn't help. He watched her lean against the counter as she poured the whiskey. Sliding a glass toward him, she then lifted hers, her expression becoming somber. He realized there was more meaning in her eyes than he wanted to see.

Her voice was too throaty for comfort. "Here's to us.''

He sure wished she wouldn't talk like this. "Us?''

The way her shaded blue eyes bored into his stole his breath. "To what could have been, Luke.''

He suddenly wanted to protest, to say it wasn't too late. His voice sounded rough as he lifted his glass. "Claire,'' he said simply in an answering toast.

He watched as she quickly knocked back the shot, not even flinching, then he took the toothpick from his mouth, just long enough to toss his back. He felt the hot whiskey sliding down his throat, warming his blood every bit as

much as she did. Maybe it was only because the raw heat
of the drink felt so good on such a cold night, but Luke
was seized by another wild urge to claim her. He saw
himself grabbing the bottle, flinging her over his shoulder,
carrying her upstairs and laying her down on the bed—
Clive Stoddard be damned. Luke wanted to undress her
slow, to lap the hot, burning whiskey from her navel and
lick it from her thighs. Emotion reared up inside him, making him want to roar. This was supposed to have been their
house. He'd helped her with the plans, and Clive didn't
even like the place. Besides which, Claire wasn't acting as
in love as an engaged woman should.

Abruptly, Luke stood. He had to get out of here. Turning
away, he picked up his jacket and shrugged into it. Out of
the corner of his eye, he saw Claire grab her parka.
"That's all right," he said. "I'll go alone. But thanks for
the drink."

"No, I'll come."

Experiencing the closest thing to real temper he'd felt
all day, Luke clamped his teeth down hard on the toothpick, biting back a quick retort. Sometimes a man needed
to be by himself. But no, Claire would never leave him
be. It was probably why she'd gotten under his skin so
much. There were plenty of folks Luke liked in this world.
There was no woman with whom he couldn't share a triv-
ial flirtation; no man with whom he couldn't ride. But only
Claire had her hooks in him.

Luke headed through the kitchen door, letting it slam
behind him. Outside, alone in the cold, he felt his mood
darken further as he began slowly, carefully circling
Claire's dream house. The night had turned unusually still.
The high winds had tapered, and the temperature had risen.
Moonlight reflected on the Lazy Four's miles of rolling
snow.

"Damn you, Claire," Luke suddenly muttered, the chill night breeze blowing long strands of dark hair against his face, making him wish he'd remembered his hat. But he'd been in too much of a hurry to get outside. The whiskey had warmed him, but it had also opened the door on emotions he'd carefully tamped down all day, releasing the darker, more passionate part of him he'd prefer Claire never see. The part of him that wanted to go back inside and possessively plunder those soft, plump lips, that wanted to drag her up that spiral staircase, take her hair out of that braid and rake his fingers through it until the soft, straight strands loosened. He wanted to devour her, to brand her in the house—the bed—that should have been theirs.

Not that Claire would ever understand why he didn't. He wasn't even sure *he* understood. But he feared he wasn't capable of the kind of love she needed—the kind her big loving family had taught her and that came to her so easily that she took it for granted.

Suddenly, he came to a stop. There it was again. Something he couldn't quite name pulling at his mind. It had plagued him ever since he'd laid eyes on the front gates of the Lazy Four, where he'd never had occasion to visit before. His eyes narrowed as the winter winds rose again, and he scanned the rolling snow-blanketed land. A stand of trees surrounded Claire's house, their dark boughs bending under a heavy weight of snow; closer, icicles hung from the eaves. But the memory still wouldn't come. Cocking his head and still worrying the toothpick, Luke waited, as if the past might come to him in a sound.

And then he caught a glimpse of yellow. It was only moonlight dancing on the snow, but it reminded him of a memory he'd had at other times. It must have been summertime, he thought now, because the woman beside him was wearing a yellow dress, printed with powder-blue flowers. In the memory, Luke couldn't see much of her, not even her face, just her side and part of her arm. Was that because he'd been a young boy, standing beside a woman? Who was she?

Thoughtfully sucking the toothpick between his lips, he started walking again, his boots crunching where the snow near the house was less powdery, packed and hard. He'd finished circling the house and was nearing the back door when Claire caught up to him.

"Find anything out here?" She peered from the raised hood of her white parka, the coat's color blending with the snow, her lovely face shadowed by a dark fake-fur ruff.

Luke shook his head. "Just snow." *And memories.*

Frowning, he glanced around again distractedly—over the long driveway leading from the front gates to the main house, then at the trees surrounding them. Claire had left the storm door open and now soft yellow light mixed with moonlight, spilling from the interior across the deck and onto the snow. Luke's eyes lifted, settling on the stars that glittered in the clear sky, then he realized Claire was watching him. Sending her a sideways glance, he felt whatever anger he'd had toward her completely disappear. "Don't get much more country than this," he commented, his breath clouding the air.

Her voice seemed unusually vibrant in the crisp, still night. "Nothing like Lightning Creek, Wyoming, on a night like tonight, huh?"

With everything in him, he wanted to fight the quiet intimacy, but he couldn't lie, "Pretty as a picture out here, Claire."

"Cold, though."

"They said it's warming up soon."

She chuckled. "Warming up to thirty degrees, maybe."

He shrugged. "This year's been milder than most."

They stood for a moment, side by side, staring up at the moon and stars in the soft black sky, and Luke found himself wondering if Claire was thinking about last summer, too. The night after the bachelor auction, the sky had been dark and clear like this. Unusually deep somehow in its very blackness, it had looked like the richest, softest velvet. Everything seemed so quiet that Luke was half relieved when Claire leaned and plucked the toothpick from his mouth, breaking the mood.

He grinned. "Give me that toothpick. That's my thinking toothpick, Claire." Without it, he'd never find Clive. And for a second, Luke decided he didn't really want to.

Claire laughed, stepped back a pace, then turned and simply ran, her boots kicking up loose, powdery snow. Catching her in two easy paces, he grabbed the back of her parka and simply hauled her to him. When she tripped, they both went down, sprawling into the snow.

"Guess you can't think now," she said with a breathless chuckle.

She was right about that much. Rational thought fled the second Luke pinned her to the ground. "I came here trying to help you," he protested, fighting his response as she began squirming beneath him, her yielding flesh feeling as soft as the snow.

"You owe me!" she exclaimed.

Swiftly grabbing her wrists, he told himself that the sooner this tussle was over, the better. Thrusting her arms high above her head, he slid his gloved hands over hers and stretched his body out on hers as he futilely pried at her balled fists. "I don't owe you," he said. "We're even."

"You were bought and paid for, Luke," she taunted, shaking her head. "You're my slave now."

"Slave?" he shot back, soft laughter escaping his lips. "Sorry, darlin', but I'm on top of you."

"Not for long." With an undignified giggle, she struggled to escape, but he merely leaned harder into her body, his weight pressuring her. Breathless and flushed, she shot him a mock glare. "Can you think yet?"

"Yeah. And I think you're in trouble," he warned as she feinted right, then left, forcing him to wrestle her until he was panting as hard as she.

Gasping, she said, "Lose track of which hand your toothpick's in?"

Hands. All Luke could think about was where he wanted to put his. The way every sweet inch of her was twisting beneath him made him remember how intimately he'd once touched her. Old memories turned his voice rough. "Claire, you can't win against me."

She wrenched away. "I'm doing pretty good."

But she wasn't. She was losing. Against his cheek, her quickened, excited breath was hot, smelling of rich, expensive whiskey, and her gorgeous mouth was too close, a scant inch from his. Long strands of his black hair lay against her pale cheeks and against her lips, so as she spoke, she was tasting them. Something about that—about seeing his dark hair in her mouth, touching the pink spear of her tongue, suddenly fired his blood, making him unbearably hard. He groaned as she bucked and writhed, then he let her win for a minute. Struggling on top, she straddled him, her thighs squeezing his hips as the parka rode up around her waist. Staring down at him, laughing and victorious, she looked more beautiful than he'd ever seen her.

His heart pounding out of control, Luke suddenly became aware of the cold, wet snow bunching behind his neck. Their hips were locked, and she had to feel how aroused he'd gotten. He could feel her heat, and it took away his remaining breath. Knowing he shouldn't, he caught her waist and swiftly rolled again. Pulling her beneath him and settling masterfully on top, he let his legs fall between hers. He brought his lips close. His voice was husky. "Men can be dangerous when they're not thinking, so you'd better give me that toothpick, Claire." As if it hadn't been lost in the snow long ago.

Beneath him, her chest was heaving. "You really think you're dangerous, Luke?"

"Right now? Definitely."

They were cheek to cheek, and she was lying flat on her back, her head nestled on the lining of the flung-back parka hood. Just beyond the hood, the snow was glistening like white gemstones. Luke's eyes roved over her face. Suddenly, they weren't playing anymore. Stray strands of his long hair had fallen across her mouth again, and when she licked at her lips, they caught on her tongue. Snow had dampened their jeans, too, and their body heat was starting to melt it. Chill air knifed to his lungs as he brought his lips a fraction closer, and when he shifted his weight on top of her, it brought desire flooding into her eyes. Suddenly, Luke couldn't remember why he was here. To hell with the bed, he thought vaguely. He wanted to take Claire in the soft snow. He didn't give a damn about her wedding.

"Luke." The whisper sounded somehow raw. "Luke."

A soft groan was torn from his lips, but her voice brought him to his senses. Thwarted, frustrated desire made pure temper course through him. "Why can't you ever leave well enough alone, Claire?" He bit the words out, forcing himself to move his hands beside her shoulders and push himself up.

She hopped up just as quickly, dusting the snow from

her behind. "*You* attacked *me!*" she declared with sudden, breathless fury.

He didn't bother to respond. He couldn't afford to. Right now, any kind of passion, even anger, might take him over the edge. Despite her engagement, he'd make love to her right now, if he wasn't careful. Fearing he'd do something he'd sincerely regret, Luke stormed toward the house. He was almost there when he felt a hand clamp down on his shoulder. He turned, and almost wished he hadn't when he saw how truly gorgeous she looked. Desire and anger had turned her eyes a flashing violet, and melting snow was sparkling in her hair, the crystals gleaming.

"Okay, maybe I started that," she admitted. "But before I get married, you owe me an explanation."

His heart was still beating too hard, less from exertion than from the unrelieved pangs of the amorous state she'd left him in, and the reminder she was marrying Clive was the last thing he needed right now. "For?"

Her gaze was dead serious. "For why you've never wanted to be with me, Luke!"

Luke tossed his head, fighting the gusts of wind that lifted the raven locks of his hair, blowing them against his cheeks. Attempting to ignore her honest anger, he told himself she was a rich rancher's spoiled daughter. "I don't need a reason," he said. "And you've no right to be mad because I didn't happen to fall all over you just now." Knowing he'd already gone too far, he gentled his voice. "C'mon, Claire. Be honest. Why would you want to be with me?"

Her cheeks were flushed, by temper, embarrassment or the cold—probably all three. "The passion, for one thing," she said, her glittering eyes making her look more alive than anyone he'd ever seen. "And the way we talked to each other that one summer." She paused, swallowing hard. "I always thought it would grow to be more between us, Luke. And when we saw each other after the bachelor auction…"

The kiss convinced her the passion was still alive. His chest suddenly aching, Luke stepped closer, giving in to the unwanted emotion she always stirred in him. Stripping off a glove, he ran a caressing finger slowly down her cheek. "Take a good look, Claire," he said, glancing around and allowing himself to trace her sculpted jaw for one brief second. "The Lazy Four's your future. It borders your pa's property, which means it'll become one of the biggest spreads in this part of Wyoming. Clive'll give you the kind of life you were born to, the kind of life you deserve."

She leaned away from his finger as if she'd been burned. "You're telling me what I deserve?" Her voice shook with quick, unchecked temper. "Do you actually think I consider *property* when I think about men?"

His voice was husky, maybe even seductive, but he did at least manage to keep it even. "You're talking like a girl, not a woman, Claire. Don't be naive."

"I used to be naive," she shot back, "but you made me grow up a long time ago."

"It *was* a long time ago, Claire."

"People don't change all that much."

"We can't always get what we want."

"Is that it!" she exploded. "You think I'm so privileged that you get satisfaction from seeing me want something I can't have?"

This was Luke's worst nightmare; the conversation had gone too far. How had he wound up standing here in the freezing cold, with her mad and him throbbing with desire? His jaw set. "I just came here to help you out."

"I don't want your help! I wanted—oh, never mind

what I wanted!'' Whirling around, Claire marched toward the back door. He watched her tawny-colored braid twitching on her back like a riled rattler.

And then he followed her. If nothing else, Luke told himself, he still had no choice but to give her a ride home.

"CAN I TURN ON SOME MUSIC?" Claire glanced toward Luke, who was driving, even though just looking at him made her heart hurt all over again. Her eyes settled where darkness cast strong shadows across his hard, unforgiving profile as she remembered how the strands of his long blue-black hair had swept her mouth, feeling as fine as corn silk. The near kiss had sparked such fire in her. Fire, she thought now, that no other man could ever tend. Fire that not even her engagement had squelched. Angrily, she toyed with her engagement ring. What was she going to do? She'd tried to forget Luke and move on with her life, but now her husband-to-be had vanished. Feeling another rush of emotion, she wished Clive had at least called her. Didn't he know she was worried? Besides, it wasn't fair to imply the wedding was off and then run. "What?" she suddenly asked, realizing Luke had said something.

"You said you wanted music. Go ahead and turn it on."

Just hearing his voice threatened to make Claire spitting mad all over again. She didn't budge, other than to purse her lips and stare through the windshield. Over the forest-green hood of the Jeep, she gazed where the high beams were barely penetrating the black, snowy night. The pavement needed to be plowed again, and slushy snow was churning up under the tires.

She glanced at Luke again. When they were playing in the snow, he'd forgotten himself for a minute and simply let his passion take over, acting on his feelings for her. And he definitely had feelings. Even his most casual glances were ravenous. The roughness of his voice and the tightly coiled stance of his body said more than a thousand words. Earlier, when he'd followed her inside the house at the Lazy Four, she'd been prepared for more fighting, but he'd simply said it was high time he took her back to her folks.

"Change your mind about the music?" he said.

She shrugged. "We're almost there, anyway." She tried to tell herself she was glad, too. Fact was, she hoped she never saw Luke again. She'd been a fool to track him down at the mall. She could find Clive herself. With the wedding so soon, cold feet were to be expected, but Clive would come around, and their wedding on Christmas would be beautiful.

Lifting a hand from the steering wheel, Luke leaned and flicked on the music. Van Morrison's voice blasted through the Cherokee. Bending swiftly, Claire turned down the volume, then still feeling petulant, she switched from the tape to the radio. She wheeled the dial until she found Bing Crosby singing *White Christmas*.

If her choice bothered Luke, he didn't say anything.

After a moment, she wriggled on the seat. "I can't believe your car has leather seats with in-built warmers." She couldn't help but add. "And you think *I'm* spoiled."

"I never said that."

"You thought it."

"Maybe."

Crossing her arms, she sighed. What did she expect? Maybe she *was* spoiled. And he was right. She hadn't left well enough alone, had she? She needed to find Clive, but Luke was the last person she should have asked for help. Really, though, she wasn't all that worried about Clive. He was famous for not accounting for his time, just as she'd told Luke. Not that Clive was irresponsible. But his pa,

Evander, was ill, and his three brothers, all of whom had businesses in town, didn't care to hear endless reports of a cowboy's comings and goings. Work kept Clive busy and he was always on the move—fixing fences, herding cattle, trading and buying equipment and animals. Someone usually knew where he'd gone; it just wasn't always easy to find that particular someone.

Claire seriously doubted Clive was interviewing small farmers, and she couldn't imagine that he was with another woman, either. No, he was simply lying low. He hadn't been entirely rational during their fight, but he'd said some things that made her feel sure he wasn't in love with her, that he was marrying her because the Stoddards wanted to merge their ranch with the Stop Awhile. But maybe Claire was wrong.... She hoped so. Thinking of the wedding preparations and of the gowns her mother was still hemming, Claire suddenly felt her heart wrench. Luke turned off the main road, going slower along the straight driveway leading to the main house. "Think you've got enough Christmas lights?"

It was the first amiable thing he'd said, and glancing up, Claire almost smiled in spite of her mood. The massive rambling log house before them had a green roof, views of a creek and meadows, and was nestled in a thick stand of pines that blinked with colored lights. Parts of the house and some of the corrals dated all the way back to the early 1800s.

"Tex always thoroughly wires the place," Claire explained, taking in the lights bordering the windows and the rough-hewn rail of the wraparound porch. Even the satellite dish in the side yard was decorated. Life-size figurines depicting Santa and his reindeer were in front of the house, next to a snowman that Tex and her sisters had made yesterday.

"Your house looks like it's under a strobe light," Luke said.

The smile tugged harder at the corners of Claire's mouth. "Mama likes to joke, saying it looks so much like a Vegas motel that we should put out a vacancy sign and advertise to do weddings, but she secretly likes the lights. We all do." Claire shrugged. "Besides, when we tease Tex about his questionable taste, he only threatens to leave the lights up year-round." Claire chuckled softly. "This morning Mama said she was afraid the airplanes'll mistake the house for the airport and try to land. She told Tex he best be prepared to forget about cattle and get himself a new job in air traffic control."

That got a smile out of Luke.

"Then Emma Jane said it's so bright we can forget airplanes. She says we should be looking for UFOs."

Luke chuckled.

"And *then* Mama said if we're lucky, maybe the hand of God Almighty will simply swoop down, do everybody in Lightning Creek a favor and unplug our house."

Now Luke laughed full-out. But the sound only made Claire sad. She wished he'd opened up years ago and admitted his feelings for her. Oh, Luke knew how to shoot the breeze with people, but he never really joined in. Didn't he know that his eyes started sparkling like Tex's Christmas lights when she talked about her family? Didn't he know he craved a family of his own?

As they neared the house, colored lights filled the Jeep, throwing mosaic patterns against Luke's skin. "So, do you like the lights?" Claire asked.

Luke hesitated a moment too long, then he shrugged. "You know I never much cared for Christmas."

Frustration coursed through her again. She knew he'd been found on the doorstep of Lost Springs on a Christmas morning; he'd told her that years ago. And if anybody sympathized with his suffering, it was Claire. Even now, she was spending extra time with Brady at Lost Springs. He'd just turned six, and more than anything, he wanted Santa to find his folks, so he could spend Christmas with them.

But Luke had to move on.

Oh, he could choose to be alone; that was a man's right. But Claire was certain it was only fear that kept him to himself. Years ago, hadn't he understood that she'd come from a big loving family? That maybe she could help him work through his feelings? Not that it mattered now. Claire had to move on, herself. She had to find Clive and address his last-minute doubts. She wanted a family now. Babies. It was time.

Inside the Stop Awhile, lights were on in the living room, and through the window, Claire could see the decorated tree, as well as Tex's collection of game mounts, which her mother professed to like even less than the Christmas lights. Her four sisters were sitting in the window seat, and as Luke pulled up near the porch, Emma Jane cupped a hand around her mouth and yelled, no doubt telling Tex and Mama that Claire was finally home.

When she realized Mama had probably held dinner, Claire's heart pulled. There was nothing like family. And despite his reservations, she thought Clive was ready for one. He'd said he wanted to have kids while he was still young, exactly mirroring her feelings. Besides, for years, the Buchanans and Stoddards had shared more than just a fence line, and there was already so much shared history between the two families....

She glanced from the house to Luke. "Thanks for doing what you could to help locate Clive," she said as Luke parked his Jeep next to hers. By now, Luke had probably guessed she wasn't nearly as worried as she'd professed. Maybe he'd even guessed her fight with Clive might affect the wedding. "I shouldn't have asked for your help," she said. "I'm sure Clive will turn up. He always does."

"I'll keep looking."

"Please, Luke. Don't." She started to tell him the truth about the fight, but she couldn't stand to let Luke know Clive might not want her. No more than Luke had.

Leaning over, Luke grasped her hand, and she felt the foolish clutch of her heart again. That's when she knew it was utterly hopeless. She'd keep wanting this man to love her until the bitter end.

His gloves were off, and she could feel how his warm, dry hand pulsed with life. She liked the strength of his dark fingers so much, how easily they closed over hers. His eyes searched hers. "Claire…" Emotion she couldn't quite read crossed his features. "I know things are going to work out for you and Clive. You're going to be real happy."

"Thanks," Claire managed to say, gazing for a long moment into eyes that looked as black as midnight in the darkened car.

A sudden shout broke the silence, and Claire realized Emma Jane, Rosie and Vickie were running down the steps of the house, bundled in parkas. They stopped, ogling her and Luke through the Jeep's window and pounding on the glass. Claire reached for a hand crank since her windows were manual, but Luke powered down the passenger window a crack for her.

"Can't you all leave me alone for two seconds?" Claire said with a perturbed sisterly sigh, squinting against the sudden rush of freezing air. "And where's Josie?"

"She's in her room with a broken heart," Vickie said practically. "But she'll be down for dinner." This morning

Josie had broken up with her first boyfriend, a relationship of two weeks' duration.

"Mama says you'd better bring in whoever's in the car," Rosie continued. "We're gonna feed him. And you'd better hurry, 'cause dinner's getting cold."

"We had to wait for you," Vickie huffed. "And we're all starving! Mama says she could eat an armadillo! And Tex picked up one of his boots and said he was gonna start gnawing on it!"

Luke chuckled and leaned toward the passenger side. "You girls tell your mama thanks, but I—"

Emma Jane whirled toward the house. "Mama!" she called, cupping her hand around her mouth. "It's Luke Lydell. The man we bought last summer at the bachelor auction. He says he won't come."

"I'm starving!" Vickie reminded him again.

Mama shouted down from the porch. "Claire Lynn Buchanan," she warned, "you know better than to bring anybody home at this hour without offering dinner. There's plenty, and it's almost on the table."

"She's a good cook," Vickie encouraged.

Don't do it, Claire, she thought. *Quit pushing.* But that damnable light was in Luke's eyes again. He'd begged off, but he'd always secretly wanted to meet her boisterous family. While the ranch was Tex's birthright, it was a little known fact around Lightning Creek that Claire's mama was born on a two-acre farm where they'd always struggled. It was why Mama never let a guest leave without a hot meal.

"Guess you'd better come." Claire shot Luke an apologetic smile as her sisters whirled around and bolted for the house. "Otherwise, I'll get into trouble. Or worse, Mama'll send Tex down to invite you personally. Since he's probably immersed in the livestock paper right now, you'll already be on his bad side." Claire eyed Luke a long moment. "Please understand," she warned. "Tex's bad side isn't someplace you want to be."

With that, Claire got out of the Jeep and slammed the door. She was pretty sure Luke would follow.

And she was right.

CHAPTER FIVE

"HOLD STILL, CLAIRE LYNN," said Mama, cocking her head and critically surveying the hem of the white velvet gown.

"I haven't moved a muscle." As her mother knelt in front of her, Claire stared down at the top of her light brown bun.

"I should have finished this last week," Mama murmured, shaking her head as she began repinning the hem. Raising her voice, she added, "And please go wash off that green eye shadow, Josie."

"But it matches our bridesmaid dresses," Josie protested. Leaning toward a floor-length mirror on the back of a closet door, Josie batted her eyelashes, admiring her handiwork. Her voice caught with excitement. "Since everybody else gets to wear makeup at the wedding, Tex promised I could, too."

"Josie, you're still only fourteen," huffed Vickie, who was sitting ramrod straight in a wing chair while Rosie practiced pulling her hair into a French twist. "And that eye shadow looks tacky."

Josie tilted her head this way and that, still admiring herself in the mirror. Suddenly, she giggled. "If it looks tacky, Tex'll love it."

Mama chuckled softly as she plucked a straight pin from a tomato-shaped cushion; obvious affection was in her voice. "Your pa most certainly will. He's the tackiest man alive. If he doesn't take down all our Christmas lights soon, everybody in Lightning Creek will probably file suit.''

"Why?" encouraged Josie.

"For lack of sleep," joked Vickie.

Rosie nodded as she continued fiddling with Vickie's hair. "All those blinking lights definitely keep me awake at night."

Vickie laughed. "I haven't had a REM phase in days."

"Me, neither." Josie whirled away from the mirror, her blue eyes sparkling. "If Tex gets sued, will he go to jail?"

Emma Jane chuckled. Fresh from the shower, she was still wearing a bathrobe, and a towel was wrapped around her head like a turban. She'd been stretched lazily on the bed in the guest room, and now she peered over the top of a paperback book, the cover of which depicted a man in a loincloth embracing a woman with a heaving chest and waist-long honey-colored hair. "Well," continued Emma Jane with a sigh, fanning herself with the book. "Dreaming is definitely important. So, it *would* seem fair to sue for a lack of sleep."

"You don't dream, Emma Jane," Claire couldn't help but put in dryly. "You fantasize. That's different."

Rosie laughed. "Well, if Tex goes to jail, I guess we'll just have to call off Claire's wedding and break him out."

At that, the girls burst into gales of laughter. "I don't know about you-all," continued Vickie, "but as much as I love Pa, I refuse to mess up my pretty green velvet dress by carrying explosives."

The idea of engineering a jail break while wearing their bridesmaid's dresses caught on, and more bubbling laughter filled the room as the girls discussed it.

Claire merely listened to the chatter, barely able to join in. Instead, she gazed guiltily down at Mama, who was trying so hard to finish the gown Claire probably wouldn't even wear. The gown itself was beautiful, with a full, flowing skirt, a fitted bodice and puffed sleeves. The fluted edges of a high collar ruffled under her chin. Taking a deep breath, Claire wished she could muster the nerve to tell Mama and the girls about the fight with Clive, but they were all so excited. It wasn't right to worry them when Claire wasn't sure if the wedding was canceled. Clasping her hands worriedly in front of her, she wished Clive would at least call. Since he occasionally traveled on ranch business, her folks hadn't been particularly concerned he hadn't been around, though they had cast some curious glances Luke's way.

"Quit fidgeting, Claire Lynn."

"Sorry, Mama." She realized Emma Jane was watching her carefully. She frowned. "What, Emma Jane?"

Emma Jane merely yawned and stretched, then lazily set the book aside on the bed. "Where'd you and Luke go yesterday?" she asked with deceptive casualness.

"We were right here, having dinner." Silently, Claire cursed Emma Jane for being so concerned with everybody else's love affairs. Especially since Claire had had such a good time last night. After dinner, they'd all danced while Tex played his fiddle, and Claire had given Luke a tour of the house.

"I mean, where did you go before dinner?" prodded Emma Jane. "I saw you drop off your Jeep here. Then you left again with Luke."

Claire's heart missed a beat. Without wanting to, she could still remember how he'd felt on top of her in the snow, how the weight of his body shielded her from the wind, and how dampness soaked through her jeans, cooling the backs of her thighs. Even now, she could feel the warmth of his breath on her cheek. It had made the core of her ache, and she was still longing for the kiss that had never come. "I ran into Luke in town," she found herself saying. "He's...working over at Cross Creek, but he's thinking about taking a job at the Lazy Four. Since I had things to do at the new house, Luke and I naturally decided to share the ride over...." Hadn't she explained that last night? Or had she and Luke said something else, to cover the fact that he was helping her find Clive? All Claire needed now was for Emma Jane to catch her in a lie.

"Naturally," Emma Jane echoed.

Claire winced. What she'd said had sounded lame. And she hated lying. While she wanted to shield her family from the fact that the wedding might be canceled, at least until she knew for certain, she felt as if she was...covering up her activities for reasons concerning Luke.

Emma Jane gazed at her thoughtfully. "I thought you two being together might have something to do with the bachelor auction last summer."

Claire fought the telltale heat rising in her cheeks. "I don't know what you're talking about, Emma Jane."

Fortunately, Tex appeared and leaned in the doorway, grinning broadly. Plucking an unlit cigar from his mouth, he shoved his other hand deep into a jeans pocket. "I was just heading to the porch to smoke a cigar when my ears started burning. You girls weren't talking about me again, were you?"

Josie released a bright peal of laughter. "We're afraid everybody in town's going to sue you for putting up so many Christmas lights, and if you go to jail, we were trying to decide whether or not we'd bust you out."

"You'd better bust me out."

"Even if we have to call off the wedding?" Vickie asked, giggling.

Tex sent Claire a grin. "After all the money you girls

have made me spend, you'd better not call off that wedding. Isn't that right, Claire?''

Claire managed a smile. "Of course we wouldn't, Tex."

Lifting a hand to his chest, Tex rubbed the space over his heart, releasing an exaggerated sigh of relief. "I knew you wouldn't do something like that to me, Claire. After all, if you don't get married soon, I can't start working on Emma Jane."

"Me?" Emma Jane said.

"Yes, ma'am," Tex returned in a mock-serious tone that sent all the girls into another round of giggles. "Emma Jane's the next to go." Narrowing his eyes, Tex slowly stared from girl to girl. "And then we get rid of Vickie and Rosie and Josie...." His eyes settled on Mama. "And then you're stuck with me."

Mama's shoulders shook with suppressed laughter, and she surveyed Tex, her eyes twinkling. "Fortunately," she shot back, "that cruel fate doesn't await me yet. I've got four more weddings to plan first."

Five, thought Claire, her heart giving a nervous start. She glanced around the room at her family. Shouldn't she tell them now?

MIGHT AS WELL STOP and tell Claire what Wesley said, Luke thought later that day, half aware it was really just an excuse to see her. Vaguely he realized he hadn't bothered to change the radio station since last night, either. Listening to "Jingle Bells" as he put the Cherokee into Park, he braced himself for the cold, got out and circled Claire's Jeep Wrangler, which was parked next to the main house at Lost Springs. Pursing his lips, he eyed the wheel wells, where rust was eating away the baby-blue paint.

"Now, why hasn't Clive seen to this?" he muttered. There wasn't a man who'd grown up in Lightning Creek who didn't know how to patch a rusting vehicle. If Clive wouldn't fix it, maybe Claire could drop the Wrangler by Luke's cabin some morning. *So what if she's getting married?* he tried to reason, pushing aside his unwanted feelings about that matter. They were friends, weren't they? he thought, even though, deep down, he knew he and Claire could never just be friends. Still, the woman couldn't drive around town in a rusted-out Jeep, could she? Between the snow and salt, the rust was bound to get worse by winter's end.

"Hey there, Luke."

Glancing up, he realized Claire had been watching him from the porch. Dressed in jeans and a red-checkered sweater, and framed by the doorway, she looked like a pioneer woman on the prairie. Luke headed toward her, pausing and kicking his boots against the steps to dislodge the snow. "'Morning, Claire."

Brady appeared next to Claire, looking happier than Luke had seen him in days. "Howdy, Luke," the little boy called with a quick wave.

Coming up the steps, Luke grinned. Brady was tugging excitedly on the collar of a worn plaid flannel shirt, and his white-blond hair, cornflower-blue eyes and the smattering of freckles that covered his cheeks and button nose made him look for all the world like the proverbial hayseed farm boy. A toy gun holster was strapped around the waist of his baggy, faded jeans. "Now, ain't you a regular cowboy?" Luke teased.

"Look what Claire brought me for an early Christmas present!" Brady grinned and held up a bright blue toy truck.

"Nice," Luke returned, raising his hands as he came through the door and into the foyer. "But watch those guns. Don't shoot me, pardner." Shutting the storm door behind himself, Luke glanced at a large paper in Brady's truck-free hand. It was a white sheet, painted over in white.

"It's a painting of snow," Brady explained.

"My, you're showing real talent there." Luke couldn't help but wink at Claire. "Better watch out, Claire. This one's serious competition."

"Me 'n' Claire wouldn't never compete," Brady assured Luke, "'Cause we're both artistical."

Claire's lips twitched. "That's right. Artistical. Now, c'mon, you'd better scoot, Brady. I think you've got some chores to do."

Luke chuckled. "Better go milk them cows, pardner."

Tilting his head, Brady shot Luke a dubious sideways glance. "I'm not milkin' no cows." Pulling a tiny silver pistol from the holster, he twirled and reholstered it. "I'm holding up banks." With that, Brady whirled around and bolted down a hallway behind them.

"From now on," Luke called after him, "we'll just have to call you *Wild* Brady Spencer."

As the boy vanished, Luke's eyes drifted to the main room beyond the foyer. Wrapped gifts, mostly from people in the community, were stacked on a red felt skirt beneath the spruce the boys had decorated. Come Christmas Eve, Luke would sneak over and add countless other wrapped presents to the pile. He suddenly remembered years ago, reading a tag that had accidently been left on one such gift. *For a seven-year-old boy,* the tag had read. As if Luke didn't even have a name. Only when he'd read the tag had Luke realized that the gift hadn't been purchased especially for him. Of course, he'd been glad to get the chemistry set. Still, memories such as that had prompted Luke to start answering Dear Santa letters when boys from Lost Springs gave them to the postman. Luke wanted each boy to receive at least one special gift that was his heart's desire. It was just too bad that not every Christmas wish could be fulfilled. Luke still had no leads on who'd abandoned Brady.

Sighing, he glanced at Claire, forcing himself to crack a smile. "You sure put Brady in a good mood."

She nodded. "For a while, anyway." She shrugged ineffectually, her eyes clouding. "But he's having such a rough time right now. The holidays leave him hurting." A soft smile suddenly curled her lips. "It's clear you spend a lot of time over here with the boys, though. And Brady adores you. You know that, Luke? He talks about you all the time."

Vaguely, Luke wondered if Claire had been keeping up with him through the boys and the gossip chain in Twyla's. *Oh, c'mon, Lydell. She doesn't care. She's getting married this week.* He allowed himself a teasing glance. "That so?"

"He says you taught him to throw a lasso, and that you're trying to fix things so some boys can take an overnight trip to Cheyenne next summer for the Frontier Days rodeo."

"That damn Brady," Luke bit out, playfully narrowing his eyes. "So, he's telling womenfolk about all my evil doings, huh?"

Claire chuckled. "Only sweet lil' prairie gals like myself," she assured him. "And anyway, I found out even more of your secrets last night."

Lifting off his Stetson, Luke hung it on a peg behind him, slicked his hair back with a hand, then turned to Claire again, raising an eyebrow. "Secrets?" he asked, trying not to notice how much he liked flirting with her. "Such as?"

"You're a good dancer."

"Your old man ain't bad with a fiddle, either."

Their eyes met, holding shared memories of last night. The Buchanans hadn't been a bit like Luke expected. Despite a passing acquaintance, from seeing one another around town, they'd never spent any real time together. While Luke had anticipated the Stop Awhile's impressive interior, with its spacious entryway, cathedral ceilings and polished paneling, the simple hominess of the rough-hewn log furniture and wood floors had come as a surprise as did the fact that he and Tex shared a common interest in Native American and pioneer artifacts.

At Tex's urging, Luke had been given a full tour, including Claire's attic quarters, and he was stunned by the hunger with which he'd collected intimate facts about her—that she kept her bathroom messy, the temperature low in her studio and sketch pads piled by the simple iron bed where she slept. "To draw things I see in my dreams," she'd said in such a husky voice that Luke had found himself wishing he'd figure in those nocturnal ramblings. For a long time, he'd studied a painting she'd done that hung above her bed; it was of a log cabin in the woods that looked much like his own.

"I had a good time last night," he found himself saying.

"We enjoyed having you. Tex, especially. He likes you, Luke."

The news made Luke feel better than it should have. He'd liked Tex, too. Luke had always imagined it would be impossible to fit in with the Buchanans, but given Claire's lack of pretension and the behavior of her sisters at the bachelor auction last summer, he should have known better. "Your folks are more down-to-earth than I expected," he admitted.

"What?" Claire laughed. "Did you think Mama fed us our grub on fine china and with sterling silver just because we've got a lot of land?"

"Something like that." Instead they'd eaten steak and potatoes on paper plates, since Mama Buchanan said she was saving up all her culinary wherewithal for tonight. She said she'd be too excited about the wedding to cook on Christmas Eve, so she was making the annual turkey dinner early this year. Last night, as they ate, the girls squabbled merrily, and Tex made a show of ordering them around. In turn, they made just as much show of ignoring Tex, right until they fell all over themselves trying to please him. After dinner, Luke had helped Tex push back the living room furniture so the group could dance near the Christmas tree. Tex fiddled and shouted square dance calls, while Luke, the only eligible male, wound up dancing nonstop.

At one point, Claire's mama had asked, "Why isn't Clive here for dinner, too?"

Claire had elbowed Luke. "He's away on some business, Mama. But don't worry, he'll be back tomorrow."

In addition to the concern with Clive's whereabouts, signs of the wedding had been everywhere, and the girls had chattered about it constantly during dinner. Upstairs, Luke had seen a basket of neatly tied net bundles of seeds, and Claire's unhemmed wedding dress hung in a guest room.

Obviously, the wedding was utmost in their minds, but Luke could tell it hadn't overshadowed the other things mentioned at dinner—Josie's breakup with a boyfriend, the stray calico cat Emma Jane had rescued and that was now living in the stables, Vickie's stellar report card, which was apparently a first, and Josie's pleas that she be allowed to wear makeup.

"Think they're strange?" Claire asked now.

"Your folks?" Luke shrugged. "I figured everybody would be going crazy, what with it being both Christmas and your wedding day so soon. In a way you do seem strange, I guess,'' Luke continued. ''Not bad strange,'' he quickly corrected himself. ''But you've obviously got your special ways of doing things.''

Claire smiled. ''That's what makes us a family.''

Luke surveyed her a moment. ''Did Clive call?''

She shook her head. A second passed. She glanced down the hallway where Brady had gone, then lowered her voice. ''In addition to worrying about Clive, I can't get Brady off my mind. All he talks about is meeting his folks. But…the police found him when he was just a baby in a motel room in Douglas, so you know his folks are never coming for him.'' Anger touched her voice. ''Brady even told me he wrote Santa, asking him to find them. Now he says Santa didn't do so last year because Brady sent the letter too late. This year, he's convinced himself that Santa's going to come through.'' Claire's usually soft blue eyes hardened with growing fury at a world that could be so cruel. ''I really think that's why Brady paints things like snow.''

Luke narrowed his eyes, not following her train of thought. ''Snow?''

Distractedly, Claire lifted the braid that lay on her chest and tossed it over her shoulder. ''He's really painting the emptiness he feels inside,'' she continued, her voice catching. ''That sweet little boy's got such a horrible feeling of emptiness….'' Her penetrating eyes lifted to Luke's, and he suddenly shifted uncomfortably, realizing she was analyzing not only Brady, but him, too. ''How can you feel right when you don't know where you came from?'' she asked. ''How can you know where you belong?''

Luke was reminded of Claire's uncanny powers of perception, and how she used her artistic skills to help counsel the boys. He thought once more of her painting of Lost

Springs, and of how those silhouetted boys reached for the sky. He sighed. "Maybe you can't, Claire."

Her eyes had turned watchful. "I don't believe that, Luke. Not for a minute. Even if you don't know your folks, you can find yourself."

Find love. That's what she meant. "Maybe, darlin'," he conceded. "But the emptiness never goes away." He could vouch for that, and it was the most honest thing he'd ever admitted.

Sudden fire came into her eyes. "But I think it *can* go away, Luke."

"I think," he returned gently, "with a family as loving as yours, it's no wonder you're so positive in your thinking."

Claire didn't seem to hear. Shaking her head, she said, "Sometimes I just want to grab him and hold him tight."

For a second, Luke didn't know if she was talking about Brady or him, but many times he'd wanted more for the boys who lived here. "I know what you mean."

She surveyed him a long moment, then she said, "Well...I'm about done here. I guess I'd better get my coat."

Luke reached before she could, lifting the white down parka from a peg where it hung beside his hat and countless little-boy coats. Holding it open for her, he watched as she turned gracefully, slipping into it. Driven by an urge to touch her, Luke skimmed a hand beneath her collar, his fingers grazing her satiny neck. Gently tugging her braid, he freed it, laying it down the back of her coat.

When she turned in his arms, she was too close for comfort. Her voice was a tad too soft and inviting. "Thanks, Luke."

He managed a nod. Was she crazy, taking that seductive tone with him? Didn't she realize she was walking down the aisle in a couple of days? Sighing, he started once more to tell her about the call he'd received from Wesley, but he found himself saying, "I've been looking for Brady's folks." Claire was the only person he'd told.

Surprise came into her eyes. "You've been what?"

Luke shrugged, then explained what he'd done during the past year. "No leads, though," he concluded. "And anyway, even if Brady's folks did turn up..."

There was a long silence, then gently Claire said, "Whoever abandoned him left him in a motel room, Luke. You can't forget that."

Whoever Brady's folks were, Brady might be better off without them. Luke's chest felt strangely tight. Even as unwanted emotion touched him, he couldn't quite bring himself to shut out Claire's perceptive eyes. Somehow, she instinctively understood the deeper things that drove him. It wasn't logical, but Luke identified with Brady. Somehow, he felt that finding Brady's folks would be like finding his own. Like Luke, Brady had been abandoned when he was too young and defenseless to care for himself. Wordlessly, Luke gazed at Claire, his attention drifting from her kind eyes to her lips, and back again.

"Who knows?" she said, her voice low as she rested a hand on his jacket sleeve. "Maybe you will find them, Luke."

He nodded, then he glanced away, wanting to change the subject. "Meantime, Wesley ran down that number we gave him last night." Wesley had also said one of his buddies passed a black Ford Explorer on the road, and that the driver could have been Clive, but Luke withheld that information. He couldn't yet rule out the possibility that Clive was seeing another woman. If so, Claire would have to know, but Luke hoped to minimize the damage.

Relief had flooded her features, and now she withdrew

her hand. "Good. You said Wesley would check the number."

"Turns out the phone's disconnected, but it was in an office at some stables on Elmer Green's property."

Claire started digging gloves from her coat pockets, and as she slipped her hands inside, Luke admired their long-fingered elegance, thinking they were an artist's hands. "Elmer Green," she said, frowning. "That name's familiar."

"He owns one of the places Clive mentioned to Wesley."

"Can we run out there and look around, Luke?" The sudden catch in her voice made Luke realize she was getting genuinely worried. She said, "Clive's been gone two nights now...."

"What time's the wedding Saturday, Claire?"

"Two in the afternoon. After morning church services." She darted her eyes toward a window, as if expecting night to fall suddenly like a stage curtain. "It's so close to Christmas, Luke. Yesterday, I figured he'd turn up. But now..."

Luke felt more torn than ever. He'd do anything for Claire, but the more time he spent with her, the less he wanted to see her and Clive reunited. *Rein it in, Lydell. Their wedding's on Christmas.* Last night, Claire had freed him of any obligation by saying she no longer wanted his help, but Luke couldn't stay away. Unbuttoning his shearling jacket, he reached inside and dug a finger into his flannel shirt pocket. His frown deepened when he found only his notebook, and then he realized Claire was watching him.

"There're some in the kitchen," she said.

He raised his eyebrows, feeling distracted. "Hmm?"

"Some of those toothpicks you're looking for. You know, the ones that help you think."

He smiled. "What? Do I look confused?"

"Very."

He felt that way, too, when he remembered how she'd snatched away the toothpick in his mouth last night. Unwanted warmth settled in his lower belly, and a sudden pull of desire made him ache. Drawing a quick breath, he tried to quit thinking of how close he'd come to kissing her. That had been the very least of what he wanted to do to her, too. "Well...if you really want me to find that fiancé of yours, I guess I ought to get myself a toothpick."

He reached for his hat and put it on, releasing another sigh. Last night, he'd driven out to Cross Creek after leaving the Buchanans. Dealing with cattle had occupied his mind until bedtime, but later he'd found himself lying in his underwear in the dark, thinking about Claire until he was hard and wanting. He'd thought of the picture he'd seen above her bed of the log cabin in the woods, and he'd imagined sharing it with her. All night, alone with his fantasies, Luke kept feeling that it was he, not Clive, who was the lost man. *I think the emptiness can go away,* Claire had said. Deep down, Luke wanted to believe the love of the right woman would make him complete, and that the emptiness he and Brady felt would disappear.

Dammit, Luke cursed silently. Every time he encountered Claire he found himself thinking this way, but Claire was marrying Clive. Yesterday, when she asked why Luke had never returned her affection, she was probably just curious, nothing more. Luke's gaze returned to hers.

She was watching him thoughtfully. "Ready for that toothpick?" she asked.

"Something in particular you want me to think about?"

She shook her head. "No, not really."

"A man's thoughts should be his own," he agreed mildly. But he had the distinct impression he should be doing some more hard thinking about his relationship with Claire.

CHAPTER SIX

A FEW HOURS LATER, they were standing in Elmer Green's stables. The double doors at the far end were off their hinges, leaving an opening big enough to drive a truck through, and freezing air was racing inside the barn, tunneling through the rickety structure. Claire surveyed some charred stains where fire had licked up the wood walls, completely destroying a tack room and office, then she glanced beside her at a shaky-looking wood-plank ladder that led to a hayloft. Sniffling, she tried to ignore the dank mustiness of the place. She was allergic to hay, and her nose was already starting to run and twitch. "Well," she said with a shiver, "now we know why the phone was disconnected."

Luke removed his gloves, shoved them into the back pocket of his faded jeans, then continued poking around. "Elmer Fudd ought to run an ad and sell whatever hay's left in that loft."

"Elmer Green," Claire corrected him, glancing upward toward the loft where icy air blasted through the large, uncovered square window of the hay chute.

"The guy was more like an Elmer Fudd." Lifting his eyes from where they were searching the ground, Luke glanced in her direction. "C'mon, it wouldn't kill you to smile."

"I can't under the circumstances." Claire was getting too worried about Clive. What if she was wrong, and he hadn't disappeared because of their fight? Her eyes scanned the hayloft another moment, then she thought of the bales outside; they were stacked behind the barn covered with snow, near where Luke had parked the Jeep. She sniffled again, crinkling her nose and wishing she could sneeze, just to get it over with. "Clive was looking to buy some hay," she added, chill air pulling down into her lungs with the words. "Maybe I'll tell him about it." Under her breath, she continued, "If we ever find him."

"We'll find him."

She glanced up, eyebrows raised. "You've got good ears."

Luke didn't say anything but merely nodded. If anyone could find Clive, it was Luke. He was carefully walking around the barn, his boots creaking on the frozen ground, his straight black hair tucked behind ears that were halfhidden by the black Stetson. She studied his easy movements and the rigid set of his jaw. As he peered into each of the empty stalls lining the walls, his eyes intently scanned the hard-packed dirt floors strewn with frozen hay. Claire slipped the camera from her pocket and snapped a quick picture of him, even though there wasn't really enough light. "Elmer said all the horses made it out of the fire, right?" she asked.

"Elmer said they were fine," Luke replied. "He got an offer right after the fire and sold 'em. Of course, since he's a horse trader, his business is ruined until he rebuilds the stalls. If he can afford to, which I doubt. But he said nobody's made an offer on his property."

"They still could," Claire said, glancing around. "You think somebody torched the place?"

"It's likely." Luke offered a curt nod. "And curious that the Lazy Four had a barn fire this year, too." Coming closer and lifting his gaze to hers, Luke observed her from beneath his hat brim, his eyes piercing the shadowy darkness. Using his tongue, he shoved the toothpick to the side of his mouth. "Is there anywhere he's supposed to be tonight?"

"You mean Clive?" Claire shook her head. "We talked about us and the Stoddards having a turkey dinner together before Christmas Eve, but Tex said he wanted to eat at home, since it's the last Christmas season…before I get married." She sighed, thinking of Tex, who kept acting as if he'd never see her again. Tex…who'd taken to Luke like a fish to water. Guilt flooded her, and she wondered if she should tell Luke everything. Were they wasting time, looking for evidence that Clive had been here?

Eyeing Luke, she suddenly wished he hadn't fit in so easily with her family, too, and taking in his shoulders, she couldn't help but remember how good it felt to mold her hands over them last night while they'd danced. The touch might have been innocent enough, but Claire's thoughts hadn't been nearly so tame. Nor, she figured, had Luke's. But how she could even think about Luke when she and Clive hadn't completely settled things? What kind of person was she?

"The Stoddards usually have a dinner on Christmas Day," she suddenly continued, crossing her arms and hugging herself to ward off the cold. "But they're skipping it this year because of the wedding. Mama invited them to the Stop Awhile tonight, but then Jenny—that's Clive's mother—said she wanted to tend to Clive's pa, since he's sick. And Evander said he wanted to rest, so he'd have more energy for the wedding."

"I heard Clive's pa's ailing. What's wrong?"

"Leukemia. It's an unusual type for adults to get, but things are looking up, and he's responding to treatment." Claire sighed, her heart hurting for the man who'd been a second father to her. "Anyway," she continued, "Clive said he'd probably come to dinner, so I just assumed he would. Anyway, it wasn't really definite...."

Claire's voice trailed off. The bothersome twitch of her nose returned, and she drew in some breaths without exhaling, preparing for a sneeze that never came.

"Luke," she began again suddenly, rubbing an index finger beneath her nose to satisfy the itch. "My mind's starting to run so wild with ideas about what could have happened. Yesterday, I was only a little worried. But what if Clive had a wreck? Or got run off the road in this weather?" She glanced outside, where snow was falling again in thick white flakes.

"He keeps provisions in his truck, doesn't he?"

That much was true. Everybody in Wyoming knew to carry flares, shovels, salt and sleeping bags. "Of course he does, but the roads..."

"I figure he's got studs and chains, doesn't he?"

"He does."

"So, I'm sure he's fine, Claire."

She sighed, then followed Luke's lead and began pacing, scrutinizing the frozen dirt floor around the hayloft ladder. "What are we looking for?"

"Anything," Luke returned. "The match cover Clive wrote the office number on looks new. Chances are, Clive called here before the fire, day before yesterday. The phone here's been disconnected less than twenty-four hours."

Claire shoved her hands into her pockets, both from frustration and a need for warmth. "Too bad Jim-Bob's gone," she said. "Guess we can't get any help from him." The man who'd occupied the office, Elmer Green's only hired help, hadn't returned since the fire, and now he'd left town for the holidays. No one had a number where he'd gone. Cold was seeping through Claire's jeans, and she stamped her feet to get her circulation going again. "What else did Elmer say?"

Luke shrugged. "Not much."

Claire had basked in the warmth of Luke's Jeep while Luke talked to Elmer on the porch. Now she suddenly muttered, "This place is so creepy!" She shuddered as she stared through the open end of the barn again. The barn was isolated, perched on a plateau, surrounded by pines, cottonwoods and aspens. Endless snow blanketed the dirt road and meadow that were visible through the entryway, and next to the evergreens the bare trees seemed fuzzy and muted, their branches against the snow-filled white sky looking like dark capillaries fanning out beneath pale skin. Just outside the barn, limbs of snow-laden gnarled trees twisted like candles left in the sun, making it seem as if the trees had melted in the barn fire. Slipping a hand into her pocket, she curled her fingers around the camera, then changed her mind about taking another picture; there really wasn't any light. She blew out a long sigh.

And it's almost Christmas, she thought. Her heart lurched as she stared at the ground, redoubling her efforts to find something showing Clive had been here. "Think we should talk to Clive's folks again?" she asked.

"Up to you," Luke said.

Clive had been staying at the new A-frame, and without alarming his folks, Claire had already discerned that they hadn't noticed his disappearance. Clive was grown; they hardly kept tabs on him. The cowhands figured Clive was stuck in Laramie, Douglas or Cheyenne, and since he was the boss, they hadn't bothered to check up on him, either. As her eyes roved the earth floor, Claire suddenly became aware of the pulse ticking in her throat. For a second, the soft beat of it reminded her of a clock, and she felt that time was running out....

She and Luke had to find Clive.

But was he really going to call off the wedding? And should she fight for a marriage to which her fiancé might not be completely committed? Maybe they weren't deeply in love, but she'd always thought she and Clive could share a solid future. Wouldn't it be foolish to throw that away? Eventually, everyone had to grow up, she thought. Relationships were all about compromise, weren't they?

Her eyes slid to Luke. Just looking at him made her realize that a part of her didn't want to grow up and compromise. Luke's head was bent low over a tangled mess of exposed electrical wires, and his hat brim cast interesting shadows over his chiseled face. Nothing about him moved except for the toothpick in his mouth.

Suddenly, he glanced up. "Recognize this?"

She squinted as Luke stood and headed toward her. "What?"

"This."

She still couldn't see. Inadvertently dropping her gaze, she let it drift over the jeans hugging his legs. Her pulse leaped when her eyes settled at the apex of his firm, muscular thighs and the strong curve of his maleness. Blowing out a surreptitious breath, she turned her attention to the silver object dangling from Luke's finger. It was a sterling charm depicting a cowboy on a bucking bronc. "That's Clive's key chain."

"Found it over by the power box. There're no keys attached."

"The keys were on the chain the last time I saw him," she said, thinking back.

Luke considered that a moment, then suddenly glanced over his shoulder toward the doors, his eyes turning flat and watchful.

Claire barely noticed. Her gaze was too busy drifting all

the way down Luke's lean, long body, from the Stetson and the warm tan shearling jacket, to the lovingly worn jeans and boots. He was the living image of the Wyoming cowboys she loved to paint, she realized, as her eyes returned to the hard, pragmatic set of his chin and took in the dark skin that probably came from his native heritage. Someone in his family had been Cheyenne, Claire guessed. Maybe Crow. Countless boys from Indian reservations around the state had wound up at Lost Springs over the years, their mothers too poor to adequately care for them. Luke was hardly the first.

"Somebody's coming," he said.

She turned toward the doors. "I don't hear anything."

"You will," Luke assured her, eyeing the ladder beside her. "We'd better get to the loft."

As she hazarded a glance upward, Claire's nose tickled again, and she crinkled it, fighting a sneeze. Her eyes flitted to his. "Are you sure?"

He offered a long, unwavering look. "Trust me."

But maybe he was just being paranoid. The creepy, isolated barn would do that to anyone. "It's bad enough down here," Claire protested, knowing she'd never survive being so close to that much hay. "Heaven only knows what's up there, Luke. Probably mice. Wild cats."

"If there're cats, there're no mice," Luke stated. "C'mon. This is no time to turn into a priss."

"I am *not* a priss."

"The truck's coming up the road," he said, "so he won't see the Jeep around back."

The last place Claire wanted to go was to that hayloft. Even down here, the scent of hay was stealing her breath, making her nose itch uncomfortably. "Oh. Now you know it's a truck? As opposed to a car or Jeep?"

Luke surveyed her a long moment, his eyes starting to

look lethal from beneath the hat brim, his lips locking together. "You'd better start scurrying, darlin'," he warned darkly.

Suddenly the rumble of an approaching motor cut through the silence. Luke had the ears of a born tracker. "You really think it's somebody..."

"Dangerous? Probably not. But Clive's been here recently, and we're trying to figure out why, Claire. So, let's see whoever it is before he sees us."

Darting her eyes to the hayloft again, Claire rested her hand on a rung of the ladder, her chest squeezing tight with an impending sneeze. "It could be a *she,* you know."

"He or she—" He shoved a frustrated hand in his back jeans pocket. "I don't think it matters right now."

He had a point. "But he'll see our tracks," she protested, even as she grasped and tested the rickety-looking rungs of the ladder.

Luke blew out an exasperated sigh. "Would you just move? And he won't see the tracks. The snow's already covered them."

The motor was rumbling closer, so Claire started climbing. Taking shallow breaths as she ascended, she fought the urge to sneeze. Suddenly, her foot slipped. Quickly jamming her boot heel over the frosty rung, she caught herself. Realizing Luke was right behind her, she gasped. "This ladder can't hold us both."

"It'll have to, Claire. The truck's almost here."

Wrenching around, she stared over her shoulder, just in time to see an aging red pickup truck lunge over the crest of a hill. Hitting the snow-covered dirt road, the truck headed straight for the barn, snow spewing from beneath the wheels. Her fingers froze around a rung. "He can already see us, Luke!"

"Not yet," he growled from beneath her. "It's too dark. But we've got to hurry."

She scrambled upward. "I'm hurrying."

"Not fast enough."

Suddenly, she felt his hand clamp onto her backside, the warm heel of the palm curling right beneath her female center. Shooting blazes of heat licked through her, feeling as dangerous as the fire that had destroyed the barn. Censure touched her voice. "Luke!"

"Oh, c'mon." A sudden hard push sent blissful awareness through her body as she tumbled into the hayloft. "You know you liked it, Claire."

"Did not," she returned, feeling so flustered she could barely speak. With just one stolen touch, the man had completely frazzled her nerve endings. As she crawled away from the ladder, she could still feel Luke's hand, alive and pulsing beneath her. Even worse, she wanted to feel his warm touch there again, this time with no clothes between them. Yes, she wanted Luke touching her, flesh to flesh. She wanted him to finish what he'd only started years ago in the woods at Lost Springs. Her heart hammering fiercely, she managed to shoot him a furious glance.

He had the nerve to smile back.

With a long-suffering sigh, she rolled over between two bales of foul-smelling hay. She stared down, toward the floor of the barn. "There's one thing I forgot to tell you," she whispered as Luke nestled beside her, and lifted off his hat so it couldn't be seen over the loft's edge.

Instead of responding Luke silently set aside the hat and riveted his gaze on the red truck that was now entering the barn. Rapidly blinking her eyes, which were starting to tear, Claire did her best to ignore the pungent, moldy smell of the hay only inches from her nose. She followed Luke's gaze. Two men were in the cab, but they weren't close enough that she could make out their features. The truck circled, pulling around so that it faced the doors. Squinting, Claire could make out a bucking bronc on the license plate, so they were from Wyoming. Closing her eyes, she committed the numbers to memory.

When she opened her eyes, she glanced anxiously over her shoulder, taking in the unbroken square of white sky framed by the open, floor-to-ceiling hay chute. The chute wasn't but twenty feet behind her and Luke, and just imagining the treacherous drop-off beyond it made her dizzy. She'd gotten colder, too, she realized, since she'd quit moving. Clamping her teeth together stopped their chattering, but it didn't ward off the chill. Beneath her belly, frigid air seeped through her parka from the hard wood floor.

It was too bad Elmer Green hadn't closed the chute, but he must have been moving bales before the barn fire. Claire sighed, wishing enough air would gust inside to relieve her hay fever, then she shivered again, so violently that her shoulders shook. "I'm getting frostbite because of you," she whispered, her eyes returning to the truck.

"You came to me for help," Luke whispered back in a husky reminder, his low voice sounding close to her ear, warming her. "Remember?"

As if this was all her fault. "You know you wanted to help me," she returned, her gaze settling on his lips.

He raised an eyebrow. "Why would I want to do that?"

"Because you think I have a way with men." She suddenly narrowed her eyes, still not entirely forgiving the abrupt and very warm feel of his broad hand between her legs, nor the storm of desire the touch had sent through her body. "Not that my charms will matter, once I freeze to death," she added.

"Here."

Just then the two men got out, circled around the back of the truck and began to confer near the empty bed. Luke scooted closer. Claire fought back a shudder of another kind as the heat of his side warmed hers. Soundlessly reaching under himself, Luke unbuttoned his jacket, opened the side, then stretched the warm shearling across her back, leaving his arm around her. Claire snuggled closer, liking the heavy feel of his arm across her back.

"Better?" he whispered.

"Better," she agreed.

She realized Luke was gazing down at her, with what she could swear was the light of tenderness in his blue eyes. "Now, shut up," he mouthed, the strong curl of his fingers around her shoulder taking any sting out of the words.

Nodding, Claire stared down at the men again. One was about thirty years old. A hand was thrust into the pocket of his navy parka, and he was fiddling with the bill of a black baseball cap that was printed with a company logo. The man doing most of the talking was closer to fifty, overweight, with a full beard and a cowboy hat. Despite the cold, only a jean jacket hung over his army fatigue pants. Peering down, Claire couldn't see their faces, just the tops of their hats. She watched as the heavy man with the cowboy hat lifted a hand and pointed toward the doors, seemingly giving the younger man directions. Straining toward the murmuring voices, Claire tried but couldn't make out the words. Luke leaned so close that she could smell mint from a flavored toothpick.

Plucking it from between his lips, he whispered, "Now, what did you forget to tell me?"

Suddenly, she inhaled. Another swift intake of breath followed. She grabbed Luke's shoulder with one hand and used the other to pinch her nose, not caring how ridiculous she looked.

Luke was squinting at her. "What are you doing?" he demanded in a hushed whisper.

Drawing an involuntary breath, she suddenly sneezed. And then she hissed, "Sneezing. I'm allergic to hay."

"Now she tells me," Luke muttered.

Below, both men's heads jerked up. Claire watched in horror as the younger man slowly unzipped his parka and slipped a hand inside. "He's going for a gun," she whispered in panic, her heart thudding wildly. The older man in the cowboy hat turned, headed for the truck cab and returned with a rifle. "Not very promising," Claire added shakily.

"Sure isn't," Luke whispered.

The man in the cowboy hat aimed the rifle at the hayloft. "Who's there?" he called, turning to the younger man. "Jack," he continued, his voice still raised. "You'd better take a look."

"Will do, Ham."

Jack and Ham. Claire would have felt safer if they'd had other names. Together, the two sounded like *jackhammer.* Her watering eyes widened as she watched Jack reach deeper inside the unzipped parka, this time pulling out a handgun. Claire knew guns. Tex collected them. And she knew that Jack's personal choice of weapon rated more than average on the scorecard for lethal. As her eyes locked with Luke's again, Claire found herself fighting against another tickle of her nose. Then she swallowed against the dryness of her throat. The blood running through her veins was turning to ice water.

Downstairs, Jack was rattling the rickety wooden ladder to the loft. Sensing movement, Claire glanced over and realized Luke was quietly lifting his jeans leg and sliding a hand into his boot. "When I say 'jackrabbit,'" he whispered, "you'd better start running, darlin'."

Her eyes darted around the hayloft. "Run where?"

Luke jerked his head toward the hay chute.

Her eyes widened just as the Colt Pony Pocketlite appeared, the tiny handgun nothing more than a quick flash of silver in Luke's dark hand. Claire sucked in another involuntary breath and sneezed again. Uttering a low curse under his breath, Luke spoke around the toothpick in his mouth. When she didn't move, he urged, "Claire, run!"

"You were supposed to say 'jackrabbit,'" she couldn't help but whisper, despite the circumstances. "Not curse at me."

"Jackrabbit," Luke whispered back pointedly. And then, glancing away, he raised his arm, took aim and started firing.

Claire flew toward the hay chute, barely aware that the rush of air she heard was from a deflating tire. Ducking her head, she cringed as one of the men gave a yell. A second later, return bullets pinged, spraying into the wood above her head. Crouching near the chute, Claire edged closer, glanced down and winced at the hay bales far below.

No way! It was a country mile to the bales. Wild horses couldn't drag her over the perilous edge of the chute. Forget worrying over her wedding; she'd be dead if she jumped. Soulfully, she eyed Luke's Jeep, which was a mere ten feet from the bales. Then she turned from the icy air buffeting her face and stared at Luke again. He was still on his belly, carefully taking aim, his expression so unconcerned that he could have been target-practicing with soda cans. As he scooted back, he lightly lifted his Stetson from the floor with his gun-free hand and snuggled it onto his head.

Suddenly, he rose, turned and bolted toward her. "Jump now, Claire!" he commanded, shoving the Colt into his waistband.

She didn't even have a chance to respond.

"Hang on to me, darlin'," he said, wrapping an arm around her waist. One hand on his hat, he jumped, pulling her with him. She was swept right off her feet and jerked through the chute. In midair, Luke's arms were wrenched away. Her heart pounded, her braid flew upward, and she began flailing her arms. The air was frigid, and she felt as if she were tunneling down through a chute of liquid ice. Scarcely aware of the cold wind stinging her tearing eyes, she saw a dark falling shape in the periphery of her vision that must have been Luke. *Cool Hand Luke,* she thought illogically

Whoomph!

"What are you trying to do?" she snarled with her first breath. "Kill me?"

"That sounds like projection to me," Luke said. "Right about now, you're probably the one who wants to kill me."

"I'm the one with the psychology degree."

"Just get in the Jeep."

"What did you think I was doing?" On a rush of adrenaline, Claire scrambled to her knees and shimmied down the stacked bales, knowing Luke could take care of himself. She hit the ground already moving. Her boots slipped on ice, then got traction. As she ran, her throat burned, feeling raw, and her heart hammered so hard she thought it would explode. Reaching the Jeep, she wrenched open the first door she came to, on the passenger side. Luke was right behind her, ripping the toothpick from his mouth and tossing it into the snow.

For the second time that day, his hand settled on her

backside, this time pushing her into the driver's seat. "Drive!"

"Quit bossing me around!" Her shaking hands fumbled at the ignition; her insides felt like jelly. "Where are the—"

"Here." Just as Luke shoved a key into the ignition, her hand closed over his, and she registered a shock of heat and electricity as she helped him turn the key. It was hardly the best time to feel physical attraction.

The engine didn't start.

"I got the license number," she gasped.

"I shot out one of their tires, too," Luke returned, looking over his shoulder. "But they'll probably follow us, anyhow. Won't it start?"

"I'm trying," Claire muttered, her heart racing as she turned the key in the ignition again. She just hoped it wasn't vapor lock. Low atmospheric pressure combined with high engine temperatures could make gas evaporate in the fuel lines.

One of the men suddenly shouted, "There they are!"

A bullet pinged off metal.

They were shooting the Jeep! "Please," Claire whispered, hunkering down and waiting for a bullet to shatter the back windshield. Panic overwhelmed her as she tried the key once more. Suddenly, the radio blasted and Dolly Parton's voice belted out "Joy to the World." Hearing Christmas music under the circumstances was jarring, but the Jeep roared to life, so Claire threw it into gear and floored the gas pedal. Lunging forward, they bounced on rough, slippery terrain. Instinctively, Luke grabbed his hat.

Suddenly, Claire realized she couldn't see anything. "Snow!" she gasped, her eyes riveted on the whitened windshield. "Luke! Where are the windshield wipers!"

Already, Luke had leaned over, his hand gripping her

knee for support as he flicked a button. A second later the windshield wipers pushed aside the snow—giving Claire enough visibility that she was filled with renewed terror. They were about to plow into a stand of cottonwoods and pines.

"Look out!" Luke warned.

"We're okay." Out of the corner of her eye, she could see Luke bouncing up and down. "We'll just go over this hill."

He gasped. "Through those trees? Are you crazy, Claire?"

"Right over this hill's the road we took to get here," she shot back breathlessly. "Right?"

"Right! But this isn't a plane, Claire, it's a land vehicle."

She'd about had it. "Luke, if you want to be a backseat driver," she said, "then get in back." She lifted her eyes from the fast-approaching trees just long enough to glare at him. "This is an off-road vehicle, right?"

"Yeah, but—"

"I know, I know," she muttered as the Jeep suddenly dived between two cottonwoods and into scrub brush and brambles, "it's not a plane."

Luke didn't respond. He was probably too busy calculating their chances of survival. She winced as branches raked down the vehicle's sides, destroying the paint job. But there was nothing she could do. Especially not when the Jeep nose-dived, heading southward, down a steep hill. Hanging on to the steering wheel with all her might, Claire white-knuckled it, dodging pines and aspens, her fingers curling ever tighter with each bend in the road. Her concentration was so intense that even Luke seemed to vanish. Everything seemed silent. And then the Jeep burst through the trees toward a roadway, its tires leaving the ground completely, spinning in midair.

"And now," she heard the radio D.J. say as the Jeep's front wheels connected with the slushy, snow-covered pavement, "this next one's from Clint Black. Hope you enjoy his Christmas ditty called "'Til Santa's Gone.'"

"Santa's gone?" muttered Luke. "*We're* goners."

The back wheels had hit solid ice.

"Turn into the spin," Luke said.

"I'm trying!" But the car was on its own, sliding in a wide, slow-motion arc. "Is anything coming?" she gasped. All they needed right now was a truck bearing down on them.

"Nope."

Suddenly, the Jeep simply stopped. It had spun almost full circle in the road, and Claire managed to maneuver it into its lane. The sudden feeling of safety was so unexpected that Claire uttered a breathless, stupefied laugh, feeling downright triumphant. Shaking her head in disbelief as she stared through the windshield, she shook her head. "Can you believe that?" she remarked, her heart still pounding rapidly with both fear and excitement as she caught Luke's eyes. "Am I good or what?"

Luke stared back, taking his hand off his hat and the roof. "Good?" he echoed, pulling the Colt from his waistband and sliding it back into his boot. "Good at *what*, exactly, Claire?"

Her eyes widened. "I know we're still in the middle of an icy road," she returned defensively, "but I got us out of there alive, now, didn't I?"

"That remains to be seen," Luke replied dryly. Lifting his feet from the floor, he pretended to be checking for broken bones. Then he shot her one of his slow killer smiles, just a flash of white teeth in his dark skin. "Guess I'm still in one piece."

One very good-looking piece. "I knew it." He felt exactly as she did. Lucky to be alive. His blue eyes were shining brightly with the exhilaration of having survived the close call. "Admit it," she challenged. "I *am* good."

He tilted his head as if considering.

"I can't believe your lack of gratitude, Luke!" she exclaimed. Still feeling strangely high at having escaped, she leaned swiftly and playfully punched his shoulder. Just as her fist connected with hard muscle, Luke caught her hand. With a quick tug, he brought her right to his mouth, so close that strands of his flyaway blue-black hair teased her jaw. "You're good," he assured. "Very, very good, Claire." And then, without warning, his lips covered hers, feeling cold and soft, then warmer and harder, then hotter and more demanding. She melted against his mouth, parting her lips for him, and as his tongue dueled with hers, she felt tingles spread across the surface of her skin and prickle inside her. Pressing her upper body against his hard chest, she felt her breasts ache for his touch. All pressure and dampness, the impulsive, wet-tongued kiss suddenly felt like a prelude to sex, and it left Claire staring at him, wanting more when he was gone.

He winked from the passenger seat as if it hadn't even happened. "Mind if we go somewhere safer?" he said. "Some place where I can think?"

Fighting to recover from the welcome assault of his mouth, Claire managed to dig a hand coolly into the back pocket of her jeans. Withdrawing a toothpick, she handed it to him. "Think away," she said. "Might I suggest the Roadkill Grill?"

CHAPTER SEVEN

"COME AGAIN, YA HEAR?" As the proprietress left Claire and Luke's change on the table, she beamed into the cozy, intimate booth. "Hope you don't mind me saying so, but you two look so good together." Releasing a soft laugh, she wiped her hands on a red-and-green apron printed with holly leaves. "I'm divorced myself," she said. "My man flew the coop, so to speak."

Luke smiled. The Roadkill Grill had been packed, and Main Street was crowded with shoppers, so Luke had suggested this hole-in-the-wall diner that had just opened near Little Creek Road and Pine Street. It was called Nora's Nest. "You don't sound too broken up about the divorce, Nora," Luke said now, sending Claire a quick wink.

Nora chuckled. "I got enough money from the settlement to move out west and open this place. Besides, when one love affair doesn't work out, it always means a better one's in the making. You can trust the good Lord on that. I'll never quit believing in love, no more than I'll quit believing in Christmas. How could I, when folks like you are the living proof?"

Luke caught Claire's helpless expression. "Glad you think we make a good couple, Nora," he said.

As Nora headed to the kitchen, Luke decided Claire did look as if she was in love. Her eyes were bright and her skin was flushed, but he doubted the kiss they'd shared in the Jeep had much to do with it. More than likely, Claire was still exhilarated from escaping Jack and Ham. Luke still couldn't believe the side of Claire he'd just seen—fearless and wild. Somehow, watching her drive through those cottonwoods had made him want her more than he ever had. "Sorry." Luke smiled. "But I didn't want to destroy Nora's delusions."

"About us?"

Luke nodded. "Wouldn't want the woman to quit believing in miracles."

Claire's eyes on his seemed too direct, too intense. "Love's not a miracle," she said with a sudden soft catch in her voice. "It happens every day, it really does."

Luke had no answer for that. "Well, Nora was right about one thing. You do look a little…" Luke searched hard for something other than "in love," and settled on "kind of wild, Claire."

Claire laughed. "What's that got to do with love?"

His eyes drifted over the stray, haywire tendrils of hair that had come loose from her braid. "Everything," he said simply, reaching across the table to pluck a bit of hay from her tangled tawny strands.

"You've got a point there."

Did he? His chest tightened as he thought of how easily he could tongue her body, how soft and yet full of fire her eyes might look as they climbed the heights of desire together. As if already feeling the warmth, Luke unbuttoned and flicked up the cuffs of his flannel shirt, rolling them on his strong, dark forearms. He managed a smile. "Looks like gunfights and car chases suit you, Claire."

"You think?"

"Sure do." Seeing her so excited was almost worth every bullet that had whizzed past his ears. At least it would have been if Claire hadn't been in danger. And if the paint job on his new Jeep hadn't been destroyed.

Reaching over to where his Stetson rested next to an empty coffee cup, Luke snagged a fresh toothpick from a dispenser and popped it into his mouth. "Now, before we hit the road again, are you sure you're all right?"

She was whirling a cinnamon stick around in a stoneware mug, stirring the remains of mulled cider. "Never felt better. You?"

"If you want the truth," he admitted, giving her a quick, pointed look of censure, "I was scared. And you should have been, too."

Her sexy lips twitched. "Right," she returned dryly. "I could tell you were quaking in your boots by the way you kept shoving bullets back into that automatic weapon."

"They're magazines," he corrected her, running a hand through his sleek black hair, pushing it behind his ears, his mouth curling with humor. "You know that." He shrugged. "Whoever said I don't know how to show a girl a good time?"

"I can't imagine. No girl in her right mind would say that."

"Only the crazy ones, huh?"

Claire sent him an endearing lopsided grin, which was at odds with her more usual, serious demeanor. "Well, I must be crazy," she said. "Because I thought it was great. For my first gunfight, anyway."

"And your last, if I have any say."

Even as he said the words, Luke knew he'd made a mistake. He sounded too possessive. But given the way she'd kissed him in the Jeep, it was hard to remember they were looking for her fiancé. During the awkward silence that fell, Luke glanced around, taking in the mistletoe hanging in the front entry, then the foot-high plastic trees on the tabletops. Instead of stars or angels, birds were perched atop the trees, and looking closer, Luke realized they were partridges in pear trees. Through the holiday messages sprayed in canned snowflakes across the windows, he could see that the snow had tapered off again.

Claire lifted the mug, finished off the cider and leaned back in the booth, against her open parka. She said, "I just wish we knew what those guys were doing out there."

And what I'm doing in here with you, Claire. "Me, too," Luke said, still feeling the tantalizing softness of her mouth. He shrugged. "Elmer said he'd never seen anybody who answered Ham and Jack's descriptions." Before coming to Nora's, he and Claire had driven to Elmer's, then they'd called Sherrif Hatcher and Wesley on the Jeep's phone to fill them in on what happened at the stables. Wesley said he'd run the truck's license plate number as soon as possible. Now Luke sighed. He just wished he knew if Clive was involved with the men who'd shot at them. Since they'd found Clive's key chain, Luke had a gut feeling there was a connection.

"Ham and Jack," Claire said, thoughtfully tapping the cinnamon stick against the mug. "I wish I'd used the camera in my pocket to get their pictures."

"There wasn't enough light," Luke reminded her.

She shuddered. "Well, Elmer wouldn't be likely to forget such unsavory characters. And Wesley says I shouldn't file a formal missing persons report on Clive, right?"

"Won't do much good yet. Clive's an adult, and he did have business out of town. They'll want to wait a few days." Leaning back, Luke stretched his legs under the table, accidently nudging Claire. "Sorry," he murmured.

"No problem."

Since it wasn't, Luke left his long legs stretched next to hers. "You really think something's happened to Clive?"

Claire sounded as if she'd reached the end of her rope. "I just don't know, Luke," she said. "I really thought he was upset and avoiding me. But now I'm afraid something's wrong."

Thoughtfully, Luke rolled the toothpick across his tongue. "You keep saying Clive goes off on his own."

"He always has. He's been boss of the Lazy Four for the past few years, and he doesn't answer to anyone."

"His pa's got a reputation for being..."

"Reclusive." Claire dropped the cinnamon stick in the mug and thoughtfully chewed her lower lip. "Even though I never heard any gossip, I always got the feeling—" she shrugged, as if searching for the words "—that Evander had some tragedy in his past."

The pale, dusky flush that appeared on her cheeks made Luke wonder if she felt awkward discussing her future in-laws. However wrong, Luke felt talking about them intruded on the intimacy he and Claire were sharing, serving as a bothersome reminder that they were only together because of Clive. "You get along with Evander?"

"Yeah." Sudden warm emotion came into her eyes, and seeing it, Luke realized that Claire and the Stoddards shared a bond transcending her relationship with Clive. It shouldn't have given Luke pause, but it did.

"He has four sons, including Clive, but he always wanted a girl, so he treats me like a daughter." Her eyes narrowed as if she were studying a knotty problem. "Like I said, I think Evander harbors a secret that eats away at him. He knows I suspect it, too."

Luke didn't follow. "You think that's why he likes you?"

Claire nodded. "Maybe. People with problems are drawn to perceptive people. They secretly hope the person can help solve their difficulties."

Do you think that's why I like you? Luke thought, fighting that aching, undeniable tug of his heart. Didn't he secretly believe Claire understood his buried fears about loving? "You're definitely a perceptive woman, Claire." *A caring, loving woman.*

When she looked at him, her shadowy eyes seemed to melt. Her voice was just as warm. "Thanks, Luke." After a moment, she continued, "As I was saying, Clive's had a free rein for years."

Luke nodded. "Lucky man. The Lazy Four's a beautiful spread. I've always dreamed of running a place like that."

"You could. You've got plenty of experience."

Luke shook his head. He'd never give his heart to another man's land, not if he couldn't fully enjoy the fruits of his labor. Being a right-hand man to someone such as Clive would have made Luke feel illegitimate, like the bastard child he probably was. He didn't want to feel second in importance to sons who stood to inherit property, whose ancestors' sweat and blood had drawn wealth from the earth. Call it uncompromising—or the pulse of his proud blood—but he'd settle for nothing less than his own land. Unfortunately, big spreads like the Lazy Four weren't usually bought and sold; they were handed down for generations. Since fate hadn't given Luke the birthright he craved, he'd chosen to work small ranches like Cross Creek, giving back to the land what little he took from it.

He realized Claire was studying him. He said, "Well, I guess we'd better go over to the Lazy Four. We'll tell the Stoddards we think Clive's really missing."

Looking worried sick, Claire stared into her cider mug. For a long moment, Luke merely watched her, lowering his gaze from her face to where the collar of her red-and-white-checked sweater was open, exposing the creamy neck he'd so often imagined kissing. Her lips were still rouged from the chill winter air, and he wanted to stroke those, too, using both his fingers and tongue, but it was her eyes that most captured him. The haunting shadows around them made her look sad in a way Luke longed to soothe. *She really loves him,* Luke thought. And then he felt a sudden rush of emotion so foreign that it took him a full minute to identify it as panic.

She started fiddling with the edges of a paper place mat, seemingly reading the Christmas dinner menu printed on it. "I hate alarming the Stoddards if we don't need to," she finally said. "Especially not Evander. He's sick."

"It's not up to you to protect your in-laws," Luke forced himself to say. And although he knew he had no right, he found himself adding, "I want you to stay out of this, Claire. It could mean trouble. We got shot at today." Seeing bullets dig into the wood near Claire's head had about done him in. He'd had clear aim at both Ham and Jack, and as far as Luke was concerned, both men were damn lucky to still be breathing.

She mustered a smile. "And I didn't think you cared."

"Darlin'," he said sighing. "You know I do. Clive could be somewhere on business, but just in case..."

She suddenly gulped. "I didn't tell you everything, Luke." Leaning closer, she rested her elbows on the table. "The Stoddards' ranch is in trouble."

Luke stared at her. "Claire, you should have told me. What kind of trouble?"

"They've lost money lately. Clive's a great rancher, but he's had setbacks. Things like that barn fire last year."

Luke pushed the toothpick to the side of his cheek. "I figure that fire's connected to the one at Elmer's."

"That's what I think, too. But...what I wanted to tell you is that once Clive and I got engaged, Evander and Tex started talking about merging the Stop Awhile and the Lazy Four. And the other day when we were arguing, it was clear Clive feels he has to marry me now, to help put

the Lazy Four back in the black." She blushed crimson.
"It didn't start out that way, but..."

Luke could only stare. He'd known Claire was withholding information, but not this. Clive might not love
Claire? All along, Luke had figured the Stoddards and
Buchanans would combine assets, since it was sensible,
but this news hurt. More than hurt, Luke realized. It was
killing him. Ever since last summer, when they'd spent the
evening together after the bachelor auction, Luke hadn't
been able to get Claire out of his mind, and when she came
to the mall, he'd been secretly hoping she simply wanted
to see him. But now it seemed as if she really wanted to
find Clive. He, not she, was having second thoughts about
marriage.

But Claire didn't kiss as if she was in love with Clive.
Luke managed a smile he hoped would smooth over her
embarrassment about her relationship troubles, then he
found his voice. "The Stoddards'll make out," he supposed. "But Tex has got a lot to gain from this deal, too?"

She nodded. "Tex has liquid capital, but the Lazy
Four's got more land, more cattle, more contacts...." She
blew out a long sigh. "Anyway, the pressure got to Clive.
He told me he never wanted to work the Lazy Four, but
since his older brothers were pursuing other job prospects,
he had no choice. Especially since his pa's sick."

Luke's mind was still reeling. He'd been a fool. If Claire
was in love with Clive, that meant she'd asked for Luke's
help simply because he was the best man for the job. And
how could Clive not want the Lazy Four? All his life Luke
had lusted after land such as that, almost as much as he'd
lusted after Claire. He could almost see the spread, how
lush it would look in summer with cattle roaming the
grasslands, or in early autumn, when the turning leaves
would burn against the sky in bright yellow sunbursts and

orange fire. Some people didn't appreciate their own good luck. Clive had both Claire's heart and the Lazy Four, but he wanted neither. Luke couldn't help but say, "I'd kill for a spread like that." *And you, Claire.* The thought came unbidden. *Dammit, I'd kill for you, too.* The power of the thought rocked him.

Claire shrugged. "Clive wanted to work with computers. He's good at it, too, as near as I can tell."

Luke could merely shake his head.

"I thought he was off somewhere, hashing out his feelings," Claire rushed on. "At least until we ran into Jack and Ham and found Clive's key chain. And now..." She looked positively stricken.

Luke's chest pulled as he recalled kissing her in the Jeep, how warm the pliable, yielding softness of those full lips had felt beneath his mouth, how she'd responded. As his mouth had moved greedily on hers, an unstoppable hunger to possess every inch of her had churned in his blood. He'd wanted to thrust himself deep inside her, claiming everything she'd offered him years ago in the parking grounds at Lost Springs. Now anger he knew was unreasonable threatened his control. But dammit, Claire had no right to let him kiss her like that, not if she wasn't thinking of breaking off with Clive. *You didn't give her much choice, Lydell.* Feeling disgusted with himself, Luke could admit that much. "Look," he forced himself to say. "We'd best head over to your..." *In-laws.* "The Stoddards'. If they know we're thinking Clive's disappeared, they'll be worried, but they'll think harder about where he might have gone."

"I'm ready," she said.

As he helped her with her parka, Claire's eyes settled on the Christmas menu printed on the place mat. Turning, she rested a hand on Luke's forearm, her long, artistic

fingers making the bare skin beneath tingle with awareness. "Why don't you come for dinner after we go to the
Stoddards', Luke? Mama's making a turkey." Claire offered a smile that didn't meet her worried eyes. "No matter what happens in life, we still have to eat."

His heart tugged because he usually ate alone, and suddenly, he felt as if he could happily dine with the Buchanans every night for the rest of his life. But he couldn't
afford to get any closer to Claire, not if it was Clive who
was getting cold feet. Besides, Claire had been free all
these years, and Luke hadn't pursued her, now, had he?
Obviously, her unavailability was somehow attracting him.
"Thanks, Claire," he said, "but no thanks. We still need
to get your Jeep from Lost Springs, and I've got some
work to do at Cross Creek. I know how anxious you are
about Clive, so I'll check in with the sheriff later. I told
him I'd make a statement about what happened at the barn,
anyway." Luke still hadn't wrapped the gifts for the boys
at Lost Springs, either.

Lifting his hat from the table, Luke tried to ignore the
wounded expression in Claire's eyes. "Are you sure you
can't come for dinner, Luke?"

"Afraid not."

She nodded. "I understand."

But she didn't, not really. She had no idea how much
he wanted her, no more than she understood the near-
physical sensation of loss he felt when she withdrew her
hand from his arm. "C'mon." He put his hand on her
shoulder, feeling powerless but to restore the physical con-
tact. "Let's go."

CLAIRE GLANCED AWAY from the windshield. "Luke?"

"Yeah?" His eyes narrowed as he drove beneath the
arched iron gate leading to the Lazy Four. Something he

couldn't put his finger on was bothering him again, and it was more than the fact that Claire was apparently truly in love with Clive. Why that should surprise him, Luke really didn't know. She was engaged to the man. Still, when Luke kissed her, her response said she was available. Sighing, he scanned the long, straight driveway. It had been cleared with a plow, and the blacktop was nearly visible under a light coat of white. Gripping the steering wheel, he pulled onto the driveway's shoulder, the Jeep's tires churning easily through piled drifts left by the plow.

Leaning, Claire reached above the car phone and lowered the radio volume. She glanced around, her eyes crinkling with concern. "What's wrong?"

He shook his head. Letting the engine idle, he watched flurries stick to the windshield and half listened to the music, a country-western cover of "Away in a Manger." "Claire," he suddenly began, glancing away from the windshield. "It's the damnedest thing. Last night, when we came here, I started getting the strangest feeling. Like I'd been here before. I doubt there's anything to it, but..."

"You feel like you've been to the Lazy Four?"

He nodded. Lifting off his hat and resting it on the compartment between the seats, Luke turned and stared at the gate again. Four rods of black wrought-iron rose from the ground on either side of the driveway, and as they neared the top of the arch, they twined together, fusing into the number four. Two man-size decorative candy canes were crisscrossed in front of the "four" and tied with a large red bow. "I swear I've seen that gate before." He wriggled his tongue against his inner cheek where a toothpick rested, as if that might help him remember.

"You've definitely driven past it."

He shook his head. "Never this close to the house. The gate's not visible from the main road."

"So?" she murmured.

At the urging of her concerned eyes, Luke thought even harder, staring outside at the rolling, snow-covered hills, and then, with another shake of his head, he told her how preoccupied he'd felt, both last night and now, and about how he kept remembering the woman in the yellow dress. "It's like something's got hold of my mind and won't let go," he concluded. *Like you, Claire.*

"You grew up in Lightning Creek," she said helpfully. "So, it stands to reason you've been here. Maybe you just don't remember it."

"Maybe...but I don't know." Claire was watching him carefully, but she said nothing more, just let him chew on the toothpick, trying to think. Vaguely, he registered the words to the song on the radio. *Away in a manger, no room for a bed.* And he found himself imagining the cold chill of the dark, snowy Christmas morning when he'd been dumped on the porch at Lost Springs. Now he felt as if *he* was the child with no place to go. But why was he thinking about that now? Hadn't he dealt with that pain years ago and gotten on with his life? Why would it come flooding back when he pulled onto the Lazy Four?

Feeling suddenly warm, Luke flicked open the buttons of his jacket. Claire did the same, unzipping her parka and shrugging out of it. "Maybe you came here as a kid," she continued. "Is there anyone you can ask?"

"Slim Struthers, I guess. Years ago, before he became head honcho at the Rambling Rose, he'd worked at Lost Springs. He was around for most of my growing up."

"You used to come to the feed store with him on Saturdays."

Luke nodded. Of course she'd remember him. "I figure he knows more about me than anybody." That feeling stole over Luke again, as if lost memories were hiding in his mind. "And last night," he suddenly added, "I think I even dreamed about this place." Hadn't he dreamed of a man and woman—no, a whole family—getting into a car and driving through the gates? "I remember a car...."

"What kind?"

He shrugged. "An old red one. Not beat-up old," he added. "Old, like it was a classic. With a shiny paint job and tail fins."

"A Cadillac?"

Maybe she was thinking of the one Tex used to drive. Luke could only shake his head again, feeling frustrated. "I don't know."

Claire leaned closer, resting an elbow on the lid of the compartment between the seats, next to Luke's hat. "Can you remember anything else?"

She was watching him with what looked suspiciously like professional interest. "I'm not crazy, Claire," he said.

"Of course not." Her all-seeing eyes became even softer, and as she reached a hand toward him, Luke's heart nearly stopped. His breath caught as her fingers slid into his hair, gently raking through the strands and against his scalp, stoking a fire low in his belly. "There's no such thing as crazy," she assured him.

A caress like that sure won't convince me, Claire. He didn't say the words because he didn't want it to end, but she withdrew her hand, anyway, and he sighed softly.

She nodded toward the car phone. "Why don't you call Slim?"

Staring up the Stoddards' long driveway, Luke felt something inside him catching. Was it fear? Whatever the emotion, he didn't entirely understand it. "Right now?"

"Why not? It'll take five minutes."

Who could deny the coaxing pragmatism in her voice? Leaning over, Luke punched in Slim's number, leaving the phone on the speaker option. "He's probably not even there," Luke said as he and Claire listened.

On the fourth ring, somebody lifted the phone. "'Lo."

Just hearing Slim's voice made Luke chuckle softly. "Hey there, cowboy."

"'Lo, there," said Slim. "Guess I should have said, 'Ho, there.' Happy holiday, Luke."

"Same to you."

"When are you coming out to sit a spell with me 'n' the wife, boy? We got a whole turkey waitin'. If you can't come Christmas Day, how's about leftovers the day after?"

"Sounds fine, Slim. Say, six?"

"Six is good."

Leaning an elbow against the steering wheel and half turning toward Claire, Luke said, "Slim, I mostly called because I've got a quick question. I'm over at the Stoddard place."

"The Lazy Four?"

"Yeah. And, anyway…" Feeling awkward, Luke went ahead and told Slim everything he'd just told Claire. "Slim," he said, speaking more candidly than he usually did. "Maybe it's just the time of the year. To be honest, I always wind up thinking back to how you-all found me that Christmas." Luke shook his head, feeling dull anger. "What kind of people would leave a baby on a doorstep?" he muttered, blowing out another sigh. "Anyway, I just wondered if you ever brought me over here, to the Lazy Four."

There was a long pause. During it, both he and Claire stared down at the phone. Then Slim said, "Uh…I sure don't recall taking you to the Stoddards'. Doubt you ever went, neither. First off, Evander Stoddard ain't much for company. Everybody knows he keeps to himself. The hands' bunkhouse is nearly two miles from the main house, you get to it by a separate road, and nobody from Lost Springs ever did any business out there. But Luke..."

Disappointment coiled inside him at Slim's words, leaving him to wonder what he'd expected Slim to say. Lifting his eyes, Luke locked them on Claire's. Registering the sympathy he saw there, he managed to crack a half smile. Damn. How could she have fallen in love with Clive? Now that Luke knew it was the truth, he simply couldn't accept it.

"Luke..." Slim began again.

Luke sighed. "Yeah?"

"I'm not sure how to tell you this, boy, but I found something in what you said to be mighty disturbing."

Luke frowned. "What's that?"

"Well...you weren't found on no doorstep when you were a baby."

Everything in Luke went still. "I wasn't?"

"Sorry to tell you this, but we found you on the steps, sure enough. And it was a Christmas morning, that's true. But you was three or four by then. You sure weren't no baby."

Luke's heart pounded. Claire's hand suddenly settled on his shoulder, squeezing tight, and without thinking, he let his palm slide over the back of her hand, his fingers falling between hers. His voice lowered, turning hoarse. "Three or four, you say?"

"You was shiverin' in a too-thin coat, and you had that blue-and-white-checkered blanket wrapped around your shoulders. You know, the one you still have?"

Luke nodded. The blanket was the only thing left from childhood, and it was folded in a trunk at the foot of his bed.

"The blanket had your name sewn inside it," Slim continued. "At least we figured Luke Lydell was your name. We called the sheriff right off, but on account of how scared you was, the authorities was real easy on you. Nothing they said could drag any information out of you. Anyhow, nobody'd seen any strangers in the area who could have left you there that morning. And it was clear you was..."

"I was what?" Luke was still staring into the soft sea of tender blue that was Claire's eyes. His hand tightened over hers. Did she know how much her touch meant to him right now? How could he have been so wrong about his past?

Slim grunted. "To be blunt, you was...not wanted, boy. Oh, darnit, Luke," Slim suddenly added, "I don't even want to talk about it. I like you too much, and I hate seeing you hurt. But you know how many kids get left at Lost Springs every year. So many that some wind up in other homes in the state."

"Can you tell me anything else?"

"Anything I know, you know, Luke."

Keeping his eyes on Claire's, Luke listened while Slim offered every detail about the Christmas morning Luke had been found. Luke had always known there was no record of his birth, since he'd asked; like most kids at Lost Springs, he'd thought of looking for his folks. It was why Brady touched Luke's heart, and probably why he'd studied law enforcement, so he could learn to search for missing persons. But now Luke knew he'd never asked the right people the right questions.

"Talk to me," Claire said simply when the call ended. Slipping her hand from beneath his, she lifted it, gliding her fingers through his hair once more, stroking the strands and tucking them behind his ears.

Luke wasn't used to talking like this, and his voice was

rough with suppressed emotion. "I can't...I just don't know what to say, Claire."

Her eyes were more tender than any mother's could have been, and Luke realized with a dull thud of his heart, they were brimming with something that had to be love.

Her lips were so close he could feel her breath. "You never asked these questions before, Luke?"

He shook his head. "I...just thought I knew."

"Deep down, you must not have wanted to know everything," she continued gently. "A lot of folks at Lost Springs could have told you that you weren't a baby when you got there. Sounds like you've avoided the truth and repressed some memories."

"A scary thought," he murmured.

"It's okay," she whispered.

Needing to hold her, he slipped an arm around her shoulder and pulled her to him, his heart aching as she sank against his chest, her cheek and palm resting there. Gently, he smoothed a hand over the top of her pulled-back hair, and they sat like that a long time, with him staring up the Stoddards' long driveway, wondering at the gaps in his life. Was the woman in the yellow dress who haunted his dreams and memories his mama? And was the family in the red car his own? Luke needed more time to think, to process this. Maybe tonight, he could kick back and chew on it for a spell. He sighed. "Guess we'd better get up to the house. We've still got to talk to the Stoddards about Clive."

Claire nodded, inching slowly up from his chest. Her eyes settled on his again, so sweet and soft and blue that Luke wanted nothing more than to pull her to him again. Her voice was low with emotion. "Whenever you're ready to talk, Luke...*if* you're ready, I want you to know I'm

here for you.'' Her voice suddenly caught. "I've always
been here, Luke.''

Not anymore. Luke was sure she was in love with Clive.
His throat felt tight. "Thanks, Claire.''

"Never thank me,'' she added with soft urgency. Reaching, she threaded her fingers deeper into his hair and pulled
herself up, close enough to kiss him. Right before her lips
brushed his cheek, she whispered, "I'd do anything in the
world for you. You know that, don't you Luke?''

CHAPTER EIGHT

I'D DO ANYTHING FOR YOU, LUKE. The words were echoing in Claire's mind hours later. Flexing her fingers on the Wrangler's steering wheel, she squinted anxiously into the pitch darkness. Even in the best weather, trees encroached on this forgotten corner of Lost Springs, their gnarled roots sprawling onto the narrow dirt-and-gravel road, making it scarcely navigable. Now winter had claimed the road, too, burying it beneath ice and snow while the canopy of trees blotted out the moon. So far, she'd gotten stuck twice. Fearing she'd have to walk, she'd spread kitty litter and salt beneath the tires, until she got traction again. It was definitely too cold to hike to Luke's cabin from here, besides, there were bobcats and wild dogs.

Suddenly she saw a flash of soft tawny hide and white back legs. Gasping, she slammed on the brakes just in time. "A deer," she murmured as it disappeared into the woods. Her heart thudding against her ribs, she slowly pressed the gas again.

At least she knew this was the right road. Claire was loathe to admit it, but she'd wound up here countless times over the years, never intending to come, but always secretly hoping to see Luke. Each time, she'd kept her camera slung around her neck and practiced what she'd say if he caught her sniffing around his territory. "Just doing a little off-roading," she'd say casually. "Taking pictures to paint from.'' She'd always imagined pointing at her paint box, which she kept plainly visible in the front seat.

But she'd never seen Luke.

''And now I'm lost.'' She was truly beginning to believe it when she saw a light glimmering through the trees. Moments later, she was parking her Jeep behind his. Icy air seeped through the open vents as she turned off the engine, chilling her stocking-clad knees. She stared through the thick snowflakes melting on the windshield, toward the one-story log cabin.

Feeling a sudden attack of nerves, she reminded herself that she'd come here because Luke was hurting. He was still processing the conversation with Slim, and spending time with the Stoddards this afternoon probably hadn't helped. No matter how it seemed sometimes, Luke's occasional, impulsive gestures of affection said he cared for her; sometimes she could swear he felt much more. Seeing how well she'd bonded with her future in-laws couldn't have been easy for him. Not that Claire could profess to know what went through Luke's impenetrable mind. All she knew was that the complexity he tried to hide drew her to him, just as the light shining from behind the cabin's closed curtains pulled her like a moth to a flame.

Well, maybe she hadn't come only to comfort Luke. Or to find out if he'd heard any news about Clive. Those things were true enough. She was worried sick about Clive, but if information was all she'd wanted, she could have called. She hadn't needed to come out here, or to change from jeans into a skirt. Or to wear makeup and let her hair flow loosely around her shoulders.

Inside, Luke's shadow moved across a curtain.

Before she lost her nerve, she grabbed a bag from the passenger seat, tucked a painting she'd gift-wrapped under her arm, got out and slammed the door. There was no porch light or sidewalk, so she squinted, forging a path to the cabin, her best Justin boots sinking in the snow. As she reached the door, she could hear Van Morrison howling "Rave On." She was taking a deep breath to steady her nerves when the door swung open.

Luke's strong, dark sleek body filled the frame. His hair was slicked back, tucked behind his ears, and he was bare-chested, wearing faded jeans and intricately beaded, hand-sewn moccasins. He looked so overwhelmingly male that Claire's insides jellied. If the cold temperature worried his naked skin, he gave no indication. He merely gazed down at her from an elevated step, not looking all that happy to see her.

"I was just about to knock," she said.

He nodded curtly, his breath clouding the dark, moist air. "I thought I heard somebody drive up."

She bit back a shiver. "It was me." *As if he hasn't figured that out, Claire.*

His eyes seemed to peer past her, as if he was checking to see if she'd brought company. "Looks like it."

Suddenly, she felt idiotic. "Luke," she found herself saying, wondering how they'd backtracked from the intimacy they'd shared earlier. "I just drove two miles through the wilderness to bring you dinner, and it's freezing out here. Are you going to invite me in or not?"

When he glanced over his shoulder, Claire wasn't prepared for a sudden, murderous jolt of jealousy. Was he pushing her away because there was something inside—or worse, someone—he didn't want her to see? Another woman, she decided, her heart fluttering with panic. *As if you've got some claim on him.* Technically, she was still engaged, at least until she talked to Clive again. Fighting an embarrassed flush over her own double standards and suppressing her guilt, she shifted the bag on her hip.

"Mama thought you might want some dinner." *As if Mama would really send me miles into the woods on a snowy night just to deliver a plate of turkey.*

Seemingly coming to his senses, Luke stepped aside. "Uh...come on in."

At this point, she couldn't exactly turn around gracefully and leave. Besides, facing that treacherous road again without at least a hot drink would be too brutal for words, so she brushed past Luke, the close proximity of his half-clothed body sending a wave of unwanted awareness through her. He so obviously didn't want her here that she barely noted the cabin's interior, though she realized the living room, dining room and kitchen were combined, and that the glowing hardwood floors were covered with Native American rugs. A fire crackled in a brick fireplace in the living area, casting long, fuzzy shadows and making the polished blond wood of the paneled walls shine.

"Here." Taking the bag, Luke lightly kicked the door shut, then he spun a knob somewhere that considerably lowered the volume of the music. "Can I take your coat?"

For a second, she didn't move, the cozy intimacy of the cabin making her further realize he'd been holed up for the night. "Luke," she began suddenly, even as he helped slip the coat from her shoulders, "I really should have called first. You obviously weren't expecting company, and I shouldn't have—" Switching topics, Claire started rambling about how Mama had had dinner leftovers, and how Claire figured maybe she should drive out, anyway, to see how Luke was feeling after his conversation with Slim, and because she was wondering about Clive.

Luke held up a staying hand. "Sorry, no news. I take it you haven't heard from him?"

She shook her head. If Luke's raised hand hadn't stopped her from jabbering, the smoldering look in his eyes would have. In the dim light near the doorway, the blue irises seemed to have darkened, turning to liquid midnight. She watched the powerful roll of his shoulders as he turned away from her, hooked her coat on a peg, then turned to face her again, his naked chest lit with burnished gold. She caught a whiff of him then. A faintly tangy scent of woods and soap that stirred her senses, heated her body and muddled her thinking. The unmistakable way his eyes drifted over her sent her reeling, too, reminding her that she'd worn her favorite outfit just for him—a pale blue sweater with a buttoned-up front and a brown calf-length skirt that was flecked with blue. When his gaze lowered, unmistakably grazing her breasts, everything inside her went tight—her belly constricted, her nipples hardened beneath her best lace bra, chafing and almost hurting with the awareness of him.

"It's okay that you're here, Claire."

"Are you sure?"

His rock-hard shoulders lifted in a shrug. "You surprised me. That's all."

"It's nice out here," she said.

"Thanks," he returned. Before she could take a good look around, his eyes locked on hers, capturing all her attention. "C'mon." Sliding a hand beneath her elbow, he urged her toward the kitchen. "I've got a pot of coffee made. Want some?"

She nodded. "Sure." As she stared into his eyes, the unbidden thought came that if she and Luke had babies, they'd have blue eyes. She found herself wishing they'd have his hair, not hers. Luke's was so sleek, like buffed black satin. Today, as she'd felt it sifting through her fingers, she'd had to force herself not to kiss him. God only knew what he thought of her, kissing him when she was supposedly engaged. Claire watched him circle behind an oak counter separating the kitchen and dining areas, and she decided he looked like a proud native warrior who could have lived centuries before. She slipped the package she'd been carrying onto a dining chair. If Luke noticed the gift, he didn't let on.

"Coffee?" he said again, setting the bag she'd brought on the tiled floor beside the refrigerator. "Or something else?"

"Coffee sounds great. I could use something warm."

Fortunately, some of Luke's usual humor seemed to return. "If I'd known your mama was going to send you all the way out here with dinner," he said, opening the refrigerator door and transferring Tupperware containers onto the shelves, "I wouldn't have had scrambled eggs and fried potatoes earlier."

Relief moved through her at the change in tone. Relaxing, she put her elbows on the countertop and watched him. "Don't worry. Everything'll keep."

Surveying the containers, he said, "Looks like the works."

"Turkey and ham both, dressing, homemade cranberry sauce and biscuits," Claire rattled off.

He read the scribbling on a strip of masking tape Mama used to label things. "Cheese grits?"

"Tex won't eat any meal without grits."

Luke glanced up. "Not even Christmas dinner?"

"Nope."

Luke whistled softly, turning back to the food. "Big portions, too. Your mama must think I have an appetite."

Claire, of course, had packed the food. "Mama did notice how much you ate the other night."

"Hope she took it as a compliment to her cooking."

"She did." As Luke shut the refrigerator door, Claire smiled, enjoying the power in his movements—the slow ripple of muscles on his back and the view of fine black hair softly curling between his pectorals. She smiled. "Besides, Mama thinks you're a starving bachelor."

Leaning against the refrigerator door, Luke tilted his head thoughtfully and ran a light palm over his washboard-flat belly. "Do I look like I'm starving?"

She considered. "Maybe." Strange lights were in his eyes, scarcely veiling male greed that made her aware of herself as a woman.

"Claire...thanks," Luke continued, smiling as he used a bare shoulder to push away from the refrigerator. "It was nice of you to drive all the way out here."

"Are you kidding?" The corners of her lips curled. "Driving hours in the snow is every girl's idea of a good time."

His eyes drifted over her. "I mean it. I can't remember the last time I had turkey in my refrigerator on Christmas. I tried to cook one once, though." He reached for mugs and began pouring their coffee.

"It didn't turn out so hot?" she guessed.

Luke shook his head ruefully. "Oh, it was hot, all right, darlin'. I burned it. I'm only good with things you can fry. If it goes in the oven, forget it."

He offered an almost sheepish shrug that didn't suit the raw power he carried in his shoulders, and Claire's heart tugged. If she'd only known, she'd have brought him turkey dinners every year. Finding her voice, she said, "I brought you a present, too, Luke." She nodded toward the dining chair where she'd left the painting.

Setting down the two mugs, Luke leaned across the counter, his eyes capturing her straying attention. "You're a present in yourself." The tone was light and teasing now, but the gaze was a bold caress that loved every inch of her. "You look nice."

"We dressed up for dinner," she lied.

"I don't care why you dressed up," he returned, though his appreciative expression said he'd guessed the truth, that she'd dressed for him. "You look...sexy."

Hearing the words made her realize how much she'd craved them. "Sexy. That's even better than nice." Their eyes met again and held, this time for so long that she became aware of things she'd rather not notice, like her racing pulse and the jittery, excited breathlessness that told her how much she wanted this man. Suddenly, her knees felt weak. Her lips wanted his hot mouth, her hands wanted his smooth shoulders, her breasts wanted to be crushed against that naked chest. A song called "Moondance" began to play, and she could hear her heart pound over the airy, romantic background flutes. Drawing a steadying breath, she said, "You want to open your gift?"

He merely leaned closer, ran a finger lightly down her sweater sleeve and smiled. "Open it before Christmas?"

A soft chuckle released some of her tension. Between her worry over Clive and her reaction to Luke, her body felt too wound up. "I won't tell Santa you were bad," she promised solemnly.

Luke grinned, his white teeth quickly flashing. "Not even if I *am* bad?"

She just couldn't help herself. "How bad can you be?"

"How bad do you want to find out?"

"How bad do you want to show me?"

His chuckle made her wonder how serious he was. "Bad."

Should she circle the counter and move into his arms? Wasn't that what she wanted? Wasn't that why she'd really come? Suddenly, the small, cozy, fire-lit space felt too intimate. Feeling heat rise in her cheeks, she glanced away and squinted. She hadn't noticed before, but unwrapped toys were stacked everywhere—on chairs, on the floor and on a dining table strewn with decorative paper and rolls of ribbon. Wrapped packages were stacked a few feet away. Her gaze returned to Luke's, full of questions. "All these toys…"

As his firm mouth twisted into a secretive smile, his eyes crinkled at the corners. "They're for the kids at Lost Springs," he admitted.

She could only stare. Everyone in Lightning Creek knew someone delivered gifts to the ranch every Christmas Eve. But it was Luke? "It's really you?"

He surveyed her with mock soberness. "I can only tell you if you'll take the secret oath."

Despite her surprise, she managed a playfully sage nod. "A blood oath?" she guessed.

"That's only for blood brothers."

"Well, we can't be brothers since I'm a girl."

"Woman," Luke corrected her. "Which means there's only one solution, darlin'."

"Which is?"

"This." Leaning, Luke swept his mouth across hers. Barely pressuring her lips, he brushed his mouth back and forth with a kiss that should have only been casual, but wasn't. "I shouldn't have done that," he murmured, pulling back.

"It's okay," she said guiltily, knowing he meant because she was engaged. "I guess I can't tell Santa you were bad…."

"Not if I *am* Santa," Luke agreed, his voice holding a trace of huskiness. Moving as lithely as an animal in the wild, he lifted the coffee mugs and circled the counter, his eyes holding hers as he carried their drinks to the dining table. "John Garret gives me the boys' letters," Luke explained, licking his lips absently, as if he were still tasting hers.

"John? The postman?"

"Yeah." Luke stared down at the mess of wrapping paper, then at the stacks of boxes. "In all the excitement," he continued, "I've gotten a little behind. It'll take all night to finish the wrapping." He ran a ragged, work-callused hand through his hair. "I wrap about like I cook turkey." His eyes met hers, suddenly sparkling as he raised his big hands. "All thumbs."

Claire was still stunned. She thought of all the hours Luke must have spent shopping for the kids, and as her eyes drifted over the packages again, her heart swelled with emotion. "I still can't believe this."

"I guess I don't much look like Santa." His smile broadened. "You know, heavy with a white beard and mustache."

"You have the eyes."

"Ah," he replied. "So you noticed."

Staring into them, she nodded. "What woman wouldn't?"

"Thanks for the compliment," he teased, "but now that you know I'm Santa Claus, maybe you're trying to flatter me into bringing you better gifts tomorrow night."

"Could be." She sighed. "Luke, I really can't believe you've been helping me when you had all this to do. The least I can do is help you now."

"A wrapping partner," Luke said, pulling out a chair and seating her with her back to the living area. "This is even better than your bringing me dinner." Seating himself, he slid a toy truck and a square of silver paper across the table. "Have at it, woman." Taking a sip of his coffee, he continued, "Does anybody know you're here, in case Clive calls?"

"I call-forwarded my phone. I hope you don't mind."
She often came and went without much fanfare at the
ranch since she didn't like to be disturbed when she was
working, and she kept a separate phone line.

Luke shook his head. "I don't mind at all."

"Before we start wrapping..." She lifted Luke's gift
from the chair beside her and handed it to him.

His expression was hard to read. Apologetic, Claire decided, since he had nothing for her. Taken aback, maybe,
since he hadn't expected a gift. But mostly he looked
moved as he gently turned over the package she'd wrapped
in gold foil paper and tied with a green ribbon. She
watched him glide a finger beneath the tape. "I had you
pegged for the kind of guy who tore presents open," she
commented.

"Me?" Luke's steady eyes lifted again, blazing into
hers for the briefest moment as he shook his head. "No
way. Gifts have been too few and far between, Claire."

Emotions she didn't even recognize tore at her. Didn't
he know she'd long wanted to give him the greatest gifts
of all—her body and heart? Her love? "Glad I brought
you something, then."

He'd opened the painting from the back, and now his
lips parted as he slowly lifted out the canvas, turning it
over. "The picture from above your bed." He gazed down
for long moments, his eyes absorbing the details: the hominess of the log cabin, the billowing smoke from the stone
chimney, the lone set of elk tracks in the snow. His voice
low, he said, "I sure appreciate your bringing it, Claire.
But this...I mean, this was hanging above your bed. I can't
accept this."

The picture was a favorite, one of the rare few she'd
ever bothered to keep for herself, and it had felt so right
to bring it to Luke tonight, maybe because years ago she'd

imagined sharing a home with him someday. A place like this, or the one in the painting. "I saw you admiring it the other night, in my bedroom," she finally said. "Don't you like it?"

"Like it?" Luke looked flabbergasted. "It's incredible."

"You'll keep it, then?" she urged.

"Yeah," Luke amended softly. "I'd like that."

She smiled at him a relieved moment. He smiled back, his face shadowed in the firelight, his eyes tender as he watched her pick up the truck and position it in the middle of the wrapping paper square. Occasionally glancing at the painting, Luke also began wrapping gifts, both of them sipping coffee and working in companionable silence. At one point, Claire glanced up from where she'd been tying a red ribbon around a children's book, and found him watching her.

"Thanks," he said.

"For the painting?"

"And Christmas dinner."

She smiled again. "Give me your finger, Santa Claus."

"Sure." Leaning over, he pressed a finger where the red ribbon crossed, enabling her to tie a bow, and she noticed his big, strong hands. She liked their calloused sturdiness, the rough darkness of the skin. As she looped the ribbon around his finger, she thought about tying ribbons to fingers for remembrance. She glanced into his eyes. "How are you doing?" Now she was thinking about his conversation with Slim.

"I'm handling it."

When he offered nothing further, she began wrapping a board game while he cut lengths of ribbon. She smiled again, her worry over Clive almost leaving her for a moment when she saw how Luke threaded the ribbons through his fingers like reins. "Ride 'em, cowboy," she teased.

He glanced up. "What?"

"Nothing." As he worked, she glanced around again, seeing the living room for the first time. A couch and chairs were arranged around the fire, and a small planted pine was perched on a table, decorated with blue lights. There were four or five wrapped gifts beneath it, along with a holiday basket of fruit. Claire tried, but she couldn't imagine spending Christmas alone, without a household of chattering siblings. And then she wondered where she'd be at this time next year. Probably alone like Luke, she thought, sudden sadness curling inside her. Just days ago, she'd pictured herself with Clive, maybe pregnant with their first child....

All at once, as her eyes settled above the mantel, she drew in a sharp breath of surprise. So, that's why Luke had hedged about bringing her inside, hustling her toward the kitchen and seating her with her back to the living room.

Claire was on her feet before she could stop herself. Crossing the room, she stood before the fire, gazing up at *Blue Sage Dreams*. She hadn't seen the almost photographic landscape for years, and although the painting had been offered as a limited print and was said to be her best, she'd never known who'd bought it. Luke had framed it beautifully, in a simple gold frame; above the frame hung a small, gold-shielded fluorescent bulb that illuminated it.

He'd bought the painting of Lost Springs, too, and the fact took her breath away. Her heart slamming inside her chest, Claire turned and stared at where it hung above the couch. Luke would have no way of knowing that the day she'd asked him to make love to her had inspired it. Even now, she could remember how she'd felt that day, all jan-

gling adolescent emotions and raging hormones. She'd felt
scared, too, especially when Luke's dark hands glided between her legs. Now warmth suffused her as she recalled
how she'd returned that intimate caress. But he'd rejected
her, she reminded herself. It wasn't wise to forget that, not
even now. Especially not now, she amended, not when
seeing him was rekindling her feelings.

Staring at the painting, she remembered that day at Lost
Springs. As she was driven away from the parking
grounds, crying her eyes out in the back of Tex's big black
Cadillac, she'd seen that young boy, wandering in the summer twilight, his arm outstretched. "Whoever you're having troubles with will come around," Tex had vowed furiously, knowing only that she'd been rejected, though
never guessing the extent of it. "No boy on earth couldn't
want to go steady with my best gal," Tex had proclaimed.
And then Tex had driven like a bat out of hell, hurrying
to get Claire home to Mama, whom Tex felt was better
equipped to deal with such troubles.

Now Claire wished Luke understood that he'd inspired
the picture, that it wasn't the boy, but she, who'd been
reaching for the sky, wanting to touch what she could
never have…to touch Luke. The image of that boy had
stayed with her for years. It was another summer—the last
before she'd finished graduate school—when Claire finally
painted him. She'd done so quickly, barely sleeping or
leaving the studio until the picture was complete. The second the paint was dry, she'd dropped off the work at a
gallery in Cheyenne, never wanting to see it again.

Now the same soul-crushing longing Claire felt years
ago on the parking grounds at Lost Springs threatened to
overwhelm her again. Luke came up behind her, his bare
chest feeling warm behind her back, his breath close to

her ear. "You've bought two of my paintings," Her voice was unsteady.

"Secret collector," he returned, striving for casualness and wholly missing the mark. "Now you know why I'm so happy to get another."

Suddenly, Claire wanted to scream. Or punch him. Something. Dammit, she'd seen the glimmer of raw, heartfelt emotion in his eyes when he'd opened the picture of the cabin, but now he was pretending none of it meant anything. Tears burned in her eyes, hurting like fire, and as she turned toward him, desperately fighting to control her emotions, her attention was caught by the Christmas tree. His gaze must have followed hers, because he leaned over, touching the top of the fruit basket. "Cross Creek gave them out to the hands," he commented. "Nice of them, huh?"

She felt stung. How long was he going to deny his feelings? And where was Clive? What was going on? It had been a long day. She and Luke had been shot at earlier, for God's sake, and the drive out here had been treacherous. Didn't Luke understand that she was human? That underneath it all, she, too, was a mess of tangled emotions right now? She'd agreed to marry Clive—to *marry* him!—and not only was he missing, but as soon as he resurfaced, Claire was probably going to confront an uncertain future. She tried to hold back the tears, but suddenly, it was all too much. She had to escape, to sit down somewhere and cry. "Where's your bathroom?" She guessed it wasn't what he expected her to say.

"Uh…last door at the end of the hall."

She headed blindly toward it, eyes filling, vision blurring. She tried to tell herself she hated Luke, that she was better off not wanting him, better off forgetting how she'd felt at Lost Springs. Luke's every breath had always been a denial of their potential love, and no matter what she did, no matter what happened, he'd always be too scared to try.

She'd nearly made it to the bathroom when a light caught her eye. Turning, she found herself staring into Luke's bedroom.

A rough-hewn log bed was covered in a quilt, and polished hardwood floors were laid with hand-woven wool rugs. There wasn't much other furniture, just a bedside table with a telephone. Two saddles and a pair of snowshoes had been left carelessly beside the door, and a trunk was at the foot of the bed. But it was the painting above the headboard that had captured her attention.

A Crow chief in full ceremonial dress gazed down, his dark eyes all-seeing. Transcending earthly knowledge, those eyes seemed to hold the sacred wisdom of revered, hallowed spirts. The chief was a study in rich colors—clay reds, mustard yellows and royal blues—and with his sharp cheekbones, high forehead and straight blue-black hair, the man could have been one of Luke's forebears. Claire had called the painting *Love Warrior,* and it was the very first painting she'd ever sold.

Looking at it, she remembered the thrilling rush of heady excitement when the gallery owner called from Laramie, saying she'd sold a piece. Though faded now, the first dollar he'd counted from his strongbox remained tacked to her easel. After that, the man had commissioned more work, and other galleries started calling, wanting to tour her studio. Now her pictures were available throughout the state, but before selling *Love Warrior,* Claire didn't think she had a professional prayer.

And Luke had bought it, secretly helping her fulfill her dream.

Tears flooded her eyes as he slipped behind her again,

his moccasined footsteps soundless as nightfall, soft as the legions of warriors from whom he was descended. His wide hands settled on her shoulders, suddenly seeming too strong for the gentle goodness he tried to hide, too callused for his tenderness. Slowly, he turned her to face him. Her heart aching, she stared defiantly into his eyes, no longer caring that he'd see her cry. "You feel for me," she said, "I know it, Luke. You can't hide it anymore."

"I do." His blue eyes were dark as midnight, and suddenly his hands were thrusting up, stroking her neck and driving greedily under her hair, his long fingers raking possessively through the strands. "I fill my house with your art," he said, his low voice almost hoarse. "I fill my house with you, Claire—" He released a long sigh. "And when you come here, looking like this—" He brushed hair from her forehead and stroked it back, smoothing it all the way down to her shoulders. "Looking so beautiful..." His voice trailed off. "Don't you know how many times I've wished you'd come here?"

A hot tear splashed down her cheek, and she shook her head. "Why did you never...?"

Lifting a hand, he splayed it on her collarbone, stealing her breath and making her heart beat wildly. Her knees were suddenly too shaky and her breasts ached, tightening at the tips; something slid like warming honey from her core.

"I used to think you deserved better, Claire," Luke said simply, edging his body so close that his beginning arousal pressured her belly. "That's what I thought for years."

She whispered, "And now?"

"Clive's missing." Luke glanced away. "I figure he'll be back. But under the circumstances, I..." His roving eyes turned smoky as they fixed on her lips. "I can't take another man's woman."

"Take me?" The murmured words caught in her throat. "You can't take me. I don't belong to anyone."

His eyes captured hers. "No?"

She knew she'd lied. She belonged to him. Fresh tears blurred her vision, and her throat ached. "I painted Lost Springs because of you. That day we were in the woods together, I saw that boy. He was the image of what I felt, but it was you I was reaching for, Luke."

He pressed his forehead to hers, his voice barely audible. "You almost caught me, Claire."

Her breath hitched. "I did?"

"I ran after you that day, but you were already in the car." Leaning back a fraction, he brushed a thumb beneath her eye, as if expecting to catch the tear teetering on her eyelid that never fell. "Do you love him?"

"Clive?" Her heart hammered. She was still absorbing the fact that Luke had run after her that day at Lost Springs. Slowly shaking her head, she was somehow sure her whole life would depend on Luke's reaction to the next thing she said. "Clive's a good man. I thought we could share a life. And I love him. But never in the way I've always loved you, Luke."

CHAPTER NINE

"YOU LOVE ME?" Luke whispered. Before Claire could even answer, his mouth covered hers, his strong hands plunging deeper into her hair. Suckling the warm length of her tongue, he nipped and widened his mouth to take even more. Wicked heat flooded his groin, making him swell with need, and his blood roared as her hands kneaded his bare shoulders, then slid down his arms.

Pulling her against the doorway, Luke knew they were going to finish what they started all those years ago at Lost Springs. Dark as night, his hands fell down through the pale strands of her hair, flowing to her arms and molding her skirt. He squeezed her hips, his fingers tightening and digging into her flesh as their lower bodies connected. As he deepened the kiss, he ground himself gently against her, rubbing back and forth. He wanted her desperately, but just by being, Claire gave him so much, so he held back. He kissed her slower...then slower, his tongue moving with lapping strokes until she moaned from far back in her throat. Against his chest, he could feel the soft tease of firm breasts he couldn't wait to taste, and as he sucked her lower lip between his teeth, he hoarsely said, "Claire, I've wanted to hold you like this for so long." Curving his hands lower around her bottom, he drew her close again, urging her to arch against him and feel the muscular flex of his response, and she complied until the sweet pressure did him in.

Her voice was ragged, clinging the way her body clung. "You never let me give to you. Let me love you, Luke."

The sincerity of her words tore at his heart. "You are loving me, darlin'," he murmured, his lower body feeling thick with desire, his eyes drifting down to the mouth his kiss had left slick and swollen.

"No, Luke," she said. "I'm not."

It sure felt like it to him. "You're not?" he returned huskily.

"No, but I'm about to." Tenderly, she pressed her lips to his cheek, the soft, feathery touch stealing his breath, making his mouth go dry and his heart pound out of control. He was powerless to move when her mouth didn't stop but nibbled down his neck, then between his pecs. Her tongue circled a taut nipple, then the other, leaving him with a kiss that almost burned before she lowered her mouth to his ribs and belly. Her tongue felt strangely cool and warm flickering on his skin, and for a second, he closed his eyes, wishing this would never end. As she opened the snap of his jeans and dipped a hand inside the waistband of his underwear, he gazed down, drawing in a sharp breath as her fingertips brushed the tip of his rigid sex. Fighting the urge to press her hand there, he let her do what she wanted, not about to control this moment.

Down the hallway, the CD stopped, and another of his inhalations sounded in tandem with the slow rake as Claire tugged down his zipper. As she slid it over the curve of his erection, Luke reached down and found a breast. He squeezed lightly, lovingly, palming from the side and fondling her through the sweater. Beneath the soft fabric of her top, he could feel a tightening nipple pressing through the lace of her bra, and he worked it, caressing with his thumb until she whimpered. He was desperate to make her whimper so much more. He wouldn't finish, he thought, until she was completely his.

"What?" Luke whispered in sudden raspy stupefaction, his dark hands threading through her loose hair. He urged her back to him when he realized she'd crouched lower before him, but she only stared up, looking defiant, her eyes full of fierce challenge that said she meant to claim him.

Luke's voice caught as her chin brushed his naked skin. "C'mon, Claire…" She didn't have to prove herself to him. He'd never rejected her because he didn't want her, never that. Did she really think so?

He released a shuddering sigh as her determined lips seared his belly, feeling hot and tender, then thoroughly maddening as she tongued his navel. Something cried out—his heart or a word, he wasn't sure which—and when his hands fisted, her hair teased the tender spaces between each finger. "Claire," he gasped again as she pushed his jeans down onto the straining muscles of his thighs. His eyes glazed as he watched her; his hands trembled in her hair, the need to feel the liquid heaven of her lips making him shake. "Claire," he whispered again roughly, not knowing what else to say as the point of her sweet tongue flickered, then butterflied around his aroused flesh. He groaned. The tendons in his neck pulled, and his heavily lidded eyes nearly drifted shut with the excruciating pleasure of it, and yet they stayed riveted on the beautiful swollen lips that slipped back and forth over him, feeling like velvet. Senselessly, he smoothed her hair until he was hanging on to the last vestiges of control. "Claire, stop," he suddenly said. "Come here."

"Where?" He loved hearing the tremor in her voice, knowing their lovemaking did that to her.

"Here." Holding her hand, he drew her to the bed.

"Where I can give you what I wanted to years ago." He cupped her chin and offered a gentle kiss, just the soft, hot brush of his lips across hers. He'd never felt so worked up, but even as he throbbed with need, emotion welled within him. "Last summer," he began huskily.

"Last summer?" she echoed, swallowing hard and watching as he slipped out of his moccasins, stepped out of his pants and stood naked in front of her, luscious and fully ready to love her. "Since the bachelor auction," he continued as he slid beside her, "I haven't been able to get you out of my mind, Claire."

"Really...I mostly wanted to see you when I came to the mall," she said, her voice low and tremulous as she laid back on the bed, her loose hair cascading onto her blue sweater, her skirt fanning on the covers. He moved closer beside her, nude and aching, and when her hungry, smoky-blue eyes lowered, he found her hand and brought it to where she'd kissed him, letting her feel the length and strength of him as his free hand labored to undo the small buttons of her sweater. Unclasping her bra from the back, he gently pushed up the cups and gazed at where her long tawny hair curled on her small breasts, framing the silken nipples.

"Let me see you," he whispered. "It's been so long."

Her voice was almost a whisper. "I'm yours to see, Luke."

Feeling in the throes of agony, he edged a dark, hairy thigh over her lighter one, gliding a hand up her pale tummy before he cupped a breast. Gently, he pinched both stiffened nipples, his work-roughened fingertips thoroughly exploring them before his hungry mouth decidedly attached to one.

"Finally," Claire gasped, feeling unbrooked need course through her as he suckled. Luke's intimate taste was still with her, and she cried out, arching and melting as she thought of how all his hard, dark heat would soon be inside her. "Luke…" Her raw throat made the name raspy while her heart ached with this victory. So many lonely nights, this was all she'd wanted. After all these years, Luke was loving her.

His tongue, like his hands and every other inch of him, was so marvelously strong, and the touch of it sent dizzying need through her as he glided his hands over her hips again. Tossing away her skirt and panties, he whispered something unintelligible as his hand moved between her legs. With the rush of sensation, her mind filled with memories of his past kisses. As he began to probe and stroke, she remembered that hot summer night in Casper last year, and the illicit adolescent kisses stolen in the back of the feed store when she was still a schoolgirl, tossing her mane of hair and wearing too-tight jeans, playing with fire and not even understanding what she was doing.

A whimper tore from her mouth as she twisted her hips, reaching for his finger, letting it fill her as the hot, slow suckle of his mouth took her breasts. Stupid, she thought senselessly. She'd been so stupid to think she was old and wise now and knew about love, when Luke's every kiss was teaching her she could only belong to him.

"I didn't know," she whispered. *I didn't know how much I needed you, Luke.* Her chest heaved up to where his tongue coaxed a helplessly tight nipple once more. So many times Luke had left her aching this way—in the woods, in her dreams. Years ago, in the parking grounds, he'd left her damp with a womanhood she hadn't even understood.

But she understood now. Now, she welcomed the fiery exhilaration brought by his touch. Riding the feverish intensity of it, she shattered, wrapping her arms around his strong back, then sliding her hands down to mold his firm buttocks. When her thighs closed, his hand remained, and after a moment, he stroked again, soothing her as he smiled against her breast. Releasing another whimper, she rolled with him, so they were lying on their sides, face to face.

"I always wondered," Luke whispered simply, stretching his powerful body against her, his heated shaft pressuring her thigh, reminding her of his unsatisfied need and making her heart fill with the need to offer the gratification. Swallowing hard, resting her hands on his chest, she gazed from the noble lines of his face down to where he was so eager. Like his hands, he was so wonderfully big and strong there. Powerful as a stallion. Her eyes rose to where a strand of blue-black hair had fallen across an eye. "You wondered?"

His voice was as silky as his flesh, just as seductive. "I wondered what you'd look like when you got off, Claire."

She wouldn't have thought it possible, but she felt lust again. "Was it what you expected, Luke?"

He trailed a finger down her cheek. "More," he whispered simply. "It was so much more, Claire. You looked so beautiful."

Their locked eyes brimmed with passion as Luke edged closer. Using his hand, he guided himself to her, and with a sigh of need, he pushed deep inside. Claire opened, one of her legs folding over his, her body heartbreakingly slack with acceptance. "I've always loved you, Luke," she whispered, her arms closing around his neck, hugging him.

Luke couldn't even find his voice. Gliding a hand over her hip, he used it to pull her closer, to plunge deeper. Before tonight, nobody—man or woman—had ever said that to him. *I love you.* Both arms slid around her waist. Pulling out, he wordlessly filled her again—slow and deep, in a way so loving it promised a future.

HEARING THE PHONE, Luke quickly lifted the receiver before the ringing woke Claire. Squinting, he couldn't believe they'd slept without turning out the lights. No goodnights, either. They'd simply sunk into the messy sheets and conked out, completely satisfied. After what she'd done to him, Luke could have slept standing up.

"Yeah?" Luke whispered into the mouthpiece, his throat going dry as he gazed at Claire, his eyes drifting from the tangled hair obscuring her face, over her bare back, and then to where her long legs were hidden under the covers.

"Luke?"

"Yeah," he whispered again, recognizing Wesley's voice.

Now Wesley whispered, too. "You got a woman in there, Luke?"

"None of your business."

Welsely chuckled. "Sounds like a yes."

"A woman" didn't begin to cover it. Luke's chest swelled as he watched Claire snuggle her cheek against the pillow, then sleepily brush the hair from her face. Turning over, she yawned, surveying him with a dreamy gaze and a slow, sexy smile.

Luke covered the phone. "I've never seen anybody look so gorgeous."

"Thanks," she whispered sleepily. "Who's that?"

"Wesley," said Wesley, "and Luke, you'd better tell that woman I want to know who she is."

"Were you always this nosy?" Luke chuckled. "And what time is it, anyway?"

"Ten."

Luke struggled up. "Ten?" It was Christmas Eve, so he had the day off at Cross Creek, but he still needed to finish wrapping the gifts for the kids at Lost Springs. And no one had called for Claire.

Claire's sleepy eyes fluttered farther open. "Ten?" She scanned the room, locating her skirt and sweater, which lay wrinkled on the floor. As she scooted closer, Luke pulled her to his side. She fidgeted until her warm body molded perfectly to his, and Luke let his mind float, enjoying her silken skin and the warm sheets.

Wesley did his best to sound sour. "Some of us have to work for a living. So, while you've been at home merrily doing whatever to whomever, I've been out earning my daily bread."

Luke playfully mussed Claire's hair. "Meaning?"

"Meaning I checked on the license plate to the truck in Elmer's barn. Turns out it's owned by Cheyenne Mining, a small firm out of Glenrock."

Luke was starting to wake up fast. The call was reminding him of why he and Claire had initially gotten together at the mall, to find Clive. Since it was Christmas Eve, Clive would probably show up tonight, unless something really had happened to him. Luke sighed. Supposedly, Claire's wedding was tomorrow.

Luke said, "Did you get any other information, Wesley?"

"Nope. But you might want to ask Evander Stoddard if anybody's been pressuring him to sell his land."

Luke glanced at Claire. "It's possible they're in a little financial hot water," he said. "Nothing big."

"Well," said Wesley, "maybe you can ask Evander if he's had any offers. I want to see if that truck from the mining company's got anything to do with Clive's disappearance and Elmer's barn fire."

"Elmer hasn't sold his land," Luke reminded him.

"But with his horses gone, he can't afford to keep it. You know that, Luke."

"True."

"Well, look," said Wesley, "I've got to go. I finally got some time off this afternoon, and I still haven't finished my Christmas shopping."

"I'll call you with any developments," Luke assured him before he hung up. Even though he needed to go to the Stoddards', Luke leaned over, pressed his mouth to Claire's and delivered a slow, wet kiss. When he drew away, her gaze had turned serious. "Luke," she said softly, snuggling against him. "I wouldn't worry. I really think Clive's all right."

Luke's voice was husky. "What convinced you? The way we got shot at in Elmer's barn?"

She shrugged. "No. It's just a feeling. And I trust my feelings."

"You keep saying that," he said, his body starting to feel flushed with his response to her. "And I'm glad, but are you sure you don't know more than you're telling?"

She pressed a kiss to his chin. "No."

"Good. I don't want you keeping secrets from me, Claire."

"I wouldn't. I meant what I said last night. I love you, Luke."

Hearing it again made his heart pound. "You said." And nobody else ever had. He wasn't sure what kept him from saying the words now. Wouldn't she think he was saying it because she'd done so? Wouldn't it be better to wait for another time?

"I want to...be with you, Luke."

From the way she said it, he knew she was talking about something significant, the kind of "being with" that led to marriage. He knew he should be careful—he never really trusted himself when he talked about emotions—and yet he felt compelled to say what was on his mind. "I want us to be together, but..."

His arm tightened around her, and he slid a hand into her hair, feeling the soft weight of it. "I've missed knowing you in the years since that summer...."

"Me, too."

"But you understand this is the way I live, Claire? I mean, it's a simple cabin. It's not like your folks' place, or the A-frame you and Clive built." He glanced down at where she'd curled on his chest, darkness clouding his features. "That was your dream home, Claire. I remember the summer you drew all those sketches."

Her eyes narrowed. "I remember it as the summer I fell in love with you," she said quietly.

"That's the way I remember it, too, Claire. I'm just saying I want you to think about this."

She scooted up, holding the covers against her breasts, hurt in her eyes. "I've thought about it. And...if you felt as strongly as I do, you wouldn't keep trying to dissuade me, Luke." With a sudden sigh, she simply dropped the covers, got out of bed and circled around it to find her clothes.

"You're so amazing to look at, darlin'," he murmured. He reached for her hand, but she was already dressing faster than he would have imagined possible. Was she really upset? Feeling strangely bewildered, he got up, lifted his jeans from the floor and pulled them on.

"Claire?" he said. "Would you just listen to me?"

"I've listened, Luke," she said, zipping her skirt.

He squinted. Was she really going to get dressed and leave? "Claire. I just want to make sure you understand—"

She turned fully toward him, now buttoning her sweater. "What I'm giving up?"

He edged closer, his eyes probing hers. "Claire, by your own admission, you chose Clive because you thought Clive could offer you a good future. You said you'd marry him because you loved him, not because you were *in love* with him."

She came closer, her skin suddenly flushed, her eyes turning violet with emotion. "Let me get this straight," she said. "You want me to understand that if I married Clive, it would enable a merger between the Stop Awhile and the Lazy Four? That I might miss not living in my dream house?"

"That's the simple truth," Luke agreed. "And we both have to face it."

She was clearly fighting to control her voice. "Evander has a lot to gain if Clive and I marry on Christmas, but he definitely wouldn't want us to wind up unhappy."

Luke wanted her back in his arms and in his bed, but he was beginning to fear this fight proved what he suspected, that he was no good at love. "I just want to make sure you're thinking this through."

"Luke," she said. "I'm only going to say this once. Love isn't practical. Being *in love* isn't something you can think through."

"I'm just saying maybe we should give it a while."

Her eyes widened. "What's 'a while'? Until we find Clive? Or do you mean a few months, Luke? Maybe years?"

"Months, I guess."

She drew a deep breath. "So that I can be sure I'm comfortable with the mistake I'm making by loving you?"

"I'm not saying us being together would ever be a mistake, Claire." He grabbed her hand and brought it to his chest. "But you've got to face the realities. You'd have to keep working if we…"

Her voice caught. "Have babies? Have you thought about that? Would you ever want kids?"

He'd never known how much until this moment. He nodded, his heart hammering at the seeming impossibility of raising kids with Claire. "But what if…" Something goes wrong? At the corners of his consciousness, Luke saw the woman in the yellow dress. Was she his mama? And what circumstances led to him being left on a doorstep? If he was three or four years old, why couldn't he remember?

Claire was watching him carefully. Her lower lip suddenly trembled. "Don't tell me you're afraid I might have to soil my lily-white hands with some hard work."

"That's not how I'd put it."

"Well, just so you know, I love my work, and I'd never give it up for anyone. Not that it matters, since I think I've changed my mind."

"About?"

"Wanting to try to be with you, Luke. It's just so… difficult."

Everything inside him went utterly still. He'd half expected this. Suddenly he ached to reach out, to hold her and ask her to never leave him. This whole conversation had tapped into powerful emotions that could get dangerous. He hated to be left. "Don't play with me, Claire," he said. He stepped close enough that it brought a wave of her body heat and a memory of the touch and taste of her creamy skin. "I never had folks," he continued, "and I can't imagine what it was like to be raised the way you were. Nobody ever even told me they loved me until last night. Do you understand that, Claire? You were the first."

With a strange mix of anger and triumphant satisfaction he watched her eyes widen. Good. Maybe she was beginning to get the picture. "Before you walk away from what people like me never had," he said, "I just want to make sure you know the score." Another wave of frustration washed over him. "Claire," he added, his voice turning hoarse. "I know you try to understand, you always have. You're a perceptive woman. But I'm trying to look out for you."

"By telling me how unhappy we'd be together?" Her eyes were so beautifully blue that they seemed to burn right through him. "Don't you see that approaching a relationship like that could make it a self-fulfilling prophecy? Luke, what's wrong with living right here? Last night, this little cabin was heaven for us. And I love what I do. Like I said, I'm never giving up my work. You're scared, Luke, and I understand, but all I've ever wanted to do with you is try..."

She was right, of course. But she had practice at love; she'd been raised in a house bursting with it. "I know." It was all he could honestly say.

"I'm understanding you, Luke. But getting in deep with you, then having you leave me, would kill me now. And I'm beginning to think that all the understanding in the world couldn't make you want to take a risk with me."

His heart was beating dully in his chest. "A risk?"

She nodded. "Of sharing a life someday."

"I don't know what to say, Claire."

"I know," she said simply. "Maybe I should just go. Maybe we both need to think."

Last night had changed everything. They weren't strangers who'd become lovers. They had a history, and he knew what she meant when she said she needed him to risk his heart. "Maybe so." He nodded.

Stepping back, she turned and strode from the room on those long, shapely legs. He meant to let her go, but after a moment, he changed his mind. By the time he reached the front door, she'd already grabbed her purse and parka. Outside, the Wrangler's engine was idling. Stepping barefoot onto the porch, Luke barely felt the cold. He waved her toward him, but she only returned the wave, then pulled out. Sighing, he watched the Jeep disappear under a canopy of trees, then he went back inside.

His eyes landed on the painting she'd brought him. He'd left it propped on the dining table, and now he took in the homey log cabin.

She was right about so many things.

Last night, this cabin had been heaven for them. He'd always let his personal demons get in the way of him and Claire being together, too. And while he'd been moved when she said she loved him, he hadn't been surprised. Deep down, he'd always known it. He didn't even really believe she'd given up on him. But thinking she might someday made Luke understand that he was never going to get her out of his blood. He loved her, too. But could he conquer his own emotions?

CHAPTER TEN

LUKE FINISHED KNOTTING a scarf around the neck of a snowman, then glanced from Lost Springs' main house to Brady. "Sure you haven't seen Claire, pardner?"

"Nope."

Leaning back, Luke surveyed his handiwork. Some older boys had built the snowman, but Brady had rounded up a hat, scarf and carrot nose. "Definitely more personality," Luke commented.

Instead of responding, Brady thrust his gloved hands into his parka's pockets and stared down the road at an approaching red-white-and-blue Jeep.

Luke's mind was still on the earlier conversation. "You're positive Claire didn't come by?"

Brady shook his head. "Nope. I've been out here awhile. I woulda seen her, Luke. I was kinda looking for her."

"Any particular reason?"

Brady shrugged. "We made some ornaments at school, and I thought maybe she could put mine on her Christmas tree. I meant to give it to her yesterday, but I forgot."

"She'll like that, Brady," Luke assured him. Gazing down, he realized Claire had probably developed as many feelings for the boy as he. Just like Luke, she spent a lot of time out here, and judging from their conversations, she liked to talk about Brady—his progress at school, his hopes of finding his folks. "You like her, don't you?"

"Claire?"

Luke nodded.

"Yeah." Brady's mouth quirked in a teasing smile. "What about you? Do you like her?"

"Yeah," he admitted. "I like her."

"You gonna marry her?"

Luke stared at Brady a long moment. "Right now, she's engaged to Clive Stoddard."

Brady frowned, his light eyebrows drawing together. "Can't they break up? Lots of people do."

"I guess that's possible." Already, they'd as good as done so. Late last night, between the times he'd loved her, Claire had told him all he wanted to know about the relationship. Still, Luke didn't know what she'd do if Clive came home, which is why he needed to talk to her. Earlier, when Luke had tried to call, he'd gotten her answering machine. Ever since she left the cabin, he'd been trying to decide what he wanted to say, but all he knew for certain was that he wanted to make sure he wasn't going to lose her.

"I gotta meet Mr. Garret," said Brady, his eyes following the Jeep.

"I'll go with you," Luke replied with a sigh as Brady pulled his hands from his pockets, bringing out a stamped envelope. "Another letter to Santa?" Luke guessed.

"Yep."

As they started walking, Luke grasped Brady's elbow, half lifting the boy as they traversed the deeper snow. Luke just wished Claire had been out there. She'd said she loved him, but that didn't necessarily mean she wouldn't marry Clive tomorrow if he showed up and was willing. Claire was ready to start a family, and she'd been prepared to do so with Clive. Hell, maybe she'd go through with the wed-

ding if she really thought she could have no future with
Luke.

Damn. Last summer the announcement of Claire's engagement had begun what Luke now saw as a slow process
of realizing what she meant to him. Even so, marriage had
been the furthest thing from his mind when she'd come to
the mall. Only this morning, as he'd watched her drive
away, had he understood that he needed to act. If he didn't,
there was still a chance she'd marry Clive. Luke was
ninety-nine-percent sure she couldn't, not after what they'd
shared last night. But the fear of the other one percent had
knotted in his gut and wasn't going away.

Besides which, after she'd left, Wesley had called again,
saying somebody had spotted a Ford Explorer yesterday
that matched a description of Clive's, and that had made
Luke feel vaguely threatened. He'd found himself half
wishing Clive would never show up in Lightning Creek
again. According to Wesley, the Explorer had been parked
at the home of a woman who worked at the drugstore in
town. Luke had no idea what to make of that, but after he
went to the Stoddards', he'd swing by the drugstore and
question the woman.

"Luke?"

Glancing down, he forced a smile. Brady merely stared,
his fair, freckled skin bright red from the cold, his blue
eyes suddenly looking too worried and knowing for a boy
his age. Leaning down, Luke tugged Brady's knit hat.
"Keep those ears covered or you'll get frostbite, cowboy.
Now, what were you going to say?"

"Nothing." Brady shrugged, grabbed Luke's hand and
began pulling him toward the driveway. "C'mon, or we're
gonna miss Mr. Garret."

Luke figured Brady had been about to discuss the search
for his folks, as he so often did. "Don't worry," said Luke.

"We've got plenty of time. Mr. Garret won't leave without your letter."

Brady pressed the envelope against his chest, as if to better ensure he wouldn't drop it. "I'm pretty sure Christmas Eve's too late to mail this, but I'm gonna do it, anyway."

Luke tilted his head, as if considering. Brady was old enough that he probably had doubts about Santa Claus, but right now, he looked so hopeful that Luke's heart pulled. He knew Brady was asking Santa to find his folks. And only Luke knew the trail was cold.

"Luke?"

"I doubt it's too late. I figure it'll get there."

"If it doesn't, it's okay. I sent some other letters."

"Good thinking." As Brady dropped his hand and ran toward the mail truck, Luke lifted his voice and waved. "Hey there, John."

John Garret waved back. "Merry Christmas. How you doing, Luke?"

"Can't complain. You?"

"Working round the clock during the holidays." As John leaned over and took Brady's letter and slid it into his mail pouch, Luke glanced around, suddenly reminded of a snowy landscape of Claire's that he'd seen in a gallery in Casper. He sighed again, thinking back to the summer they'd gotten to know each other. In order to impress her, he'd read about everything from Alfred Jacob Miller's drawings of Wyoming's Wind River Mountains through Remington's and Russell's portraits of cowboys, to Georgia O'Keeffe's sandstone landscapes. Since then, Luke had come to feel that it was Claire's sharp, almost photographic pictures that best captured Wyoming—just simple scenes such as this, a boy running through the snow toward a mail truck.

Claire was simply the best, in every way, Luke thought with another sigh. As Brady turned and ran toward him again, Luke told himself he'd do anything to keep her. First, though, he had to find her.

ALTHOUGH THE LAZY FOUR'S stables were heated, the air remained cool enough that Claire's breath clouded it as she cooed to Clive's quarter horse. "Hey there, Shadow," she whispered. Reaching into a stall, she smoothed a hand over the animal's charcoal coat. "Where's Clive, huh?"

With a soft whinny, the horse sidled closer, moving on sturdy legs and nudging Claire's parka sleeve. "Here, I brought you a little something." Claire reached into her pocket for a sugar cube, then felt a soft nuzzle against her palm as Shadow took it.

"Thatta boy." Claire petted the long, strong neck, letting the coarse mane fall through her fingers. After a moment, she sighed. Making love with Luke had been everything she'd dreamed it would be, but now she had to face facts. While it was hardly her style to leave as she had this morning, she knew the depth of her feelings for Luke would never change him. She didn't want him looking out for her best interests; she wanted him to see happiness as something they could achieve together.

Luke had so much love to give. How he'd claimed her physically proved it, as did his attention to the boys at Lost Springs, and the fact that he was Lightning Creek's secret Santa. But even if they were together now, she feared he'd blame her for whatever might go wrong between them. She could almost hear him saying, *If you wanted life to be different, you should have married Clive.*

She couldn't settle for ever hearing "I told you so's." Not even from Luke, no matter how many years he'd been in her thoughts. That no one had ever said "I love you" to him before last night was heartbreaking. So was the fact that his past had damaged him; she shook her head, thinking maybe she should have stayed away. Maybe trying to bring him into her life again was a mistake. When she'd decided to marry Clive, she'd been sure she'd faced the truth about Luke and moved on, but when Clive disappeared, she'd run straight to Luke, hadn't she? "And we made love," she murmured.

He'd find her soon enough, too. After screening his call, she'd headed for the Lazy Four, feeling she had no choice but to start repacking the boxes in the A-frame. Even if Clive returned and wanted to get married, she couldn't after what happened last night, no more than she could settle for a less-than-equal partner who wouldn't take his share of the responsibility for the relationship. Now everything seemed such a shame. Even the fact that the wonderful house she'd designed would probably sit empty on the Stoddards' ranch for years to come.

"And the wedding," Claire whispered miserably. Mama and Tex had outdone themselves, readying the barn for the hoe-down. Mama had cooked as well as hired caterers, the musicians were coming this evening, and Claire's sisters couldn't be more excited. Claire tried not to think of how they'd all giggled together as they'd fussed with the emerald velvet gowns, new makeup and hairstyles, and she tried not to think about facing her future alone.

She stroked Shadow's flank in a way that probably soothed her more than the horse. What if she was wrong about Clive? What if he was really in some sort of trouble? Ever since the events at Elmer Green's, Claire had found herself vacillating between being worried and reexamining her own inexplicable gut feeling that he was all right.

Hearing approaching voices, Claire glanced around. After a moment, she recognized one of them as Luke's. He said, "So, you still can't think of where else Clive might have gone?"

"Like I said," returned Evander, "I think he had business in Douglas and Laramie, maybe Cheyenne. You'd know better than me, since you went through his calendar book. But still, it's hard to say. My son's always going off on his own." Lifting a hand, Evander waved and called out, "Didn't know you were here, Claire."

As she turned from Shadow's stall, her eyes trailed from the snow-touched brim of Luke's black Stetson, down to the open shearling jacket he wore over a blue flannel shirt and jeans. His lips parted slightly—in surprise at finding her here, she guessed. She glanced at Evander. He'd once been the spitting image of Clive, tall and lean, with bowed cowboy legs and blue eyes, but illness had left him thin and pale. His sparse hair was dark now, shot through with gray, and his face was almost gaunt. He shoved both hands in the pockets of tan Carhardt coveralls he wore under a jeans jacket.

"Why are you out here?" he asked as he and Luke approached. "Something wrong?"

"No, Evander," Claire replied casually, her eyes still locked on Luke's. "Everything's fine. I'm just worried about finding Clive, that's all."

Luke was eyeing her, seemingly wishing they were alone. "When I'm through talking with Evander, mind if I have a word with you, Claire?"

She shot him a glance of censure, since his look implied he wanted to question her further about Clive's disappearance, not something personal.

"If you don't mind," Luke added.

She minded. Last night the depth of love she felt for Luke had shaken her, and now she had no intention of bringing him any closer, not unless she saw a sign that he was ready to accept the kind of love she had to offer. "Well," she said, aware Evander was watching them, his sharp blue eyes curious, "I'll try to catch up with you, Luke."

His jaw set at the lack of commitment. "I'll look forward to it."

"Me, too," she shot back, avoiding Evander's quizzical gaze. Taking long strides toward the door, Claire told herself what she had for years—that it was in the best interest of her heart to stay as far away from Luke as she could get.

SIGHING AS HE WATCHED Claire go, Luke reached into his shirt pocket and plucked out a toothpick. Popping it into his mouth, he wondered how Claire could be so distant. After last night, it unsettled him to think she might really fear—or decide—that their relationship was too problematic to pursue.

Luke was still fighting the impulse to leave Evander and follow her when Evander said, "You two know each other, son? I mean, you were together yesterday when I met you..."

Luke managed a nod. "From back in school." *And the bachelor auction last summer. And bed last night.* Leaning against the stall where Claire had been a moment before, Luke gazed into the frail old man's eyes, feeling guilty. Hours ago, the woman that this man thought was his future daughter-in-law had slept like a kitten in Luke arms. *Daughter-in-law,* he thought again. *Well, she will be if she marries Clive, anyway. Which she still might if you don't do something about it.*

In the interest of keeping his professional and personal lives separate, Luke said, "Thanks for taking the time to see me again today." Fishing the notebook and pencil stub from his shirt pocket, he prepared to write. "I've got a couple more questions. Hope you don't mind."

"Nope." Hitching his pant leg, Evander rested a boot on top of an upturned feed bucket. "Go ahead. I'll answer anything you can throw my way, son."

Son. After his exchange with Claire this morning, that was the last word Luke wanted to hear. It definitely opened old wounds. If he'd had a pa, maybe he'd understand how to better handle his feelings for Claire. Suddenly, Luke thought of how Brady had run through the snow toward the mail truck, the Santa letter pressed against his chest. Luke figured Brady would walk barefoot through the snow—or hot coals—if he thought it would bring him a man who would call him son. Funny, Luke thought now, how folks threw around the simplest words, never knowing how they affected other folks. "Like I said while we were walking over here," Luke forced himself to continue, "I was wondering if you'd heard of an outfit called Cheyenne Mining?"

"Nope."

"What about parties looking to buy your ranch? Are there any?"

"The Lazy Four?" Evander shook his head. "I'd kill 'em first. So would any of my four boys." He laughed ruefully. "Some days I think that's why we call it the Lazy Four, though. Those four boys have plenty of other things keeping them busy, besides the ranch. Not that I complain. Fact is, I wish Clive could get somebody to help him out."

"So, there're no prospective buyers?"

"Not a one, son. But there's a consortium with an interest in the area, the folks who were considering buying Lost Springs. And my neighbor to the north—that's Clayton Ford—why, I bet he'd love to get his hands on my land. But like I say…'' Evander chuckled softly. ''Fat chance.''

Luke couldn't help but smile in appreciation. ''It is a gorgeous spread.''

''Wish Clive had more interest.'' Evander sighed. ''But it's computers he loves. He spends all his spare time designing programs. Since I got sick, I know he feels he's got to stick around and run the ranch. And hell, I guess he does. But it's a shame he can't go to school in Cheyenne.''

''Cheyenne?''

Evander nodded. ''For years he's talked about taking a degree, so he can get a job in the computer industry. But he'd have to move somewhere else to do that kind of work. Anyhow, it's just talk. Now he's settling down and marrying Claire.''

Luke felt more than a twinge of guilt. ''First, let's find him,'' Luke said.

''I'm not that worried,'' returned Evander. ''Like I say, he takes good care of himself. He'll turn up. He always does.''

Luke tamped down another rush of unwanted emotion as he glanced around at the well-kept stables. The world was at Clive feet and the man didn't even seem to care. It was possible he was simply off somewhere, having a good time. Suddenly, Luke's eyes settled on a blue-and-white-checked blanket that was tossed over an inside wall of the stall. He hadn't noticed it before, and now his breath caught. ''Where did that come from?''

Evander squinted. ''What?''

Luke nodded at the blanket, his heart pounding. ''That blanket.'' It was identical to the one he'd had when he was found on the porch at Lost Springs.

''I was going to ask you…'' Evander began, then he

changed horses in midstream and continued, answering
Luke's question, "We order those blankets in bulk from a
wholesaler in Cheyenne. The hands use 'em. Don't rightly
know how that one wound up in here, though." Evander
peered at Luke a long moment. "When I heard your name
yesterday, something started niggling at my mind, and I
just figured out what it is."

"What?" Luke managed to say, his mind reeling. Obviously, someone connected to the Lazy Four had known
him when he was a boy, or had at least given him a similar
blanket. Had Luke's pa been a cowhand here? Had his
mama worked in the house?

"Years ago," said Evander, "we had a hand who went
by the name of Luke Lydell. Was your pa named Luke,
too?"

Luke didn't exactly want to go into his family history
with a near stranger, but his chest constricted and once
more he felt strangely breathless. "It's possible," he said,
trying to tamp down the hope he felt, since it would probably only lead to disappointment. "I was raised over at
Lost Springs."

Evander looked relieved. "Then he couldn't be a relation. The authorities would have known you and him was
kin."

Luke's heart sank. "Authorities?"

Evander nodded. Suddenly looking pained, the older
man simply sat down on the overturned feed bucket where
he'd previously propped his foot.

"Maybe we'd better head back," Luke said, seeing how
tired Evander looked.

The man gazed up, shaking his head. "Glad you walked
with me, from where we parked the cars. I needed to get
out, son. My wife, Jenny, has conniption fits if I go anywhere alone." Evander laughed softly. "It's nice of her to

worry so much, but I don't intend to die anytime soon. Anyhow, what I was going to say was that Luke Lydell—the cowhand we hired—wound up in the state pen. When he worked here, he was always getting tanked up on liquor, so we finally tossed him off the Four. After that, he got caught messing with the government. Some kind of mail fraud, I think.''

As the horse sidled closer, Luke ran a palm down his neck. How was he connected to Luke Lydell? he wondered. Maybe the cops had simply overlooked the connection and the ranch hand was his pa. Hadn't Luke always thought his folks might be criminals? After all, what kind of people left a kid on a doorstep?

Lydell. It wasn't even Luke's real name, just a name taken from the label in a lost blanket. Luke guessed there was no real reason for anybody at Lost Springs or the sheriff to know that the Lazy Four had mass-ordered the blankets. ''Was this man white?'' Luke suddenly asked.

Evander gazed at him thoughtfully. ''White as aspirin.''

Luke's heart sank. ''That so?''

''White-blond hair, blue-eyes.''

Luke had straight, blue-black hair and dark skin. His pa might be white, but probably not white-blond. ''In the past, did anyone ever come here, asking about one of these blankets?''

''Like who?''

''Like the sherrif?''

Evander shook his head, the focus of his eyes sharpening and becoming more curious. ''Not to my recollection. But they'd have asked in the bunkhouse, not at the main house.''

The Lazy Four was too big an operation to bother the owner about such a matter, Luke thought. And boys moved in and out of Lost Springs all the time. Maybe no one had even tried to trace the blanket. "Who would have been the boss here? Say, twenty-five years ago?"

Evander scratched his chin, thinking back. "A man by the name of Dusty Hooper, I think. But he's long gone. Mind telling me why you're asking?"

Luke shrugged. "Just a question."

"If you want to know about our blankets," Evander continued, still eyeing Luke critically, "you could check with the current cowhand boss, Jim Sanford. He works under Clive, and he keeps all the employment and inventory records. We keep pretty good track of things we give out to the hands. Jim's gone for the holidays, but he'll be back in town January 2."

"Thanks for your time," Luke said, wishing he didn't have to wait to find out what had happened to Luke Lydell's blanket. Was it possible they'd assigned it to another cowhand? Had someone other than Luke Lydell given it to a girlfriend? Or to Luke's mama?

Just as Luke was turning to go, Evander cleared his throat and said, "Before you leave, I've got a favor to ask."

As much as Luke wanted to get out of here and process the information he'd just heard, he liked this man. During the walk from their cars to the stables, they'd hit it off, talking about ranching and bull riding, and now Luke felt glad to be of use. "What can I do for you?"

"To tell you the truth," said Evander, scratching his chin thoughtfully, "I figure Clive's got a case of last-minute cold feet. He'll show up for the wedding tomorrow, mark my words. No man misses his own wedding, right?"

"Right," Luke replied.

"After you came yesterday," Evander continued, "I checked you out. Turns out you're just about the closest thing to a P.I. we've got in Lightning Creek. You used to be a cop, too.''

Luke nodded. "A state cop, out of Cheyenne."

This was no news to Evander. "I should have known about you, but...well, for years...let's just say I kind of stick to my own neck of the woods. Truth is, I haven't been off the Lazy Four since February a'fore last, when Clive talked me into riding to Cheyenne with him. Anyhow, son, I'd like to hire you."

This was the last thing Luke expected. "For?"

"Well, it's a long story...." Evander began. And then, from his seat on the feed bucket, Evander started telling Luke about a woman he'd loved but had never married. "She was a maid at the main house, a Crow woman who came off the reservation." Evander sighed. "She never did think she was good enough for me. Hell, she was backward, uneducated and unsure of herself. But I didn't finish college, myself. Forgot half of what I learned in high school, too. And I was proud of it. I was a rancher, born and bred. What did I need with a bunch of books? But all this woman could see was how much money we got from the land."

"A spread like this is worth a fortune," Luke said.

Evander shrugged. "I never gave a damn for money. All I wanted was Laura." He glanced at Luke again. "Laura Blackfeet. That was her name. Back then, my ma was still running the main house and—unlike Jenny, my wife—Ma had some real citified ways. You know, serving dinners with three forks and dressing up in fancy clothes. I tried to tell Laura she could adjust to us and learn to feel comfortable in the house. Or that we'd move away. But Laura said she couldn't take me from the land I loved, and she couldn't fit in here. Not even when she got pregnant."

Luke had been listening carefully. "She got pregnant?"

Evander nodded. "And then she took off. Just like that. Never saw her again." The old man's voice suddenly cracked. "She…" Reaching inside his jeans jacket, he pulled out a photograph. "You might think it's strange, son," he continued, "but Jenny and my boys know all about her. I couldn't hold anything back from Jenny. She's the best friend a man could ever have. And since I got sick, I wanted my boys to know they had more kin somewhere, in case my other boy never shows up." Evander held out the photograph. "Here's Laura. She was pretty, don't you think?"

Taking the black-and-white photograph by a frayed edge, Luke gazed into it, and his breath left him. It was a face he'd seen in his dreams; for years, it had haunted him. He took in the sad dark eyes, proud mouth and long, flowing hair. An image of her wearing a yellow dress filled Luke's mind while Evander continued talking, describing how an investigator he'd hired followed her trail out of state.

Was it possible Laura Blackfeet returned to Lightning Creek? Luke wondered, his heart thudding dully against his ribs. Had she come with her young son? Was he his mama? Was that why he remembered the Lazy Four? The strangest sensation washed over Luke. He could almost feel the texture of that yellow dress against his cheek. It wasn't of summer fabric as he'd thought, but of coarse wool. Now Luke was sure they'd sat together in a parked car. Hidden by a stand of trees, they'd stared down the long, snowy driveway to the Lazy Four as a shiny red car approached. A man and woman were in front, with two babies in back. Had the adults been Evander and Jenny?

"The man I hired finally found her," Evander was saying, shifting his weight on the uncomfortable-looking bucket. "But that was years after she'd gone. By then, I'd married Jenny and we'd had our first two boys. Turns out, Laura had died in a hospital of breast cancer.'' He blew out a sigh, adding, ''On a Crow reservation.''

Dead? She was dead? Luke felt oddly unbalanced. Had he found his mama only to discover she was dead? He could barely find his voice. ''What year did she die?''

When Evander named the year, Luke's heart missed another beat. She'd died shortly after Luke was left at Lost Springs. ''Which reservation?'' Luke managed to write it down when Evander told him.

''Thing is,'' Evander continued, ''one of the nurses said she kept calling my name when she died, and she was talking about our boy.''

Luke could barely believe what he'd heard. It seemed so impossible. But everything fit. Laura Blackfeet could have taken Luke Lydell's blanket when she left the Lazy Four. Maybe when she found out she was ill, she'd tried to return to Evander with their son, only to find that Evander had since married and begun a new life with Jenny. Knowing she couldn't care for an infant much longer, and probably having nothing of monetary value to give him, she'd taken her son to Lost Springs, knowing he'd at least be clothed and fed. There was no doubt in Luke's mind that Laura Blackfeet was his mama.

Luke's eyes settled on Evander. He was a white man. He looked as if he'd once had blond hair, too, but it was dark blond, like Clive's. Evander bore little resemblance to Luke, except in eye color.

''Will you take the case?'' Evander asked.

Luke managed a nod, but he already knew the answers in his hammering heart. He stared down at the man who had to be his father. He tried not to think of the wasted years—that the mama he'd never known was gone and his pa was ailing. But did Evander really want to know the

truth now, as he professed? Or was this search the normal
course for a dying man to take…a man with unfinished
business? Evander had grown sons by another woman, after all. Luke glanced away, his heart now heavy with the
thought of how easily Evander Stoddard had begun—and
lived—a full life with a woman other than the one he
seemingly loved most. Could Claire still do that with
Clive?

"You feeling ill, son?"

Son. The word pounded through Luke's head. "Fine."

"You looked a little peaked there for a minute."

"I'm okay," Luke repeated.

"Well…you're right good company, so if you're not in
a hurry, I'd love to show you some of my cars."

Luke needed to get away and think. "Cars?"

"Antiques," said Evander. "Collectibles. I've even got
an old red '59 Caddy. She's a beaut."

Feeling unsteady, Luke leaned a hand against the stall.
His heart was pounding so hard that it rushed in his ears.
Was Evander's red Cadillac the one he remembered from
his childhood? "Maybe another time," Luke managed to
say, thinking he'd sneak out to the garage and look. He
didn't want to be with Evander when he saw the car. He
wanted to be alone.

Evander slapped a hand against his thigh, as if to say
they'd concluded their business. "Will you look for my
boy by Laura, then?"

"Sure."

"Come around after the holidays, and I'll turn over the
files the last investigator left with me," said Evander.

Somehow, Luke found his voice. "Will do." Glancing
away, his eyes landed on Claire, who was standing by the
door. She'd apparently come back to the stables. She'd
overheard every word, too, judging from the fact that she
looked as stunned as Luke.

CHAPTER ELEVEN

LUKE WAS MOVING with impossibly long strides, taking the path of least resistance toward the Cherokee, ignoring a walkway and plowing straight through the snow. His shearling jacket was open, the sides flapping in the biting breeze.

"Wait a minute." Shivering as she jogged alongside him, Claire fumbled with the zipper to her parka, her freezing fingers yanking it up. "Luke, I heard everything."

"Claire, for once...I'd really like to be alone."

Feeling frustrated, she squinted against the sun that had broken through the clouds and was reflecting off the snow. For years, she'd suspected Evander had a secret past, and yet she could barely believe he was Luke's father. All the facts fit, though. Luke had been found with a blanket from the Lazy Four, he was obviously half-white, and now she could see that he had Evander's eyes. How could she not have seen the resemblance before? "I thought you wanted to see me," she ventured, the brisk wind making her shudder.

"Changed my mind." As they reached the Cherokee, he swept the hat from his head, slapped it against his thigh and turned into the winter breeze to face her, fine strands of his jet hair whipping across his chiseled face.

"Don't shut me out," she began simply. Last night proved they could be everything a man and women were meant to be, and now, one look at Luke made her long to feel his strong arms around her again. If he'd only talk to her, maybe she could take that as proof that he was willing to completely open his heart to her. Once more, she thought of last night, and despite the chill air, memories of loving him warmed her. "Talk to me," she urged. "We've known each other so long. And you need a friend."

His look was guarded, his eyes dark. She watched as he wriggled the Stetson onto his head again, the brim shadowing his face. Compressing his lips, he eyed her a long moment. "Let me handle this my way."

"Handle this?" Was he considering not telling Evander?

"C'mon. Let's not stand out here arguing."

He meant he didn't want to talk at all, but she chose to deliberately misunderstand. "Okay," she said. Turning on her heel, Claire circled the Jeep and hopped in the passenger side.

Luke got in and slammed the door. He turned the key in the ignition, and when the motor roared to life, he flicked off the windshield wipers and muted the radio. Then he turned toward her. "Claire," he continued with unusual calm as he reached and trained the heater vents on her knees. "It won't do a bit of good to announce my suspicions. At the first bend of a willow, no rational man assumes a storm's coming."

For a second, she couldn't even respond. Her eyes were riveted on the key chain dangling from the ignition; it was the laminated photo from the mall where she was sitting on Santa's lap. Only now did she recall Luke's taking the key chain from the elf's table and pocketing it. He must have put his keys on it this morning. "Evander's your father, Luke," she forced herself to continue. "He's got to be."

He stared through the windshield a long moment, his expression grim as he pulled down the sun visor. "Seems like it," he conceded. "The blanket I have came from here. And I recognize the picture of..." *My mama.* Luke couldn't quite get out the words. "Of her."

Claire could still barely process it. "Luke, you recognize the picture? Then it's true. You have to tell him."

As Luke's eyes roved over her face, fire suddenly came into them, communicating equal parts lust and anger. "Claire," he nearly growled, "I'm going to make sure of the truth before I turn everybody's lives topsy-turvy."

"Evander asked you to look," she protested. "He wants to know."

His gaze softened, lingering a long moment on her mouth. "I'm not talking to him before I'm sure."

"But you know it's true." Her voice rose. "Besides, only getting blood tests from Evander will prove it, Luke."

Luke's eyes scanned the windshield again, taking in the snow-blanketed field near the stables. "Evander and his wife have been working this ranch for years, Claire. What if he feels he has to..."

"Recognize you as his son?" Claire gasped. "That's the whole point." Oh, she thought, with mounting frustration, she was beginning to know Luke so well. "You'd risk not knowing your family better because you fear they might not want you making demands on them? Or because they might not want you to become part of life at the Lazy Four?"

His eyes had slowly dropped down, almost caressing her as they took in the length of her body, but when they returned to her face, they held molten anger. "It's easy for you, Claire," he returned, obviously fighting to keep his voice even. "You've had your needs met. You've been pampered. Cared for."

Maybe he was right, but the words stung. "Maybe it's true. Maybe it's easier for me. I admit, I don't know what it's like to be left on a doorstep in the middle of winter. But you know something else? This means your mama loved you, Luke. She left you because she was dying—" Claire suddenly drew a sharp breath. She hadn't yet pieced together the rest. "The family in the red car," she said now. "That was Evander and Jenny, wasn't it? The two babies must have been the oldest boys, Bob and Clive." Her voice hitched with excitement. "Evander said he has an old red Cadillac. He hasn't driven it for years, so I'd forgotten."

Luke looked noncommital. Fishing a toothpick from his pocket, he began chewing it with calculated slowness. "Maybe."

She tried not to react, but his attitude was starting to infuriate her. If Luke would only deal with his past, maybe they could have a future. Her voice low, she continued, "Why are you always so unwilling to confront the truth?"

His lips closed tightly around the toothpick for a moment. Leaning back in the seat, he rested a hand on the steering wheel, as if he was ready to go. "Like I said, Claire, I don't feel right, stepping in and changing everybody's landscape just because I've got a hunch."

It was the wrong time to remember how sweetly he'd touched her body last night, and how lovingly he'd kissed her naked skin. Her pulse suddenly leaped, and she shifted uncomfortably on the seat. "You've got more than a hunch, Luke," she managed to say.

"Well, I don't want to mess up other people's lives."

Her lips parted. "As if I do?"

Lifting off his Stetson, Luke thrust an angry hand through his hair. Shoving the toothpick to the side of his cheek with his tongue, he spoke, his voice suddenly sounding strangely hoarse. "You made a commitment to a man who's disappeared, Claire."

Hearing the suppressed emotion beyond the words, her heart skipped a beat. "Clive's all but broken off our engagement," she defended. "And I've got a gut feeling Clive's fine."

Luke's eyelids had lowered, and now he was watching her carefully from beneath them. "That's convenient. Soothes your nerves, I bet. I'm not as convinced."

Claire sucked in a deep breath. Luke's body suddenly seemed too close, too unforgettably masculine and powerful. The proximity was enough to warm her, and so was her rising temper. "Don't attack me because you want to push me away," she warned softly. "You're the one who's never wanted to make commitments."

He eyed her. "So, you're definitely not marrying Clive?"

"No." She stared steadily back at him. "I'm going to tell him...I have feelings for you, Luke."

He sighed. "When you were fighting, Clive might have been blowing off steam. If he comes home, that news might rock his world, Claire. Your mama and Tex have no idea you're thinking about calling off the wedding. The church is set to go. The musicians are—"

"Given our conversation this morning, my wedding's none of your business," she said, damning the way her heart was beating out of control.

Luke's eyes turned hot on hers. "After last night, it's all my business, Claire."

"I'm beginning to think you really feel I should marry Clive."

"Of course I don't want that, Claire."

Luke surveyed her with shaded eyes. The Jeep suddenly seemed too small, the heat coming through the vents far too warm. Taking a deep breath, Claire couldn't help but recall the smooth glide of their naked bodies, the raw sexual needs and emotions they'd shared. Last night, she'd said she loved him. And now, returning his unwavering gaze, she knew that would never change. "Evander wants to know what happened to you," she said, forcing herself to continue with their earlier conversation, knowing that this was the wrong time to address their relationship. In part, she feared Luke was just trying to deflect the serious talk about Evander. "If you're his son," she continued, "and I know you are, he wants a relationship. That's what you've always wanted, isn't it?"

He sighed, his eyes still boring into hers. "Things are…difficult now. Don't you understand what this means for us?"

She'd lost his train of thought. "For us?"

"All my life, I've wanted folks." Luke's eyes turned strangely hard. "And now there's a good chance Evander Stoddard's my pa. There's a chance…that Laura Blackfeet didn't leave me because she didn't want me."

"Your mama had no choice, Luke," Claire quickly assured him. "She knew she was dying. She must have come back to Lightning Creek to bring you to Evander. She probably didn't know what to do when she realized he'd started a family with another woman." Claire sighed. "If only she'd told Evander then."

"He might not even be my pa," Luke reminded her.

It was as if he didn't dare to hope. "He *is*. All the facts fit too neatly. And Luke—" She wondered if she should address the real issue "—you can let them love you. You can love them back." Her voice suddenly trembled. "Luke, you can love me, too."

"But don't you see?" His eyes fixed on hers, steady and intense. "I wanted a family all my life. What kid in my shoes doesn't? It's why we've both been trying to help Brady. Anyway, I always swore if I had them, I'd do right by them. I used to watch folks yelling at their kids, or kids disrespecting their elders, and I'd think they didn't know how good they had it. I couldn't imagine why somebody might leave a baby on a doorstep.'' The focus of eyes sharpened. ''Don't you see, Claire?''

She didn't understand. ''What?''

''Claire,'' he said slowly. ''The man you're supposed to marry tomorrow is my *brother*.''

He was right. She hadn't thought of it that way. Realizing how much strain Luke was under, guilt flooded her. She'd thought that if he understood Laura Blackfeet loved him, then surely he'd open his heart now and begin to share more of himself with her. But Clive was his half brother…a relation Luke wanted and had never known he had. By loving Claire, Luke would be going against his own blood.

Luke looked shaken. Leaning across the seat, he lifted a hand and traced a thumb along her jaw. ''See, Claire?''

She wished she didn't, but she nodded. Nothing would ever be possible with Luke until her past was put to rest with Clive, and until Luke came to an understanding with his family.

The car phone suddenly rang, startling them both. Pressing a hand to her chest, Claire said, ''The phone.''

Luke blew out a soft, irritated sigh as if to say he was sorry, since there was a world of things for them to discuss. Leaning over, he pressed the receiver button. ''Luke here.''

It was Wesley. ''Luke, I've been trying to reach you for the last hour.''

''What's up?''

"Lots. But I hear rustling. It that the same woman who was in your bed this morning?"

The car filled with warm tension at the reminder of last night. Claire glanced through the window as it all flooded back—the dampness and relentless heat, the words of love and broken cries. Now it was hard to say where their relationship was heading. She could swear she heard a soft catch in Luke's voice when he said, "Yeah."

"Howdy-do," said Wesley.

"Hi," said Claire.

"Soon as I got back from Christmas shopping," Wesley continued, "I called a couple of the places we were talking about. Gomer's Hole and the Flying Swords."

Luke glanced at Claire, the quick pass of his eyes like a soft caress of silk. "What about the Triple T?"

"Just talked to them on the phone. Thing is, Clive was right. But like to say, it's Christmas, and we didn't have much manpower. The poor folks out at Gomer's Hole are packing their bags. Seemed too scared to talk, but let's just say I've got a special way about me, and after a while, they opened up a bit."

"And?" Luke prompted.

"And it sounds like a couple of guys scared the heck out of Gomer Silvers, and Web Saunders, who owns the Flying Swords. Both of 'em feel pressured to sell their land. Turns out, the perps meet the description of your friends Ham and Jack."

Luke said, "And the Triple T's having trouble?"

"Yep. Said they had a suspicious brush fire that ruined last year's hay. According to the Cheyenne Mining Company, the red truck's theirs, too, but it's a one-man show, and the owner, B. G. Boggs, says he doesn't know which employee took the truck." Wesley paused. "Of course he's only got two employees."

"And they are?" asked Claire.

"Nicknamed Ham and Jack," returned Wesley.

"Sounds like Cheyenne Mining's too small an operation to mess with the Lazy Four, though," Luke commented.

"True." Wesley replied. "But I figure B. G. Boggs is looking to mine something in the area. Bentonite. Silver. Who knows?"

"And Clive got a line on it," Luke continued with fraternal appreciation.

"And now we've got a line on Clive," assured Wesley.

Surprise touched Luke's voice. "You do?"

Claire's fingers tightened on her knee, and her heart felt as if it was in her throat. Only then did she realize how truly worried she'd been. "Is he all right?"

"Can't say as I know." Wesley sighed. "He's definitely been to all the ranches, asking questions. Gilbert Tucker at the Triple T says he saw Clive with Ham and Jack. They all piled in the red truck and drove away together this morning. Gilbert overheard them saying something about going to Casper. And Clive looked none too happy. Now Gilbert's thinking maybe Clive was forced into the truck."

"Was there another vehicle out at Gilbert's place?" Luke asked with concern. "Clive drives a—"

"Ford Explorer," interjected Claire. "It's black."

"And it's parked on Gilbert's property. The way I figure it, Clive was spying on Ham and Jack when they caught him. Since he'd hidden the Explorer, Gilbert didn't find it until a few hours ago. He didn't bother to call it in, either. He figured somebody was fishing illegally on the Triple T's lake."

Luke frowned. "Gilbert didn't want to stop trespassers?"

Wesley sighed again. "Nope. Said it was Christmas, so

he was hardly going to shoot some poor fellow's backside full of buckshot.''

Luke chewed hard on the toothpick in his mouth. "When did Clive leave with Ham and Jack?"

"It's been a few hours now."

"I hope he's all right," Claire murmured. "And I wonder where he's been staying. This means he's been in town the past few days."

"Guess he got a line on these guys and followed up," agreed Wesley, "since we were busy. He'll have done folks a good turn, too, if they'll testify that Cheyenne Mining was harassing them. Anyhow, we called the Casper cops."

Claire felt relief course through her until Luke said, "You sure it's Casper, the *city?*"

"Come again?" said Wesley.

Luke's frown deepened. "As opposed to Casper, the mine?"

Wesley whistled softly. "I didn't think of that, but you're right. They could be staying out at the old Casper mine."

Luke was already putting the Cherokee into gear. "I'll head up there now."

"Ten-four," said Wesley, right before he rang off. "I'll meet you up there with some backup."

Luke turned toward Claire. "You'd better get out."

She stared at him, not intending to budge. "I'm coming."

He uttered an exasperated sigh. "We've already been shot at once. I really don't want you in any danger, Claire."

She didn't want that, either, but she had to know if Clive was okay. "It's noon," she returned decidedly. "So, if you hurry, I might make it home in time for Christmas Eve dinner.''

By now, Luke knew arguing with her was pointless, so he put the Jeep into gear and started driving.

LUKE EDGED AWAY from where he'd hidden the Jeep behind a stand of pines and aspens. Across a clearing was the mining shack, a rickety, dilapidated one-room cabin with a tin roof; a cinder block was in front of the door, serving as a makeshift porch step. From this distance, nothing was visible through the darkened, smudgy windows, but the red truck was parked in front of the shack, and judging from the black smoke billowing from the chimney, the inhabitants were burning coal. Next to Luke, Claire shivered, her gaze following his across the clearing.

For the first time, she sounded scared. ''Do you really think Clive's in there?''

Luke sighed again, still wishing she was safely back at the Lazy Four. ''Beginning to think you shouldn't have come?''

Her eyes narrowed. ''I'm fine.''

''You insisted on coming.''

Her eyes shifted to the shack, and some of the fight went out of her. ''That was before I saw the place,'' she admitted, nervously tugging the braid out from the collar of her parka. ''Shouldn't we wait for Wesley? Luke, it's really isolated out here.''

She had a point. Heavy snowfall had made the first road they'd tried impassable, and the drive here was longer than Luke had anticipated. The sun had slipped lower behind clouds, turning the sky gray, and on the radio, the D.J. had announced they were in for more snow. Luke squinted into the weak light, his eyes trailing over three barely discernible sets of footprints that led from the red truck to the shack, then he turned toward Claire, feeling torn up over her relationship with Clive. Why couldn't she have been involved with any other man on earth? As confused as he felt, Luke couldn't stop his voice from growing husky with concern. "You going to be okay here, darlin'?"

Her eyes widened in protest. "I'm coming with you."

"No way," he said simply, his chest constricting with sudden tension. He'd had it with her willingness to put herself in danger. He'd had it with lying awake burning with aching physical need for her, too, and with possessing every last inch of her last night, only to feel as if he had to take it slower with her now because of Clive.

"Look," he said sighing, stepping closer.

"I'm looking," she returned, stepping back and looking luscious when she leaned against a tree trunk.

"I tried calling you this morning," Luke continued, edging nearer. "And I wanted to talk on the way over here, but I'm not sure what to say. Claire, I want to be with you. If marriage is what you want, I thought I was ready. That's why I was looking for you, to tell you. I can't stand the thought of losing you. But now...what if Clive's my brother? Can't we take this slow?" The more Luke had sat with the feelings, the more last night seemed like a revelation. It was only the beginning of what he and Claire could be together. Still, he knew he wasn't offering much more than he'd said this morning.

Her eyes were crystal clear as they gazed into his. "I know things have changed now, but my feelings haven't since the summer we were together in high school. I know Clive's your brother, Luke—he's got to be—but..."

He nodded, knowing she was ready for a sign of commitment from him, one he couldn't give until he'd figured out what to do. Lifting a dark, ungloved hand to her cheek, he brushed a thumb across her cold, silken lips. She looked as if she were freezing. "C'mon. Your teeth are chattering and your lips are turning blue," he said. "And since Clive might be in trouble, I'm not going to wait for Wesley. So, why don't you get back in the Jeep and get warm?"

She shook her head. "I'll wait right here."

"Do me a favor and stay put, then," Luke warned.

Her eyes suddenly looked so trusting that all his heart-strings pulled. He just wished he wasn't so scared something might happen to her. At least her parka was white. It blended with the snow, just the way his Jeep blended with the green of the trees. Suddenly, he could no longer fight his urges, and he lightly pressed his mouth to hers.

"Luke," she whispered as he drew away.

"Stay warm when I'm gone," he said gruffly.

"Hurry back."

"I will," he promised.

And then he turned, edging around the ring of trees that circled the clearing, intending to approach the shack from the back. Moving soundlessly behind snow-heavy pines, he surveyed the place, his eyes as sharp as a hawk's. Strange time to notice, he thought, but it was beautiful out here. Despite the gray, cloudy sky, the clearing and surrounding evergreens looked quiet and peaceful.

Moments later, Luke crept behind the shack. After discerning there was a back door, he edged to the side of the building. He glanced toward the Jeep, his eyes scanning the trees. Claire was gone. Dammit. He should have known she was lying about staying put. Biting back a testy sigh, he crouched down, planted a hand on the top of his hat to keep the wind from blowing it off, and moved toward the shack's side window, wincing every time his boots crunched in the snow.

When he reached the window, he blew out a surreptitious breath, then gingerly raised himself and peeked inside. Sure enough, Clive was in there. *My brother,* Luke thought, new emotion pulling at him. Unfortunately, the situation wasn't good. Clive was sitting upright in a hard-backed chair, his hands bound behind his back with rope. Ham and Jack were both armed and pacing the room. Jack's navy parka was slung on the seat of another chair, and his shoulder holster was visible against the plaid flannel shirt he wore. Ham, rifle in hand, was talking to Clive. Knowing he had to pay attention, Luke tried to push away thoughts of Claire. But it was hard. Ever since he watched her drive away this morning, he'd been trying to find her, to tell her he loved her. He wanted to let her know he'd do anything rather than lose her. But this could cause a rift with his father and brothers, and so Luke just kept going over it in his mind, the whole thing ripping him to shreds. He sighed. At least Wesley hadn't mentioned the woman from the drugstore while Claire was within earshot. It was too soon to tell if Clive had been visiting the woman and why, and Luke wanted to protect Claire in any way he could. Shaking his head, as if to clear it of the unwanted thoughts, he turned his attention back to the window—only to find that the lapse of attention had left him vulnerable.

Jack had whirled around. The man squinted, pointing at Luke. "Ham! It's the guy from the stables! He's out there."

Ham didn't waste a second. Swinging his rifle to his shoulder, he aimed and fired. Just as the window glass shattered, a figure lunged from nowhere, flying through the air and knocking Luke to the side, "Claire," he gasped, as a bullet hissed, hitting the ground near them. "Run."

She ran.

Luke scrambled up just as Ham's thick, muscle-bound

body swung around the side of the building. He must have come from the back door, and his heavily bearded face was a mask of fury as he raised the rifle, pointing it at Claire.

CHAPTER TWELVE

"GET BACK HERE, CLAIRE!" Luke yelled.

"What do you think I'm doing!" Claire had pivoted and was now running toward the front of the shack again, snow flying up from beneath her boots.

Just as she passed Luke, Ham fired a round into the air, probably trying to scare them into leaving. Luke bolted after Claire. Lifting his leg as he ran, he tried unsuccessfully to raise his jeans leg and snag the Colt Pocket Pony-lite from its holster. Half-hopping, he uttered a curse. Ahead, Claire was rounding the corner of the shack. Suddenly, Luke looked up—and stopped in his tracks. "Great," he muttered.

Jack was leaping through the front doorway, flying over the cinder-block step, waving a pistol. Landing squarely in the snow, Jack lunged at Claire.

"Luke!" Feinting left, Claire turned toward Luke, but Jack was too fast. He swiftly grabbed her from behind, looping an arm around her neck. Jerking her to his chest, Jack brought the gun right to her head.

She gasped, clutching at the strong forearm locked across her neck. "Wha—" She didn't finish protesting because the pistol's bore came to rest against her temple.

The back door slammed, and from inside the shack, Ham yelled, "You got the situation under control out there, Jack?"

"Looks like it, Ham."

Luke's heart hammered, making blood roar in his ears. Even from here, he could see the tremor of pale skin, just inches from Claire's eye where delicate skin met blue steel. He'd kill any man who touched her, he thought, murderous rage surfacing. As Luke faced Jack, his fingers itched at his sides, his mind racing. He wished he wasn't wearing this bulky shearling jacket. Could he reach down, pull up his jeans, get the gun and fire before Jack killed him? *Doubtful.* Even if he could, Jack was using Claire as a body shield, holding her from behind. Ignoring the wild, frightened darting of her eyes, Luke growled, "Let her go."

Instead, with a flick of his wrist, Jack turned the pistol on Luke, took aim and pulled the trigger. The second Jack fired, Claire elbowed him, momentarily upsetting the aim and making the shot fly wild, but it caught the brim of Luke's hat, blowing it off his head. The Stetson rolled through the air like a tumbleweed, and as the wind took it, Luke was in the process of dropping to his belly, the soft snow cushioning his fall. His hand went straight for his boot and gun. "I was trying to save your life," he managed to say. "Not the other way around."

"No problem," Claire shot back tremulously as Jack grunted and dragged her backward, now hauling her over the cinder-block step and across the threshold, into the shack. If Jack bothered to close the door, Luke didn't hear it.

Luke watched in frustrated fury, then leaped to his feet, this time wielding the Colt. Steel flashed in his hand as he ran for the door and leaned his back against the outer frame. Resting a foot on the cinder block, he raised the Colt and swiftly swung his body inward. From inside, a shot was fired.

Luke jerked back as the bullet whizzed through the door

frame. He waited a second, his heart pounding. He was vaguely aware of the freezing-cold temperature, and of the snow-covered trees circling the clearing. There was ice on the cinder block, too, and he eyed it, hoping he wouldn't slip when he ran inside. Should he make his move now? he wondered, tossing his head to keep the hair out of his face. If Clive and Claire weren't inside, Luke would consider offering return fire, but he couldn't put them at risk. Besides, as much as he disliked Ham and Jack, he'd rather not have their blood on his hands. Cocking his head, he listened. Everything had gotten real quiet inside the shack. If he tried to rush in, there was a chance he'd be hit. From far off, he was glad to hear a car motor, then another. Help was on the way. Probably Wesley and whoever he'd been able to strong-arm into coming out on Christmas Eve.

Suddenly, he heard a thud. Claire shrieked, "Luke!"

No longer caring if he took a bullet, and not about to wait for Wesley, Luke swung around, lunged through the doorway and rushed the room. His darting eyes speedily assessed the situation: The chair to which Clive had been bound was overturned. Clive had freed himself and was fighting Ham for the rifle, and Claire was wriggling away from Jack.

"Hit the floor," Luke commanded as he flew to her rescue, ramming Jack with his full weight. The gun spun from Jack's hand, and the man went down with a thud. Luke rolled with him, then scrambled to his hands and knees. Swiping the floor, he pocketed the pistol and grabbed some strands of rope Clive had left near the chair. Jumping onto Jack's back, Luke ignored the man's writhing and tied his hands to the leg of the coal-burning stove.

"Here." Claire crouched beside Luke, her hands moving over his, taking the extra rope. "You'd better help Clive," she continued in a panic. "I'll tie Jack's feet."

Ham was definitely getting the best of Clive, so Luke was glad to hear a car door slam outside. Voices sounded, one of which was Wesley's. "In here, Wesley," Luke shouted. As he ran for Clive, Ham reared back, giving a loud belly roar. Suddenly, the burly man's beefy fist connected with Clive's chest, sending Clive sprawling. Ham whirled around in fury, raising the rifle.

Luke's heart stopped the second he understood where Ham was aiming—at Claire's head. Forgetting all reason, Luke lunged just in the nick of time, right as Ham fired. Diving through the air, he landed on top of Claire, knocking the breath out of her and shielding her body as a bullet splintered the wood floor right next to her ear.

Just as she whispered "You saved my life, Luke," Wesley barreled across the threshold. He was a big man, redheaded with a full bushy beard. "Drop the rifle," he commanded as another officer appeared behind him. "You two are under arrest."

Seeing the officers was enough to convince Ham he wasn't going to win. Angrily, he tossed down the rifle. "It's not my fault," he growled. "I work for a man, name of B. G. Boggs. He's a miner, out of Glenrock. He said we wouldn't get no Christmas bonus this year if we didn't help him buy some property around here."

"We weren't gonna hurt this guy," Jack added. "We was just trying to warn him to leave us alone!"

They'd hardly seemed like warning shots to Luke. He half listened as both men's tongues wagged, and his palm smoothed over Claire's back as he rolled away from her. "You okay?" he asked, registering the husky gentleness and concern in his own voice. *The love,* he thought.

Claire sat up looking shaken. "Yeah," she said, brushing dust from her parka, then staring in shocked horror where the bullet had marred the wood only inches from her head. Her voice shook. "Thanks."

Luke smiled, running a hand through his hair, the squint of his blue eyes making them crinkle. "I owed you one," he said, grabbing her hand and standing, helping her to her feet.

"Ever since the bachelor's auction I guess you have," Claire agreed, her body bouncing comfortably against his. "But you're all paid up now."

"That so?" Seized by a sudden urge, Luke leaned over to kiss her, and then he realized Clive wasn't but six feet away. *My brother.* Luke came up short, his lips stopping so close to Claire's that he could feel her breath.

"Lost your hat, huh?" Claire's voice was throaty.

"To hell with the hat," Luke returned, gazing deeply into the shadowy eyes he knew so well. He was only vaguely aware that Wesley was clamping a hand down on his shoulder. Luke said, "I'm just glad you're still in one piece, Claire."

"Me, too," said Clive. Without another word, he brushed past Luke, stopped in front of Claire, and then drew her into an embrace.

Luke's heart pounded. He'd always known Clive by sight, but now, when Luke looked at him, it was with the awareness that Clive was most certainly his half brother. Clive was younger, but he shared Evander's—and Luke's—blue eyes. He was lighter-skinned than Luke, too, with wavy dark blond hair and a mustache. Good-looking, Luke decided, his throat and chest feeling tight. Countless emotions welled within him, but the main one was panic. Especially when Claire wrapped her arms around Clive's neck.

Wesley's hand clamped down harder on Luke's shoulder. "Turns out it's real simple," Wesley said conversationally. "Boggs sent these two fellows to get whatever land's available real cheap. He didn't want to mine it, just to combine and ranch it. Figured if he could buy up enough small farms, he could put together a big spread, since no big ranches around here ever go up for sale." Wesley nodded toward where the other officer was reading the Miranda warning to the men. "Guess Boggs had ideas about competing with all the larger concerns around Lightning Creek. Anyway, we've got enough to file harassment and weapons charges, as well as attempted murder, since they were shooting at you. We'll recheck Elmer Green's place and the Lazy Four for physical evidence indicating that the fires were suspicious." Wesley glanced toward where Clive and Claire were still locked in each other's arms. "What a great guy. When he got interested in what was happening, he sure took the law into his own hands."

The law wasn't the only thing Clive had taken into his hands. Right now, his palms were roving over the dirt-streaked back of Claire's parka, and just watching them was making something dark and untamable course through Luke.

"Guess this is wrapped up," Wesley said jovially. "Like a Christmas gift. All those folks who were being harassed will definitely have a better Christmas." At least someone would, Luke thought as Wesley continued, saying, "Yeah. This case sure was simple."

Simple? Luke's eyes were still riveted on Claire and Clive. Wesley couldn't be more wrong. This wasn't simple. This was the most difficult moment of Luke's life.

"I'VE BEEN SO WORRIED," Claire managed to say, barely aware the two officers were in the corner, questioning Jack and Ham. As Clive stepped back, Claire glanced through the still-open door of the shack, renewed panic seizing her.

Luke was taking long strides, heading straight across the clearing toward where they'd hidden the Cherokee. He'd retrieved his hat, and the Stetson, like the rest of him, looked almost like a silhouette in the shadowy afternoon light. Although his back was turned, Claire knew he was reaching into his shirt pocket for a toothpick. What was he thinking about? And how could he leave like this, when she'd still been hugging Clive? She felt a round, hard knot of discomfort settle in her gut, and then she realized Clive was watching her carefully.

"Claire? Are you okay?"

There were so many questions in his eyes. She hazarded a glance at the officer who was leading Jack and Ham toward the door. "Guess I'm shaken up," she said. And getting more so by the minute. Outside, looking very far away, Luke was disappearing under the hanging, snow-laden bows of the trees.

"I should have called you, Claire," Clive began.

"You should have. I was worried sick."

"Sorry."

"You should be," she said with a sigh. She surveyed him a long moment, taking a deep breath. No, she realized she didn't feel the same heart-racing, soul-shattering, crazy emotions she felt for Luke, but she did love Clive. As she glanced toward Luke again, her heart pulled with a peculiar savage, unsatisfied longing. Judging from how he'd just walked away, she might as well face it. Something— and it was always something, wasn't it?—would always come between them, whether it was Luke's past or the one she shared with Clive.

"I never knew you were interesting in solving mysteries, Clive," she managed to say, turning back to him.

Clive merely raised his eyebrows. "Solving which? The

one involving Cheyenne Mining? Or the mystery of our relationship?''

"Both. About us..."

"Yeah?"

Impulsively, she pressed the back of her hand to Clive's cheek. Staring into eyes that were so like Luke's, Claire considered the fact that Clive would make a wonderful husband. He was good-looking and kind, great with kids. Someday, another woman was going to be very lucky.

Glancing away, she saw that Luke had disappeared. All that was left was the lone set of his boot prints trekking across the snow. Her heart fluttering, she felt almost as if Luke had wanted to leave her behind, to marry his half brother. And yet, Claire realized, Clive didn't even know he had a half brother. Would Luke tell Evander? She wondered now. Or would he refuse to claim his father and brothers' love, just as he'd so often refused to claim hers?

Claire's eyes returned to Clive. "Clive—'' Her voice caught. "We need to talk.''

"SORRY WE COULDN'T be alone earlier,'' said Claire hours later. They'd seated themselves on the couch in the main room of the Stop Awhile, where they'd been alternately talking and gazing at the Christmas tree.

Clive shrugged. His blue eyes that were so like Luke's settled on hers, and for a second she was tempted to tell him he had a half brother, but she couldn't, of course, since that was for Luke to tell. If he ever did. Sudden, wishful anticipation made her heart miss a beat, but she was fairly certain Luke would turn away from his father, the way he'd turned and walked away from her today. Ignoring what Evander had said, Luke would probably convince himself he was keeping silent for Evander's sake, because Evander only wanted to appease his guilt, not really know his son. Dammit, sometimes she thought Luke would rather do anything than accept the love that was all around him.

Reaching beside himself, Clive rubbed a flattened palm absently across the couch cushion. "Well," he said with a sigh, "it's not anybody's fault we couldn't sit down before now."

"Things just sort of snowballed," she agreed. Earlier Wesley had driven her and Clive here, which meant they couldn't talk in the car, and by the time they reached the ranch, Mama was serving dinner. After they'd eaten, Tex had monopolized Clive, forcing him to take a trip to the stables to see a new horse. "I can't believe no one noticed we were such a mess," Claire said.

Clive shrugged. "They probably figured I was working."

"And that I was unpacking boxes at the house." She sighed again. "If Tex ever finds out I was involved in two shoot-outs, he'll hit the roof," she continued, glancing guiltily toward the foyer and the darkened staircase. Thinking of Ham and Jack, she felt a prickle at the base of her spine. Wesley had given her until the day after Christmas to come in and give a full statement of what had happened at both Elmer's stables and the Casper Mining shack.

"Not a creature is stirring," remarked Clive, following her gaze to the staircase.

Everyone had gone to bed early, to rest up for the big day tomorrow. And now, just thinking about telling her folks the wedding was canceled filled Claire with dread; first thing in the morning, she'd have to do it. She and Clive had already established that much. Her eyes returned to the tree Tex had decorated with multicolored, blinking lights, and then she looked at Clive, now watching how the lights flickered, casting colored spots on his face. He offered a wry smile that made his mustache curl and his Luke-like eyes wrinkle at the corners. "I guess we blew it, didn't we, Claire?"

She shook her head. "No. Things just didn't work out the way we thought they were going to."

"Sure didn't." After a long, pregnant silence, Clive said, "I have something else to tell you."

"That you don't want to marry me wasn't enough?" As soon as they were alone, that's what he'd said.

Clive scanned the room for a second, taking in the Christmas tree, then her. "Be honest, Claire. Would you have gone through with it?"

She shook her head again. "No."

"I didn't think so."

Their eyes met and held, and understanding coursed between them. "I do love you, though, Clive." She smiled at him in the dim light. "I figure we'll get wistful from time to time, and wonder what our life together would have been like."

He nodded, another almost-rueful smile touching his lips. "Maybe after we've married other people…"

"And we've just had a big fight…"

"And suddenly the grass will look greener."

She gave a soft, barely audible chuckle because it all had such a ring of truth. "What else did you want to tell me?"

"I don't know if I should say this but, there's… someone I'd like to start seeing." Looking nervous, Clive slicked his hands down the thighs of his threadbare jeans, then he quickly continued, "Nothing's happened between us, Claire. But over the past couple months, when I was getting Pa's medicine at the drugstore, I started talking to a woman there.…"

Claire tried to sort her muddled feelings. Putting aside

her unreasonably wounded pride, she realized she felt relieved. She'd felt so guilty for sleeping with Luke. And wonderful, too. A ripple of awareness pulsed through her at the memory of it. "Have you been staying with her?"

Clive looked as if he were carefully considering what he wanted to say. "Yes, that's where I've been. But, like I said, nothing happened. We didn't sleep together. I just...wanted to get away from everything, so I could think, and she said I could use her couch."

Guilt tweaked at Claire again. "And now you want to take her out?"

"Yeah. Maybe I shouldn't have brought it up, especially not tonight. It may not even matter, but..."

He wanted to assure her before she saw them around town together. "Thanks for telling me, Clive."

He was studying her. "I figure I'll run into you and Luke soon enough."

Her lips parted in surprise, and she knew color flooded her cheeks because they felt so hot. "What?"

Clive shrugged. "I remember that summer, back in high school, when you two used to hang around town together every Saturday. You were inseparable. And then I saw the way you were looking at each other today."

Was it really that obvious? "Today?"

Clive's eyes captured hers. "When he was leaving, you looked like it was breaking your heart, Claire."

It was. "Well," she admitted, "I don't know what's going to happen." No more than she had years ago, when she'd first told Luke of her feelings. But now things were different. So much more complex. They were older, they'd become lovers, and what was happening between them felt like a last chance. How many times would she be willing to initiate an affair, when he wasn't ready to share a life?

She blew out a long sigh. "I really don't know what's going to happen," she repeated.

Stretching out an arm, Clive pulled her to his chest in a brotherly half hug. "I guess that's the secret, Claire," he said. "We never know how things'll turn out. Now, c'mon. Before we start getting maudlin on Christmas, you gonna help me get my coat?"

"Sure." They rose and headed to the foyer where she took a shearling jacket similar to Luke's from the closet. Dusting it off before she held it out to him, she said, "It sure got dirty." Thinking of Ham and Jack again, she suddenly shuddered. "I'm so glad you're okay. What possessed you to go after those guys?"

Clive shrugged into his jacket. "That woman at the drugstore I was telling you about?"

Claire nodded.

"Well, she's been nice enough to ask me about Pa's health, so we've gotten to talking while the pharmacist fills the prescriptions. Anyway, Sylvie Saunders—that's her name—started telling me that her family was having some trouble at the Flying Swords, so I figured I could at least try to help out. And then, after our fight, I just wanted to get away for a while, too, so…"

Claire squeezed his forearm as they headed for the door. "You don't need to explain any more."

Turning to face her, Clive shoved his hands in his jeans pockets. "Thanks, Claire."

"For what?"

"For being you."

She let her eyes rove over his face, as if for the last time, taking in the curling ends of a dark blond hank that licked his forehead, then gazing into his eyes. Clive really was one of the best men she knew, even if they weren't right for each other. "You'll tell your family first thing tomorrow, won't you?" she said.

Clive nodded. "If not tonight. I figure they'll still be up when I get home." He sighed. "Your sisters are going to be disappointed."

"I know," she said with a helpless shrug. "But they'll understand. Mama and I will call all the guests."

"No," he said. "We'll split the list."

Claire nodded again. "Okay. And maybe you can call the church."

"I will."

Somehow, discussing the particulars made everything suddenly seem very real, and she swallowed hard. The wedding she'd been planning for months was simply not going to happen. "The musicians," she murmured. "And the caterers." She suddenly groaned. "And what are we going to do with that gorgeous cake, Clive?"

"Don't worry, Claire. We'll figure it out in the morning."

She nodded as he swung open the storm door. Turning, he wedged himself between it and the glass outer door. Strange, she thought, shifting her gaze from the snow outside to Clive's eyes. It was impossible to look at Clive now without seeing he was Luke's brother. Vaguely, she wondered if she'd been drawn to Clive, in part, because of those eyes that were so like Luke's. And once more, she found herself fighting temptation. If she told him about Luke, Clive would tell Evander. Maybe the Stoddards, more than she, could convince Luke of how easy it could be to love. To be together, living as a family.

Clive's gaze had grown intense. "I'll always have feelings for you, Claire. You know that, don't you?"

Her heart swelled with warmth. "Yeah," she said. "I do." Maybe, if they were lucky, they'd both find the love they deserved. Who knew? Maybe Sylvie was the woman for Clive. And maybe Claire would wind up with Luke, somehow. Edging closer, she laid a hand on Clive's sleeve and used it to pull him closer. Stretching to her tiptoes, Claire pressed a light, sisterly kiss to his cheek.

He said, "If you need anything..."

"I'll call," she assured him.

And then Clive was gone. She watched him walk through the snow to the Explorer, which Wesley and another officer had delivered. Turning, he waved. She waved back, then went inside. Shutting the door, she leaned against it and drew a deep breath. *This is it,* she thought. *The wedding's really off.*

Her eyes drifted to a phone; it was perched on a stand near the archway that led into the living room. Slowly she walked over and lifted it. Maybe she shouldn't call, she thought, punching in Luke's number, but she wanted...to know why Luke had left without saying goodbye. And she wanted to hear his voice and tell him that her and Clive's wedding was officially canceled.

But he didn't seem to be home. She frowned as the phone rang, thinking it was too early for Luke to be delivering the gifts to Lost Springs. "He must have gone to give his statement about what happened at the shack," she murmured.

The answering machine picked up and she felt a rush of pure heat in her veins at the slow, mellow, deep sound of his voice. "Luke," she said softly when the beep sounded, "I...just wanted to call and wish you a Merry Christmas." With a sudden, sharp intake of breath, she added, "I wish we were together tonight."

Gently replacing the receiver, she crossed the foyer, seating herself on a step. Glancing up the darkened staircase, she was glad everybody was already in bed. At least she still had until morning to decide how to break the news. With a sigh, she stared through the archway at the Christmas tree. Tex had gone all out—the tree was covered with decorations, including those she and her sisters had made in school and craft classes over the years.

"Nothing like Christmas," Tex had said with a satisfied sigh as he put the angel on the top.

"Definitely not this year," Claire agreed now, and then she simply sat there, drawing her knees up and hugging them, as she began planning the words she'd use when she told her family about the wedding.

LUKE PULLED THE JEEP under a canopy of trees and stared at the main house at Lost Springs where he'd spent his childhood. Closing his hand over the ignition keys, he glanced down, then he turned over the laminated key chain. The picture was hard to make out in the dark interior, but he could see that Claire looked gorgeous, sitting on his lap, definitely a sight better than he did in a Santa suit.

"It Came Upon a Midnight Clear" was playing on the radio, and somehow, when Luke glanced through the windshield again, the fact seemed strange to him. The digital clock on the dashboard read 2 a.m., and outside, the night really had cleared. It was cold and crisp, the sky star-studded. Emitting a wistful sigh, Luke turned off the motor, got out and circled the Jeep, hoisting two heavy sacks off the passenger seat.

Suddenly, he uttered a soft curse as a neatly wrapped package tumbled into the snow. Leaning over, he tried to retrieve it, only to lose his hat again. It just wasn't his day. Ever since he'd left Claire in Clive's arms, Luke had been stewing in his own juices. Spending most of the evening giving the cops a statement about the encounter with Ham and Jack hadn't helped.

Now Luke lifted the Stetson and fit it back onto his head. Why he was still wearing it he didn't even know, since the bullet hole through the brim had ruined it. As he lifted the package and dusted off the snow, he recognized Claire's handiwork. The woman tied a helluva bow. Red-and-green lengths of intertwined ribbon stretched over the gold foil paper, looping gracefully. None of Luke's bows ever looked like that, and he suddenly wished he knew what she was thinking at this very instant and if there was any chance she'd be around next Christmas to help him. Putting the present back into the sack, Luke headed toward the house, approaching it from the side in case any young, prying eyes happened to be watching.

Reaching the porch, he paused and frowned, kicking a step to dislodge the snow from his boots. Drawing a deep breath, he looked around the place as he often did. Glimmers of the past haunted his mind, and for a second he thought he remembered his mama standing here with him, saying goodbye. Had she really been wearing a camel-colored coat over a yellow dress? And had she really told him to ring the doorbell after she was gone?

Suddenly, the sharp night air was hurting him, somewhere deep inside his chest. Or maybe it was Luke's heart hurting. Ever since he'd run into Claire again, he was getting used to dealing with unwanted emotion. Shaking off the feelings, he fitted a key to the front door lock, propped open the door with his foot, then hoisted both bags of gifts over the threshold. Once he was inside, he headed straight for the Christmas tree.

White lights ringed the bushy boughs of the evergreen, casting a glow over the worn wooden floors, and for a moment, Luke glanced over the ornaments made by the boys. Tomorrow, this room would be a madhouse, with boys climbing over one another for gifts. Luke's lips twisted into a wry half smile when he thought of the guys he'd grown up with, so many of whom he'd seen last summer at the bachelor auction. Luke could still remember them on Christmas morning, wrestling and sharing their toys.

Getting down to work, he began quickly arranging gifts under the tree, and as he did, he called himself ten kinds of a fool. He wondered if he feared Claire would come to know him better and really guess at what it meant to have nothing. *To stand on a dark porch, alone on a cold, clear Christmas morning with your mama leaving.* Slightly tilting his head, Luke could almost see the long rivers of her raven hair, falling over her shoulders as she leaned down to tell him...

He couldn't remember. Sighing, he stepped back and stared at the tree again, viewing his handiwork. As he finished folding the two empty sacks, his gaze lingered where red light reflected on some shiny gold paper.

The room was dim and peaceful—reverent almost—and now the soft lights made Luke suddenly think about how he used to watch Claire years ago, even before they'd met at the feed store. He was still in grade school then, and sometimes he and other boys were piled into a bus and driven to the Methodist church off Shoshone Highway for Sunday services, the same church where Claire's wedding was set to be held. Luke and his friends had gone scrubbed and pressed—all best bib and tucker—dressed in their newest blue jeans and freshly ironed white shirts, and they'd always taken the last pew in back. The front pew belonged to the Buchanans. Even then, in her lace ankle socks and white gloves, with a long tight braid flowing down the back of her frilly dresses, she'd completely captured his attention.

"Luke?"

The voice startled him, and he jerked his head, looking over his shoulder just in time to see a child streak through the dark toward him. Small fists rained down, pummeling Luke's thighs. "You told me there was a Santa, and he was gonna get my letter!"

"Brady," Luke whispered simply, leaning and pulling the boy into his arms. Brady was really too big, but Luke held him, anyway, even though the boy kept punching; his tightly balled fists didn't hurt nearly as much as the pain Luke knew the boy felt. Glancing down, he took in Brady's white flannel pajamas, which were printed with a sports team logo. Luke figured he'd been fighting sleep for hours, hoping to catch Santa. Unfortunately, he'd seen Luke instead.

Brady hiccoughed, his ineffectual fists opening and his small hands curling around Luke's shoulders. "There's no Santa Claus, is there?"

Luke knew what the question meant for Brady, who was hoping Santa would find his folks. He also knew how alone and abandoned he'd felt at Brady's age. Already, the world had lied enough. "No," he admitted. "But there's a spirit of giving. That's why I'm here." Brady's small arms tightened fiercely around Luke's neck, and he released such an inconsolable-sounding whimper that Luke disengaged a hand and smoothed the boy's flaxen-blond hair. "C'mon, now," he said, "cowboys don't cry."

Brady sniffled, wiping his hot salty tears on Luke's neck. "I bet you cried at least once, Luke," he charged.

"At least," Luke admitted. He tried not to think of Claire, and of how bad he'd feel if things didn't work out between them, and vaguely he wondered what to do about

Evander. Maybe Claire was right; maybe Luke should simply tell Evander what he knew to be the truth. "Brady," he said, emotion suddenly roughening words that he could only hope were right. "Maybe Santa's not going to find your folks this year, but sometimes things such as that happen. You know how I know that, pardner?"

Brady tearfully shook his head, his fine hair flying.

"'Cause years ago, my mama left me here at Lost Springs on the porch. See, I always thought she didn't even want me...."

Brady gulped back a sob, then quieted some. "She didn't?"

"Turns out she did." Evander wanted him, too, Luke realized with force. And Claire. All at once, something tugged so hard at Luke that he couldn't breathe. "Turns out my mama just got sick, Brady, and she had no choice but to leave me," he continued.

"You remember when she left?"

Luke nodded. "I was standing on the porch with her, and it was still dark." So dark that there seemed to be no lights left anywhere in the world, except through the window at Lost Springs. Luke had seen a tree, nearly a replica of this one, probably lit by these same strands of lights.

Pretty tree, isn't it, Justin?

Justin, Luke thought now, his heart welling. *That's what she named me. Justin. And for a while we lived in the mountains, on reservation land.*

Luke could see her leaning toward him again—the rivers of her raven hair flowing, the cold winter's air blowing the strands while her dark, magnificent eyes roved over every inch of him. He saw tears gather in them as she leaned closer to press her soft, cold lips to his cheek. Her lips moved, but now he could hear the words. *The spirits of the world love you. And I love you. Never forget that.* Your mama loves you. Swear you won't forget. Luke felt the words touch his heart, and he thought, *I remember now.*

"Luke?" Brady prompted.

"She loved me, Brady," Luke said. "That's what I found out today. So, I figure it could be the same with your folks."

Brady leaned back his head, his tired blue eyes settling on Luke's. "You think my mama loved me?"

"Sure, Brady." Nobody could hold this boy and not love him.

"Thanks," Brady whispered, burying his head against Luke's shoulder again.

"Wish I could do more." Some day, when Brady was older, maybe Luke would tell him the few scant facts he'd discovered on his search for Brady's folks and how the trail had grown cold. Now, staring over Brady's shoulder again at the tree lights, ornaments and tinsel, Luke felt something warm curl inside him. It was as if he'd suddenly been given an essential heat, a burning fire he'd missed all these years.

My mama named me Justin, Luke thought. *And she loved me.* Claire wasn't the first to say it, after all. But she loved him, too.

"C'mon, cowboy," he said. Gently prying Brady's hands from his neck, Luke lowered him to the floor and took his hand. "We've got to get you to bed."

Brady's voice was still strained—more by fatigue now and less by tears. "Do you gotta go be Santa to other folks now, Luke?"

"Sure do, pardner," Luke returned. "I sure do."

CHAPTER THIRTEEN

"CLAIRE LYNN," Mama yelled from the bottom of the attic steps. "What are you doing up there?"

"Coming!" Claire shouted. As she strode from the closet, tugging a comb through her hair, her eyes landed above the whitewashed iron headboard of her bed; seeing the barely visible, discolored square that marked the spot where the painting she'd given Luke had hung, Claire felt her heart ache. She'd kept the phone's ringer turned up last night, hoping he'd return her call in spite of the late hour, but he hadn't.

"Just because you're getting married today," declared Josie furiously from the bottom of the steps, "it's not fair to hold up Christmas for everybody else!"

"Hurry, Claire!" Rosie added. "We're ready to open presents!"

"Tex says come down or else!" Emma Jane threatened.

"Coming!" As she listened to her mother's and sister's retreating footsteps, Claire tugged a navy wool sweater dress over her head, slipped on opaque tights and a pair of dress boots, then headed downstairs. In the second-floor hallway, she paused, glancing into the guest bedroom at her and her sisters' gowns which hung in the open closet, wrapped in plastic. Nervously clasping her hands, Claire recalled all the pretty little speeches she'd planned last night. But how could she tell everyone the wedding was off? Mama had worked so hard, making the dresses and planning the party, her sisters were so excited, and Tex wanted to merge the Stop Awhile and the Lazy Four. Claire almost wished she wasn't the kind of person who felt inclined to take everyone else's feelings so much into account; otherwise, it might be easier to break the news.

"Claire Lynn," Mama yelled again, her voice coming from the living room. "I know you're nervous, but there's nothing to worry about. Everything's all set. Did I tell you the musicians from Laramie got here last night?"

"No, but thanks, Mama," Claire called, moving along the hallway, then down the stairs.

"Well they did," Mama assured her. "The flowers arrived, and the food's set to go... Claire? Claire?"

"I'm right here, Mama." Leaning in the archway that led into the living room, Claire gazed at the blinking lights on the tree, then at Mama, who was wearing a red-and-green apron over her slacks.

"Finally!" Josie exclaimed. Hopping up, she and the other girls began distributing presents.

"About time you came down, Claire," Tex said, waving agreeably from an armchair. He was wearing brand-new jeans and a plaid shirt, and sipping coffee. As Mama passed him, heading for Claire, he patted Mama's hand. "By this afternoon," Tex said with a sigh, glancing at Claire, "you'll belong to another man."

"Which is why we need to hurry with the presents, girls," Mama said.

Usually, the family prolonged the pleasures of the gift exchange by neatly folding wrapping paper and saving bows, but this Christmas everyone thought they needed to get to the church. *Tell them.* Instead, Claire glanced past the Christmas tree to where early-morning sunlight streamed through a window. Outside, a gorgeous day had dawned in Lightning Creek; the snow glistened like cloth sewn with diamonds.

"Couldn't have asked for a prettier day for a wedding," Mama continued, her voice gentling as she sidled next to Claire.

Claire's eyes suddenly stung, and she blinked back unexpected tears.

"I know how it is," Mama added with a soft chuckle, slipping an arm around her daughter's waist. "When I married Tex, I cried my eyes out."

"I'd cry if I had to marry Tex, too!" Josie exclaimed with a giggle as she plopped a huge, red-wrapped package at her father's feet.

"Watch it, Josie," Tex shot back with a laugh. "Or I'll remember that remark come allowance time. Now, c'mon, Claire," he continued, pointing under the tree, "open that big one."

Claire nodded. But the only presents she wanted weren't under the tree. She wanted Luke. And so many times this year she'd imagined holding babies, inhaling their baby-smell, and loving them until they were fully grown. She tamped down an abrupt flood of anger. Why hadn't Luke bothered to call her back last night? She'd wanted him to, no matter how late it had been. What had he been thinking when he'd left her and Clive yesterday at the shack?

Mama sounded worried. "Claire? Are you all right?"

She glanced at her mother. "No...I'm afraid I'm not." Her eyes swept over each member of the family with such intensity that things quieted—her sisters quit delivering gifts, and her parents watched her expectantly. "Last night, after you all went to bed," Claire began carefully, "Clive and I decided not to get married."

"Not get married!" Tex gasped. "I'll kill him."

"Tex," Claire assured her father quickly, "it was a joint

decision. And I'm sorry, since I know how you and Evander thought the marriage might make it easier to merge the ranches."

Tex rose to his feet. "Can't say I'm not disappointed, but we just want you to be happy."

Mama drew a sharp breath. "But what happened between you and Clive?"

"Clive just...doesn't want to go through with it. He's perfectly fine with the decision. We'll always be friends. And..." Claire glanced between her parents. "And I think I'm in love with somebody else," she announced.

Emma Jane swooned. Fanning herself with a romance novel she'd already snatched from her stocking, she breathlessly asked, "Is it Luke?"

"Who he is doesn't matter," Claire returned, wanting to keep her feelings private.

"But it's Luke, isn't it?" prodded Emma Jane.

Claire sighed. "Emma Jane, this is none of your business, but—"

"Luke!" Josie gasped. "Are we going to get in trouble, since we bought him for Claire at the bachelor auction last summer, Mama?"

"It was Emma Jane's idea!" vowed Rosie.

Emma Jane offered a derisive grunt. "You went along with it!"

"Just because we *bought* him, didn't mean Claire had to *do* anything with him!" defended Vickie.

"Mama," added Rosie, "it's not our fault!"

"Please," Claire interjected before the girls started squabbling in earnest. "This is no time to place blame. I don't want to ruin everybody's Christmas, either, but...but I've got to go."

"Where?" Mama murmured.

"To find Luke." The second the words were out of her

mouth, Claire felt the truth of them. There was no place on earth she'd rather be this morning than with him.

Her mother squinted at her. "What for?"

"I don't know." But Claire did. She wanted to beg him for a sign that he was ready to share a life with her.

"The church is expecting us this afternoon," offered Tex, as if reading her deepest thoughts. Coming closer, he joined her and her mother. "If you're looking for a man, you'd better go find him."

Claire leaned over and gave Tex an impulsive hug, feeling her spirits rise. "It's a long shot, Tex," she admitted. And yes, she'd probably offered her love to Luke too many times already. "But that's the best idea I've heard this morning. And you know what else, Tex?"

"What?"

"*You're* the best." Claire planted a kiss on his cheek, whirled around, grabbed her parka from a coat tree, shrugged into it and checked a pocket for the Wrangler's keys and her gloves. Running out the door, she left her family to a moment of stunned silence.

Suddenly, Tex released a low chuckle. "If Clive's all right with this turn of events, I guess we should be. And I guess our little girl's in the mood for love." He slipped an arm around his wife.

Mama snuggled against Tex. "After all these years, I know I still am."

Tex laughed. "Me, too. I just hope she winds up as happy as we are." He shook his head in astonishment. "This sure is shaping up to be one unusual Christmas."

CLAIRE WAS PULLING from the Stop Awhile's driveway onto the main road when a car nearly collided with hers. "Dammit!" she exclaimed, gripping the steering wheel and swerving, then laying on the horn. What was the person trying to do? Kill her? Fishtailing to the road's shoulder, she pressed a hand to the space over her hammering heart. A glinting flash of green glanced off her hood as the other vehicle swung around her.

"Luke," she muttered. Hopping out and slamming the door, she strode toward the Cherokee, the wind whipping against her face and hands, her boots sinking in the snowdrifts. As Luke got out of the Jeep, Claire's already unsteady heartbeat accelerated. He looked luscious. He was hatless. Without messing his side part or loosening his blue-black hair from where it was tucked behind his ears, the winter wind was lifting a few wild strands. His jeans were snug and decidedly sexy-looking, and his big dark hands hung from the sleeves of the shearling jacket. He started coming toward her on those muscular legs that had been wrapped naked around hers just two nights ago.

They met halfway between the cars.

"What are you trying to do?" she managed to say, gazing into his eyes. "Get us both killed?" Any fantasies she'd had moments ago about proposing to him left her. She simply couldn't ask for things that only Luke could decide to give.

A corner of his mouth curled in a faintly chastising, gorgeous smile. "Merry Christmas to you, too."

She eyed him a moment, thinking of how, just a few days ago, she'd run straight to the mall and into his arms. "Merry Christmas," she conceded.

"Where were you headed?"

To look for you. Claire shrugged, now thinking better of telling him the truth.

"I thought you might be headed to the Stoddards'."

"No." She shook her head. "We officially called off the wedding. That's why I called…"

"I got your message."

"Where were you?"

"I went to make a statement with the cops, then to the main house at Lost Springs. It was too late to phone you back, and I guess I should have this morning. Anyway, I figured I'd just drive over."

He'd been coming to see her? "To spend Christmas with us?"

Reaching down, Luke grabbed her hand and loosely locked their fingers, then he backed up a step, tugging her toward him through the snow. "No, I came to pick you up."

She walked toward him, unable to help the flirtatious smile pulling at the corners of her lips. "To pick me up? What for?"

"This." Swiftly tugging her hand, Luke hauled her against his chest, slanting his mouth down. Just as his nose brushed hers, feeling so freezing cold that she shivered, she also felt the perfect fit of his lips over hers, and the hot, insistent thrust of his tongue. Licking inside her mouth, Luke sent another shiver through her, this time of awareness that went to her every last erogenous zone. She curled her arms tightly around his neck while he settled his hands on her waist and drew her closer. Together they slowed the blissful pace of the kiss—as if they had all day, she thought. And as if they weren't standing knee-deep in snowdrifts. By the time Luke's mouth began closing wetly against hers, and by the time his lips kissed the tip of her tongue goodbye, she felt weak. Everything inside her had turned as hot as summer.

"Don't stop kissing me," she found herself murmuring against his cold, wet mouth, vaguely wondering if they couldn't make love in one of their cars. Why not? she wondered, her mind hazy with need. Didn't people do it all the time? Swaying in his arms, she realized she was quite simply unable to let go. She never wanted to lose the sensation of Luke's kiss, nor the feeling of his body against hers. At the juncture of her thighs, he'd become all hard pressure and manly arousal.

Gliding his hands over her hips, Luke stretched down an arm and grabbed her hand. Beside her ear, his voice sounded husky, and the nuzzle of his nose and cheek was both warm and yet cold. "C'mon, Claire."

The idea of loving him physically right now flooded her with unbrookable passion. "Where?" She'd go anywhere.

His eyes locked with hers, looking strangely determined. Staring into the irises, she noted some tiny black lines that fanned from the pupil, then threaded through the blue. He said, "You'll see."

ONLY WHEN EVANDER'S EYES drifted curiously downward did Luke realize he'd linked hands with Claire again. When she tried to pull away, he threaded his fingers through hers even more possessively. The Stoddards, he figured, would find out his intentions toward Claire soon enough. Lightning Creek was a small town.

"Clive said the wedding's off." Evander commented, tucking his thumbs through the shoulder straps of a pair of blue jeans overalls. He'd spoken to Claire, but his narrowed blue eyes were drifting over Luke.

"Yes, and I'm sorry," Claire murmured.

"Clive said we might expect to see you around town with Luke, too," continued Evander, that intent gaze of his still searching Luke's face.

A hint of defensiveness crept into Claire's voice. "Clive's also seeing a woman named Sylvie from the drugstore."

The first touch of a smile touched Evander's lips. "Yep.

He said so. Sounds like calling off the wedding was a mutual decision."

Claire sounded relieved. "It was." She quickly added, "And Tex will probably call you today about your business dealings. Clive and I'll start calling the guests soon...."

A hint of worry crossed Evander's features but vanished as quickly as it had appeared. "I figure me 'n' Tex'll work things out."

"You will," Claire assured him.

Luke hadn't told her his intentions in coming here, but she'd asked on the drive over in the Cherokee, and now Luke figured she must have guessed. Right now, she was watching him, her eyes expectant. Drawing a deep, steadying breath, Luke ignored his nervousness and the urge to fetch a toothpick from his shirt pocket. "Mind if we sit down?" Luke asked.

Evander shook his head. "Go right ahead."

Luke backed up, and he and Claire seated themselves on a small beige sofa. Neither took off their coats. Luke glanced around. It was a big homey room, with brick walls and polished hardwood floors covered with Mexican rugs. Eclectic furniture—both mission-style and claw-footed armchairs—were arranged in a casual way that gave the place a lived-in look. As Evander seated himself on a plump red-and-green-plaid sofa opposite, Luke took in a Christmas tree in the corner. Simple, hand-painted wooden ornaments hung from the thick branches, as did strung cranberries, popcorn and tinsel. From down a hallway, Luke could hear rough male voices and the occasional laughter of women and children. No doubt, some of Luke's half brothers were married with kids. *I might have nieces and nephews,* Luke thought, surprise stealing over him.

A male voice rose above the others. "Pass the syrup."

So, Evander's sons were eating breakfast. Strange, Luke thought now, to think that he, too, was one of Evander's sons.

Evander was staring over a black, oblong coffee table between the two couches. "What can I do for you?"

Luke's throat felt suddenly dry. His fingers tightened around Claire's, and he was glad for the strength he felt in her slender fingers. Since Luke didn't know where to begin, he simply said, "I think I found the son you had with Laura."

"My son?" Evander gasped. For a moment he merely gaped at Luke, then he leaned forward. "Jenny! Boys! Get in here! Forget those flapjacks!"

"Luke," Claire murmured. "I knew you were going to tell him."

Turning and seeing the emotion in her eyes, Luke was sure that no matter what happened after this, he'd done the right thing. His gaze returned to Evander. "I figured you might want to keep this private."

Evander still looked stunned. "I told you. My family knows everything."

Only Evander's immediate family appeared, and Luke watched as Jenny and three men he knew by sight—Bobby, Billy and Foster—crowded through a doorway and into the room, all of them tall and long-boned, wearing denim and flannel. Jenny seated herself on the couch next to Evander, while their sons found armchairs. Clive appeared in the doorway, then leaned against the jamb, eyeing Claire and Luke.

"What are you-all doing here?" Clive said.

Evander sent Clive a glance with a hint of chastisement, reminding Clive that he no longer had any claim to Claire's affection. "Luke says he's found my and Laura's son."

"He really found Laura's boy, Evander?" Jenny echoed. She was a large, practical-looking woman, with iron gray hair that was swept into a bun. Scooting closer to her husband on the couch, she nervously wiped her hands on a dish towel she'd brought from the kitchen, then folded it in her lap.

Luke frowned. Evander had said he'd shared information about his previous love interest with his wife and sons, but it still seemed strange. As if reading Luke's mind, Jenny prompted, "We're a family. We share everything."

Feeling unwanted emotion clogging his throat, Luke wished he were better at social graces. That Clive was in the room didn't help, somehow. There was enough subtle tension between them without Luke's announcing they were brothers.

"Well, tell me what you found out, son," Evander urged.

Son. There was that word again. And Luke was still searching for what to say. Now his already-tight throat felt as if it were closing up entirely. The hell with feeling nervous, he suddenly thought. "It's me," he said simply. "I think it's me."

There was a shocked silence, then Evander said, "You? What are you talking about?"

"He's saying it's *him*, Pa," said Bobby.

Evander stared. "You think you're my son?"

Luke nodded, knowing he needed to better explain. He felt the couch cushion shift as Claire edged closer, offering support by slipping a hand around his upper arm. The touch wasn't anything so physical that Clive might take offense, but right now, it meant everything to Luke. "I was found on the front porch of Lost Springs," he began. "Wrapped in a blanket that was once used by Luke Lydell, the cowboy who worked here. His name was sewn on the label.'' Luke's eyes met Evander's, which were so like his own. "I recognized the picture you showed me, too.''

"You recognized Laura?'' Evander asked.

Luke nodded again. "Years ago, I remember coming here with her to look at the Lazy Four, the same Christmas morning she left me at Lost Springs.''

"You didn't remember until now?'' Jenny said.

"Until yesterday. I was young. I guess the trauma of her leaving made me forget. But I know she called me Justin. I figure it's too late to change my name back, though, so I figure Luke'll do.''

"Justin,'' Evander said.

Luke continued, "The way I figure it, I turned up here long after your investigators quit looking. You'd had feelers out, but by the time I got here, no one knew to look right under their noses. If the authorities had any questions, they asked them in the bunkhouse.''

"Meantime,'' Evander said, rising from the couch and slowly circling the coffee table on his too-frail legs, "You were being raised an orphan, when your family was right here.''

"It was a good upbringing,'' Luke said generously, feeling unaccountably awkward as the man he knew was his pa came to a standstill in front of him. Somehow, Luke felt he was just too damn old and had too much testosterone to feel this uncertain and vulnerable.

"You were raised without your mama,'' Jenny said softly, rising from the couch.

Disengaging his hand from Claire's, Luke forced himself to stand. He felt embarrassed, but he was tired of backing away from love, and Claire had to see that. That was the most important thing. Since Luke was taller than Evander, he stared down, and his eyes met his father's.

"Only a blood test will really tell the truth, Pa,'' warned

Bobby, the oldest son. "Don't get me wrong," he added, glancing between his father and Luke. "We've...looked a long time, and we need to make sure."

"I understand," said Luke. He glanced assurance at Bobby, then turned his eyes to Evander's. Yesterday Luke had felt he needed more proof before confronting the Stoddards, but not now. His gut feeling was enough.

"I don't need any more proof than you." A soft light came into Evander's eyes. "You said you recognized Laura. And remember when I said something niggled at me when I heard your name?"

Luke nodded.

"It's more than the name, or your having my same eyes," said Evander. "You've got the shape of Laura's face, a similar smile. Son..." Despite his stoical expression, Evander's old eyes suddenly looked watery. "I'm a sick old man, so we'd better not waste more time. Let's just go ahead and get this over with." Closing the distance, Evander stretched his thin arms around Luke's waist, embracing him, while the remaining Stoddards got over their stupefaction and drew closer.

"C'mon, boy," urged Evander. "Just call me Pa."

It was a word Luke never thought he'd have occasion to say. "Pa," he said simply, giving Evander's frail back a pawlike pat. An awkward moment passed when Evander stepped back, then Jenny said, "I hope you'll want to get to know me some."

Luke said, "I'd like that."

Then Bobby, Billy and Foster edged closer, shaking hands. Luke glanced at Clive. Even though he'd called off the wedding, there were egos involved here, Luke's own included. For a lifetime, he'd have to deal with knowing Clive had laid hands on a woman Luke wanted to make his wife. He met Clive's eyes dead on. Without further adieu, he said, "I'll put this simply. I want to marry her, Clive."

There was another stunned silence.

"Claire." Before Clive could respond, Luke turned away, his gaze drifting possessively over her. He wanted her so much, and since Luke was sure she loved him, he was also sure it wasn't too late. "I could never let another man have you. Not without a fight. Ever since the day before the bachelor auction last summer, when you announced the engagement, I've been going crazy."

Claire sighed. "You mean it, Luke?"

"Sure do." His eyes narrowed, and he studied her more carefully. "I've got a lot to learn from you, but I think we can make it."

Her voice caught. "I think so, too." With the Stoddards looking on, she twined her arms around Luke's neck, and he held her tight, loving the feel of her long-limbed, willowy body. Sliding his hands down her back, he urged her closer. "Marry me, Claire," he whispered.

"When?" she whispered back.

"Now." It only took a second for the idea to catch hold in Luke. "I mean, today."

Leaning back in Luke's embrace, Claire searched Clive's eyes. For a moment, the man she'd almost married—Luke's half brother—continued sizing up Luke, and Luke feared he wouldn't offer a blessing. But suddenly, Clive shrugged, a slight smile curling the corners of his mustache upward. "Why not?" he said, as if it was the most natural thing in the world. "Hell, we've got a party planned."

Luke's voice lowered to a seductive drawl as he drew Claire to him again. "Guess we can wait a couple of hours." Leaning down, Luke brushed his lips to hers, the chaste kiss nothing next to what he'd take from her if company wasn't present.

"We'll need blood tests," Evander announced.

"On two counts," said Bobby, still not convinced Luke was a blood relation.

"I'll call up Doc," said Jenny, taking charge. "If he can't do the tests this morning, maybe Luke and Claire can have the ceremony and make it legal later." Her voice softened. "You okay with this, Clive?"

"Fine," Clive assured her.

Luke barely heard. He was too occupied, nuzzling his cheek against Claire's, feeling an escaped strand of her braided hair teasing his cheek. "I've got one more thing to ask," he murmured, so only she could hear. "Are you really interested in having kids?"

Excited color rose in her cheeks. "Sure. Maybe by next year…"

"I'm talking about now." Luke's expression was serious. "I'm asking if you'll agree to adopt Brady with me, if we can."

Tears sprung to Claire's eyes, and her gaze softened with more love than Luke had ever seen. Before she even spoke, he knew her answer was yes.

"I want to make sure he gets folks for Christmas," Luke added, resting his forehead against hers.

"We'll be great folks," Claire assured him with a tender smile.

"Yeah, we will." Lowering his mouth again, Luke reveled in the loving warmth as he swept his lips across hers. "Claire," he said with a sigh. "You'd better get ready, darlin'. Because I think we're going to be perfect together."

EPILOGUE

LUKE STRIPPED OFF his shirt, placed a new Stetson on his head, then he leaned lazily in the doorway of Claire's studio, toying with the bandanna slung around his neck and sliding a hand down his bare, suntanned chest. More than anything, he loved watching his wife paint. She was standing in front of her easel, her head tilted so that it nearly touched the dollar she'd tacked on there years ago, after the sale of *Love Warrior*. Her eyebrows were knitted together, and she was so intent on the portrait of their son, Brady, that she didn't even notice Luke watching her. He grinned, seeing a dab of blue paint smeared on her long, tawny braid. No doubt she didn't even know it was there. Luke's gaze drifted down to where her white blousy artist's smock hung open over a T-shirt, and when he saw the growing curve of her belly, he felt his heart stretch. No matter how often he saw the evidence, he still could barely believe they'd be blessed with another child in just a few more months, and that Brady would have a brother or sister.

After a moment, Luke glanced away. Looking through a window of the A-frame, where Clive had insisted they live, Luke took in the Lazy Four's green rolling hills and grasslands. It hadn't taken long for Clive to get Sylvie to agree to move to Cheyenne, where Clive was now studying computer programming. The only hitch had been that Clive and Evander needed someone competent to run the ranch. As much as Luke missed Cross Creek, he'd been the most likely candidate, especially after the blood tests proved what Luke had been sure of, that Evander was his pa. Nowadays, a new metal rod—this one of silver steel—had been added to those twined together at the front gates of the ranch. Not only had the Lazy Four become the Lazy Five, but they'd legally merged with the Stop Awhile. Claire was glad not to lose her in-laws, though she still couldn't believe Clive had never told her Evander's secrets.

At the Lazy Five, Luke had already made his mark, and everywhere he could see the fruits of his labor. Finally, he'd found a place to call his own, and Luke was giving his all, for the kids he and Claire meant to raise here, and for those of his brothers who might someday decide to live their lives the old-fashioned way, from the land. Just glancing at the hills, Luke strongly felt a sense of belonging. His love of the ranch pulsed through his veins as surely as his blood. And each time Luke looked over the vast terrain, he felt blessed by the words his mama had given him. *The spirits of the world love you.*

He'd found Laura's grave high on a mountain, on land belonging to their people, and he'd found folks who told him more about himself, and about the life of Laura Blackfeet. The day he, Claire and Brady had first visited the grave, they'd found a feather on it, too, and now Luke wore it in the brim of the new Stetson Claire had gotten for him, to replace the one Ham had ruined. Shortly after Claire had bought the hat, both she and Luke had testified in court and the two men, along with B. G. Boggs, had been locked away for a good long while.

"Mama!"

Claire turned toward Brady's voice, and Luke smiled at her, sighing with satisfaction.

She smiled back, setting down a paintbrush and walking slowly toward him. "What, Brady?" she called, her eyes still on Luke.

"What's Uncle Clive's e-mail address?"

For the umpteenth time that day, Claire rattled it off as she approached Luke, then she hesitated a moment.

"What?" Luke said with a soft chuckle. "You don't love me anymore?"

She gave him a dubious glance. "You're a little sweaty," she admitted.

"I'm a cowboy," he explained with a smile. "I've been herding cattle."

"Oh." She laughed. "Is that all it is?" And then she stretched her arms around his waist. His wrapped around her, and he turned with her, so they could both look at Brady, who was staring at a computer screen.

"Pa!" exclaimed Brady excitedly.

"Right here," called Luke.

"Are you really taking us to the rodeo in Cheyenne?"

"Sure thing, pardner." Luke chuckled. Brady knew the answer, but he was so excited he kept asking. The adoption had been thankfully quick, and while Brady loved his new home, he still spent time with his friends at Lost Springs. In addition to what Luke offered, he'd gotten donations from buddies he'd seen last summer at the bachelor auction to help fund a trip for the boys to Cheyenne. Really, Luke thought, things couldn't be better. Evander was starting to respond to experimental treatments, and Luke was beginning to think his pa would outlive them all.

Luke's eyes strayed to the window again, to where summer heat baked the land; long green grasses blew, waving in the wind. When his gaze returned to the living room, it landed on Claire's painting of Lost Springs. For the first time in his life, Luke knew exactly what that wandering boy was searching for. As he took in the dusky twilight and the expansive sky, Luke thought, *he's reaching for this. For a life like mine. For love that's already inside him, and that's as close as the woman in my arms.*

"It doesn't get any better than this, does it?" Claire said simply.

"Oh—" Luke leaned to nuzzle her hair. "I think it could."

Claire frowned up at him. "How?"

Luke chuckled softly. Tightening his hands on her growing waist, and he drew her closer, brought his mouth to hers, and whispered, "Like this." Then he claimed a deep, loving kiss.

continues with

THE RANCHER AND THE RICH GIRL

by

Heather MacAllister

After eight years of always doing the right thing, wealthy widow Jessica Fremont is ready to rebel. Her son Sam wants to be a cowboy—to his grandmother's horror—and Jessica's going to help him. So she bids on gorgeous rancher Matthew Winston, hoping he'll show Sam the ropes. Only then she discover that Sam's not the only Fremont with a weakness for cowboys...

Available in January

Here's a preview!

"TEN FIVE," Liz called out. "I want that cowboy."

Jessica raised the bid to eleven. It was much easier to bid with zeros removed in her mind.

"Eleven five," Liz promptly bid.

"Hey, Liz. Cut it out." Tara nudged her sister. "Jessica is bidding against you."

At that moment, Jessica nodded to Sam, who in his excitement had climbed onto the bleachers next to her. Sam jumped and waved the marker, raising the bid to twelve thousand dollars.

Tara stared at Jessica, then poked Liz. "Jessica, who hasn't shown an interest in any man since her husband died, is preparing to fork over at least twelve *thousand* dollars for this one. Let her have him."

Liz licked her lips. "She's not ready for a man like that yet," She made a kissing motion and signaled the auctioneer. "Thirteen's always been my lucky number, anyway."

"I don't know what she thinks she's doing," Tara said to Jessica in a low voice.

"Making it very difficult to explain this to my mother-in-law, that's what," Jessica whispered.

Sam overheard his mother. "How much money can we spend?" his voice carried.

Jessica raised hers. "As much as we need to, sweetie. Mommy's been saving her allowance."

Liz leaned forward. "Now, Jessica, honey, let's not lose our friendship over this."

"I agree. Stop bidding against me."

The auctioneer's voice rang out. "We have fourteen thousand going once…"

"Fif—" Tara clamped her hand over Liz's mouth.

The auctioneer clearly didn't know what to do. "Going twice…"

"Will you just call it sold already," Tara yelled, now firmly planted on her sister's lap.

"Sold to Jessica Fremont for fourteen thousand dollars!"

"Yea!" Sam jumped off the bleachers and headed toward Matt, who'd swung off his horse. "Hey, Matt, we bought you!" Jessica heard him yell.

She'd done it. Now what?

"Oh, get off me," grumbled Liz to her sister. "I get it now." She straightened her blouse, then blew Matt a kiss. "Bye-bye, cowboy." Sighing, she faced Jessica. "Why didn't you tell me you were buying him for the kid?"

Jessica was still miffed with her. Standing on shaky legs, she smiled. "Because only the horse was for Sam."

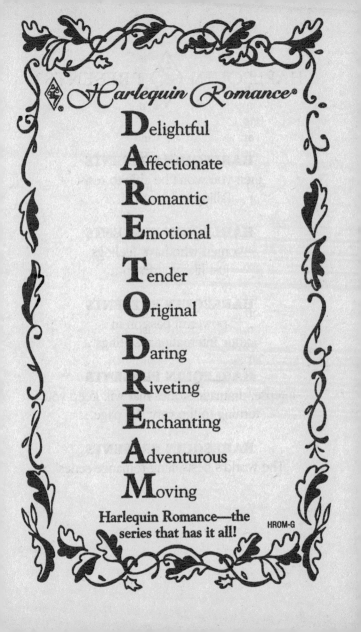

Harlequin Romance®

Delightful

Affectionate

Romantic

Emotional

Tender

Original

Daring

Riveting

Enchanting

Adventurous

Moving

Harlequin Romance—the
series that has it all!

HROM-G

HARLEQUIN ◆ PRESENTS®

HARLEQUIN PRESENTS
men you won't be able to resist
falling in love with...

HARLEQUIN PRESENTS
women who have feelings
just like your own...

HARLEQUIN PRESENTS
powerful passion in
exotic international settings...

HARLEQUIN PRESENTS
intense, dramatic stories that will keep you
turning to the very last page...

HARLEQUIN PRESENTS
The world's bestselling romance series!

**Harlequin®
Historical**

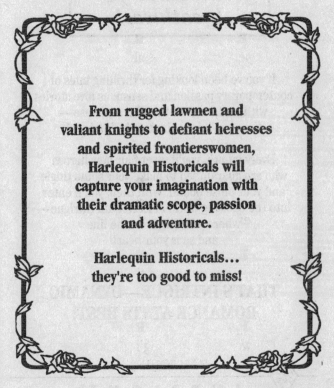

From rugged lawmen and
valiant knights to defiant heiresses
and spirited frontierswomen,
Harlequin Historicals will
capture your imagination with
their dramatic scope, passion
and adventure.

Harlequin Historicals...
they're too good to miss!

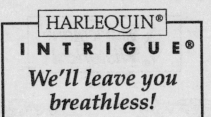

LOOK FOR OUR FOUR FABULOUS MEN!

Each month some of today's bestselling authors bring
four new fabulous men to Harlequin American Romance.
Whether they're rebel ranchers, millionaire power brokers
or sexy single dads, they're all gallant princes—and
they're all ready to sweep you into lighthearted fantasies
and contemporary fairy tales where anything is possible
and where all your dreams come true!

You don't even have to make a wish...
Harlequin American Romance will grant your every desire!

Look for Harlequin American Romance
wherever Harlequin books are sold!

HARLEQUIN SUPERROMANCE®

...there's more to the story!

Superromance. A *big* satisfying read about unforget-
table characters. Each month we offer
four very different stories that range from family
drama to adventure and mystery, from highly emo-
tional stories to romantic comedies—and
much more! Stories about people you'll
believe in and care about. Stories too
compelling to put down....

Our authors are among today's *best* romance writ-
ers. You'll find familiar names and
talented newcomers. Many of them are
award winners—and you'll see why!

If you want the biggest and best
in romance fiction, you'll get it
from Superromance!

Available wherever Harlequin books are sold.